Brian Scovell is one of Britain's most experienced and respected sports writers. He became the youngest-ever cricket correspondent on the *Daily Sketch* in 1960 before joining the *Daily Mail* in 1971 where he is the senior cricket and football correspondent. In 1990 he was runner-up in the Sports Council's award for the Sports News Reporter of the Year. He has written or co-authored eleven books on cricket and football, including the authorized biography of Sir Gary Sobers. He is married with two children and lives in Kent.

BEATING THE FIELD

Brian Lara
with Brian Scovell

CORGI BOOKS

BEATING THE FIELD
A CORGI BOOK : 0 552 14350 2

Originally published in Great Britain by Partridge Press,
a division of Transworld Publishers Ltd

PRINTING HISTORY
Partridge Press edition published 1995
Corgi edition published 1996

Set in Bembo by
Falcon Oast Graphic Art

Corgi Books are published by Transworld Publishers Ltd,
61-63 Uxbridge Road, London W5 5SA,
in Australia by Transworld Publishers (Australia) Pty Ltd,
15-25 Helles Avenue, Moorebank, NSW 2170
and in New Zealand by Transworld Publishers (NZ) Ltd,
3 William Pickering Drive, Albany, Auckland.

Reproduced, printed and bound in Great Britain by
Cox & Wyman Ltd, Reading, Berks.

I would like to dedicate this
book to my late father Bunty, my mother Pearl and
everyone else who helped me in my career.

'Cricket has always been more than a game in Trinidad. In a society which demanded no skills and offered no rewards to merit, cricket was the only activity which permitted a man to grow to his full stature and to be measured against international standards. Alone on a field, beyond obscuring intrigue, the cricketer's true worth could be seen by all. His education, wealth did not matter. We had no scientists, engineers, explorers, soldiers or poets. The cricketer was our only hero figure. That is why cricket is played in the West Indies with such panache.'

V.S. NAIPAUL, *The Hidden Passage*

CONTENTS

FOREWORD – By Sir Gary Sobers

BEATING THE FIELD

FOREWORD
by Sir Gary Sobers

THE FIRST TIME I SAW BRIAN LARA BAT WAS EIGHT YEARS AGO when he came to Barbados with his school, Fatima College, for the annual international schools tournament which I help organize for the Barbados Board of Tourism, and which they have been kind enough to name in my honour. I got a call from a friend of mine, former Trinidad and West Indies batsman Charlie Davis, asking me to come and have a look at a boy he said was something special.

It is always difficult to form an immediate impression of players so young, especially when watching from side on as I was then. The sixteen-year-old Lara was very small and could hardly hit the ball off the square, but the thing that struck me most was that he obviously loved batting. I think he got 50 or 60 odd and you could see his whole intention was to bat as long as possible. He wasn't giving his wicket away at 20 or 30 as is often the case with schoolboys. The bowler had to work for his wicket.

By the time he came back the following year his reputation at youth level was well established. He had the talent that excited old players like myself and I have made it a point to follow his progress ever since. I even played against him once, for a team of ex-players against a Trinidad side at the Queen's Park Oval.

Now that Brian has overtaken my world record Test score and developed into the most exciting batsman on the international stage, I do not think there are many who saw him from his early days who are surprised. I am certainly not. I really felt he should have been in the West Indies team a lot earlier. We had a middle order with some players failing miserably, but perhaps because the side was winning, kept their places in the team. But once Lara got there, he wasted no time in showing his worth.

What I like most about him is his approach. He is always looking to take advantage of the loose ball, and even the half-loose one. Once he gets in, he can get rid of even the good ball, which is the real sign of a great player. He will get to the stage where the bowlers cannot bowl to him because he is despatching the good, the bad and the indifferent with certainty.

That was the case during his magnificent 277 against Australia in Sydney which I was privileged to be able to watch from the stands. Only at one brief period somewhere between 230 and 250 did he seem to lose concentration and played at a few balls that were not there for the shot. But he settled down again and it was a great pity when he was run out. My record might have gone then!

He can dominate any bowling and has all the shots. He scores at a high rate of runs per ball, faster than any other contemporary player, and he doesn't need to hit the ball in the air. That is another sure sign of an extra special batsman.

Of course there have been one or two weaknesses in his technique. Before the last tour of Australia I thought he was vulnerable outside the off stump because of the positioning of his top hand. I told him I thought his top hand was too far in front on the grip, so that when he played the ball leaving him it was too weak to hold the bat in place. It meant he had to open the face to get into a stronger position, which is where the bottom hand took over. I suggested he should try and get his top hand round the handle a bit more. He said he would work on it but – intelligently, I thought – he didn't want to work on it right away. That was fair enough because you can't go making dramatic changes in the middle of a season.

I believe he worked on it later and he looks a lot more solid in defence outside the off stump. The ball is going a lot straighter, instead of flying down through gully or backward point, which is good to see. I also noticed some time ago that he started to move too far over to the off stump so that he committed himself to play at balls he would be better leaving alone. If he looked at his videos, he would have seen that he played at balls outside his off stump and you could see all three stumps behind his legs. Getting behind the ball is all well and good but only when the ball is on the stumps, not when it is wide of off. I think he worked on that to put it right.

I particularly like the shot he flicks through mid-wicket from outside the off stump, proving he is the type of player who has the ability to improvise.

From talking to him and observing him from afar, I

believe his mental attitude, so vital for sporting success, is very good. He looks to be a natural leader, an attribute recognized by the authorities who made him captain of the West Indian youth team to Australia, the B team to Zimbabwe and the Trinidad and Tobago team, all before he was twenty-one. He looks so mature. If you walked into a ground and Brian Lara was playing you would not have to ask who was leading the team. He would be obviously in charge. His movements and mannerisms show leadership qualities. He is a student of the game and there is no doubt in my mind that he is a future captain of the West Indies Test team.

I have heard it said that the responsibility of captaincy would detract from his batting and I believe that is why he was replaced as Trinidad's captain and the job given to others before he was handed it back again. That is a load of rubbish. Did the captaincy affect the batting of Bradman or Hutton or Gavaskar or Lloyd or a number of the other great batsmen who have led their countries? I hope it is not an argument that will keep Brian Lara from his rightful position.

Of course it is not only his cricketing ability that will determine whether he will become the truly great player he obviously has the potential to become in the next few years. There are plenty of pitfalls along the way and Brian will have to be careful of them all. One is hero-worship; people will get carried away and start comparing him with the greats of the past, those with long and proven records. Once he appreciates that greatness does not come overnight, and I am sure he does, he will be all right. Then there will be those looking to pull him down for whatever reason, or knocking his life-style saying that when he fails it is because he is doing this or that. I had plenty of that kind of sniping in my time. Once he understands that there are going to be the ups with the downs and learns to accept both in similar fashion, he has nothing to worry about.

Brian Lara has the world in his palm at present. He will get offers from all over the world to play and I would advise him to accept as many as he can without interfering with his commitment to West Indies cricket. He is young, enthusiastic, and the more he plays, and in different conditions, the more he will learn and the better he will get. Playing in England last summer would have helped him.

I haven't been so excited over the emergence of a young player for a long time. Perhaps I feel a certain affinity with him because he is a left-hander and a West Indian, with a West Indian approach to cricket and life in general. I have watched him from that day in the schools match and he has grown into a man who played one of the best innings I have ever seen. His luck ran out at 277 that day in Sydney and you need luck. He was on his way to the record when he was run out. I told him then his chance would come again, and even though he may have felt I was kidding, I knew I would be proved right.

When I wrote my autobiography *Twenty Years at the Top* in 1988 I said I believed my 365 would never be beaten. I based that on the theory that one-day cricket was producing a type of batsman who is less capable of playing a long innings. There were few batsmen around, I said, with the necessary concentration to stay at the crease for ten hours or more and aim for a score of 300 plus. Watching Brian in Sydney made me change my mind. It was obvious that here was a very special player with all the qualities needed to pile up really big scores.

Records have never meant a great deal to me. But as

I stood on the edge of the boundary at the Recreation Ground waiting to hand over the mantle, so to speak, I was happy that it was Brian Lara who was to become the new holder. To me, he is the one batsman today who plays the game the way it should be played.

That innings was further proof that he can become one of the really great players. He is not there yet since, as I have said, greatness is only achieved over a period of time, playing in all conditions against all types of bowlers. He has still got to prove he can do that but I am sure he will. He has always had a good technique and there is no problem with either his attack or his defence.

Perhaps what he has to worry about most now is not so much his batting, because that will take care of itself, but about how he might be used following his tremendous success and how he deals with all the attention that has been heaped on him. He has become internationally famous. So did I when I broke the record but I did not have to deal with all the commercial benefits that follow such a feat in this day and age. I got my $150 match fee and that was about it. Now Brian has to consider all the offers for endorsements, appearances and interviews. I have read that he could become a millionaire, and I believe it. I know him to be intelligent enough to handle it and go about his life without letting it interfere with his cricket.

I feel he was motivated into batting as he did in Antigua by the added responsibility of being vice-captain. Both Richie Richardson and Desmond Haynes were out injured and Courtney Walsh took over as skipper with Brian his deputy. That meant so much to him that he went out to the middle and really put his head down, especially when the West Indies were 2 wickets down early on and struggling. As he also showed when he captained Trinidad and Tobago in the Red Stripe Cup and carried them to second place, almost on his own, he thrives on responsibility, on leadership. I have always felt he would make a great captain and I am certain of it now.

I am sure he will knock off a few more records before he is through. I hope I am lucky enough to see them all.

Barbados
October 1994

CHAPTER ONE

THE WEST INDIAN WAY

THE WEST INDIAN WAY OF PLAYING CRICKET IS TO TRY TO ENTER-
tain, to be flamboyant and to enjoy it. From a very young
age boys will be trying to improve their game on the beach
or on little-used roads or bare patches of land – anywhere
they can find. And they will be doing it with some style
and charisma.

That is where I learned the game and it is where the next
generation of West Indian cricketers will learn it. Cricket
has been the number one sport in the Caribbean because
it suits the personality of the West Indian. It is more of
an aggressive game and it meets our need to impress and
show pride in performance. Football is popular too, but
lack of exposure is one of the reasons why we do not
produce world-class footballers.

Cricket was passed on to us by the plantation owners

and their workers. The West Indian labourers who took it up wanted to be different in their approach to the game from the people who oppressed them, so they were much more aggressive, using their physical strength and gift of co-ordination between hand and eye to strike the ball great distances. Just to be allowed to play cricket in those days meant a degree of freedom for them. They were playing a sport they could enjoy and that feeling lives on. The West Indian presence added a new dimension to cricket and was mainly a reflection of our culture and our need to be recognized.

If you watch an English boy playing cricket he tends to play the game in a textbook manner. He will be putting his foot towards the pitch of the ball in the approved method suggested by the coaches and trying to play straight, usually in a defensive way. A West Indian boy will be attempting to smash the ball as far as he can. He will be playing with much more freedom.

This attitude goes right through our cricket to the very top. It is the way our international players play. We, as West Indian cricketers, try our best not to be stereo-typed. Youngsters want to be the next Viv Richards or Curtly Ambrose. The great cricketers are the heroes of West Indian youth. All the leading players are individuals with their own methods. Youngsters learn from watching them on TV or in person and this will continue as long as the West Indies reigns as the best side in world cricket.

Much of my learning process about the game was conducted through a transistor radio when I was a boy. When the West Indies were playing in Australia I would hide it under my pillow and wake in the middle of the night to tune in. My father would be listening to his radio in another room and I knew he would be upset if he felt I was missing out on sleep because of school next day. My hero was the West Indies and Guyana left-handed opener Roy Fredericks who was at the height of his career at this time. He appealed to me because he was left-handed and played flamboyant shots. I was so obsessed about him and his exploits that the other boys nicknamed me Roy Fredericks. I wore my shirt sleeves buttoned at the wrist, just like him.

He was not my only hero. I also idolized Viv Richards for the exciting way he played the game. I realized that it was probably better for my own game if I shaped up like Gordon Greenidge who played straighter, but Viv had wonderful eyesight and was able to get away with playing across the line when he played on the legside. Listening to these players enthralled me. I wanted to learn everything about them and what they did.

When I was called up for the West Indian side and was introduced to Roy Fredericks I found it frightening. I hardly knew what to say. But he was very friendly and gave me plenty of advice in his capacity as a selector. When you become a public figure certain myths are created about you, and one which developed about me was that Colin Cowdrey, the former England and Kent captain, was one of my heroes. I am afraid that is not true. I was four when Mr Cowdrey played his last test in 1974 and would not have seen him play. I knew hardly anything about him except that he was a very graceful batsman with exquisite timing.

My other heroes were the four West Indian fast bowlers Clive Lloyd used so effectively earlier during his captaincy – Michael Holding, Andy Roberts, Colin Croft and Joel Garner. With my slight build, I knew I could never aspire to match them but I admired their aggression and passion for the game. The West Indies continue to produce fast bowlers because we have the raw material which is then fine-tuned. They are not stopped from doing what they like best which is running in and bowling as fast as they can. Later they learn how to hold the ball properly, how to add accuracy. If they have the talent and the desire that will all fall into place. The supply seems to be drying up just recently, especially in Barbados, the island which has traditionally produced the most West Indian fast bowlers. But one or two always crop up and often in the most unexpected places. I have no worries about that.

I do not think many of them will be as single-minded as I was about cricket because there are more distractions these days, more choices to make. When I came home from school I would do my homework and then go out to play either cricket or football. Now youngsters are just as likely to find themselves being distracted by other interests. The danger to the dominance of West Indies cricket lies in the inroads made by the American sports – basketball, volleyball, baseball and US football – which are fuelled by television. These sports appear more exciting to our youngsters and are accompanied by an easy-going life-style. I think that is sad for our culture. Schools still play cricket and will continue to play cricket. If youngsters want to reach the top in the American sports they cannot do it in the Caribbean. They have to emigrate to the USA. So cricket still offers them the more realistic road to attaining international fame.

I wasn't tall enough to play basketball so the choice for me was more limited. I didn't like running for the sake of running so it had to be a ball game. I loved to play both cricket and football and if I had been bigger I think I might have made the grade as a footballer, alongside my best friends Dwight Yorke, who plays for Aston Villa, and Russell Latapy, who plays for FC Porto in the Portuguese league.

Religion played a big part in our lives. If we showed any reluctance to attend church on a Sunday our mother would take us by the ear. I am not so sure that is the case now. With so many outside influences standards are declining, which makes it so important to hold on to what we have.

There are more signs of affluence but wages have not risen with the cost of living in most of the islands and life is still a struggle for many people. Cricket gear is expensive but West Indian youngsters have always made their own rough bats and balls and that shows no sign of changing. There are facilities to play the game at the schools, not high-class facilities but they are adequate.

West Indies cricket will always be aggressive and exciting because as people we do not like being restricted. It is no use a coach telling a young West Indian batsman to play the ball in the V between mid off and mid on, or a bowler to bowl a tight line just outside the off stump. Our batsmen want to play the exhilarating shots. The bowlers want to knock the stumps out or force the batsman on the defensive.

As the West Indies team became more and more successful after 1975 so the authorities tried to curb the use of the bouncer which has always been a part of our game. A rule was introduced limiting bowlers to one bouncer an over, but I believe it had the reverse effect to the one intended. Our bowlers had to learn to be better bowlers, concentrating more on getting batsmen out, and the batsman, knowing which ball was going to be the short one, started losing the ability to play fast bowling. We have seen a number of leading batsmen in recent years who get into all kinds of difficulty when the ball is short. I do not believe there should be any restrictions on how many bouncers a bowler can bowl. They don't say to a batsman,

'You can't play a square cut'. There are no restrictions on the batsman so why should there be a restriction on the bowler? The bowler's life is tough enough anyway with pitches so often favouring the batsman.

The batsman has all the protection he needs – the helmet, the arm protector, the chest protector, and pads and gloves. He can always move out of the line of the ball and not play it. If he keeps doing that, the bowler will realize he is wasting his energy. He will only persist in bowling short if he thinks the batsman is troubled by it.

Most West Indian batsmen love hooking the ball because it is such a spectacular shot and crowds love to see it. But it is also a shot which causes a lot of dismissals and I rarely play it these days. Similarly, I do not play the reverse sweep, an equally dangerous shot. Bowlers need to be able to exploit bouncers and I would not deny them that privilege. In India the ball often turns so much that it can pitch on leg stump and go towards second slip, making it almost impossible for the batsmen to play a stroke. Should that type of bowling be banned because it is not good for the game?

I have been hit a number of times on the helmet by short-pitched bowling and accept that it is one of the risks involved in playing the game. Malcolm Marshall once hit me in a Red Stripe Cup game and I was left with a sore head, and Curtly Ambrose hit me in England when I made the mistake of taking my eye off the ball.

I do not think the risk of injury should preclude bowlers bowling short. When you play football and you go into a tackle, you accept there is a risk of injury. Similarly in other sports. In cricket the leading sides have up to four fast bowlers and it is fanciful to expect them not to use every weapon in their armoury. Bouncers are an exciting part of the game and have long been part of the West Indian cricketing culture.

The law about intimidatory bowling still remains and it is up to the umpire to decide whether to use it. When a tailender is facing, I think it is perfectly legitimate for the umpire to intervene. There have been occasions when Devon Malcolm, England's number 11 batsman, needed this kind of protection.

Great fast bowlers have kept the West Indies on top and I am hopeful that will continue to be the case. When Michael Holding, Joel Garner and Andy Roberts retired another squad came along, Curtly Ambrose, Ian Bishop and the Benjamins, and when Curtly retires, which may well be in a year or two, I am sure others will follow behind him to maintain the line. There was a decline in the late Eighties when Viv Richards and Gordon Greenidge retired, but it picked up again in Australia under Richie Richardson in 1992–3 and the West Indies remained on top. Because of the success of players like Curtly Ambrose, Jimmy Adams and myself a new interest has been created, and more youngsters will be eager to become the future West Indies cricketing stars and not the next Michael Jordan. Cricket has been a way of life in the West Indies, a form of recognition for our people. I would be mortified if one day the West Indies were unable to produce a team capable of doing us proud.

The other feature of West Indies cricket which remains unaffected by changing society is the sportsmanship of our players. Winning at all costs it not the most important thing. There are still many batsmen in our cricket who will walk if they are out. I do myself and have always done so. I do not see any point in hanging around if you know you are out. But if I am not sure – and sometimes that is the case, as when the ball brushes the pad as you are attempting a leg glance – I leave it up to the umpire to decide. I have no complaint with those who don't walk – it is a purely personal choice.

In the early days of our cricket, when George Headley and Learie Constantine were among the most prominent players, there was hardly any money to be made from cricket. Players had to go to England to play in League cricket to be rewarded. This lack of money helped retain the sporting ethos of the game. Things usually worsen when big sums are at stake. Sir Frank Worrell, one of the great West Indian cricketers who went to play League cricket in England, and was the first black captain to lead the West Indies in a series, was the leading influence in ensuring that our cricket retained its sense of sportsmanship. He was the chief instrument in that process and he was the unifier of our cricket. Worldwide, standards of behaviour have declined in sport, which was why the ICC introduced their Code of Conduct. Not too many West Indians have been fined for indiscipline.

English boys have their bats bought for them by their parents and once they start playing they will be fully kitted out. My first bat was made for me by my brother Rudolph when I was three. I was born in the village of Cantaro in Santa Cruz, north of Port of Spain, on 2 May 1969, the seventh son in a family of eleven. I weighed 7 lb exactly. My father Bunty loved cricket and played it as a boy. He might have gone on to play it at a higher level, but after being asked to play in a regional match he couldn't get there because according to him the donkey cart that was supposed to pick him up failed to arrive. He told me once that he played in a match in which his side was all out for 6, and he made 4 of them.

My first experience of playing cricket was with the

other small boys living in our street, Mitchell Street, where my mother Pearl still lives. The other boys would borrow my bat and I usually had the soft ball we played with too. If there was no ball we used oranges. We also played cricket and football on a spare piece of ground nearby. We played until it was too dark to continue.

My love of the game was probably inherited because not only was my father a fervent follower of cricket but my grandfather Herbert St Louis was also a fanatical cricket lover. Unfortunately when listening on his radio to a particularly exciting day's play in a Test between Australia and the West Indies he had a stroke. He died at the age of seventy.

Like most West Indian boys I played 'pass out', a street version of cricket where you are out if you miss the ball. An old man, Mr Dorsey, who used to live nearby would often offer the other boys money for getting me out. It made me all the more determined to bat on as long as possible.

When the others grew tired and went home and there was no-one else to play with I used to play my own Test matches on the porch of our house, using a broom handle or a stick as the bat and a marble as the ball. I would arrange the pot plants to represent fielders and try to find the gaps as I played my shots. If I missed the rebound from the ball that was a wicket.

When I was six my sister Agnes saw an advertisement in a local newspaper inviting boys to attend coaching classes at the Harvard clinic in Port of Spain. She wrote in for details and enrolled me. We did not come from a poor family, but with eleven children my father had no money to spend on luxuries. He was a manager employed by the Ministry of Agriculture and it was one of the top jobs in the village. He had to make sacrifices to buy the shoes and clothes we needed, and the school books. Agnes, who has two sons of her own who are developing into fine young cricketers, bought me a green cap, some whites and a junior single-scoop bat and took me to the Harvard clinic on the first two Sundays. The coach there was Hugo Day.

From that time onwards, my father never missed one of my practice sessions, or any match I was playing in. I think I may have been his favourite. He wanted me to do well in the sport he loved so much and, as I grew older, he would drive me in his old Morris Cambridge to every venue. He even ran a junior cricket league for boys on a nearby ground which is no longer in use. The pitch was red clay covered with matting.

While playing in Port of Spain I met David and Michael Carew, the sons of Joey Carew, the West Indian opening batsman who played nineteen Tests between 1963 and 1972, and they became two of my best friends. When it was late and difficult to make the half-hour journey back to Cantaro I would be invited to spend the night at their home. Joey Carew would talk cricket to us for hours, we would watch videos and he would talk about what made the great players so good. I learned a lot from him and he still gives me very good advice. He is now the chief executive at the Queen's Park Cricket Club and I still meet him regularly to talk cricket. He is a kind of father-figure to me and I appreciate everything he has done for me.

Around the age of eight my targets were firmly set. I wanted to be a top-class cricketer. I wanted to play for the West Indies and break records. I remember being selected once to play cricket for my first school, St Joseph's RC Primary School, but I was demoted to twelfth-man duties. That did not bother me too much because I was attending Harvard and playing in the league organized by my father. The street games continued daily and there were a number of occasions when I broke windows and my father had to pay for the repairs.

At eleven, I was accepted for Fatima College, the leading Catholic school in Port of Spain, which has produced so many outstanding Trinidadian cricketers. I went on to obtain seven O Levels and but for cricket might well have gone on to higher education, possibly in America. Maths was my best subject, but cricket overrode anything else.

I played for each age group, usually a year or two ahead of schedule. Harry Ramdass, coach of the Under-14 side, was a great encouragement to me along with the other members of staff including the headmaster Mervyn Moore. I spent all the time I could practising and playing.

My height was a handicap. I was only five feet tall until my mid-teens, when I started growing to my present height of five feet eight inches. I remember in one match I went to the wicket with pads almost up to my thighs and baggy pants, and when I took guard there was a sympathetic chuckle behind me as one of the fielders said: 'It will be just a matter of time before this guy is out.' It *was* a matter of time, quite some time! When bowlers tried to exploit my lack of height by bouncing me it made me all the more determined to do well.

These matches started at 3.30 on Fridays and continued on Saturdays, usually on grass wickets but occasionally on matting. There wasn't much time to get a result, which put pressure on batsmen to score quickly. I did my best to oblige.

I always wanted to become a captain and was soon given the job at school. I would write down field placings on a piece of paper and discuss them with my bowlers. As captain you are more involved in the game. I liked that.

My lack of height was a greater problem on the football field. I played football regularly and represented the

Trinidad and Tobago Under-14 side in the same year as my great friends Dwight Yorke and Russell Latapy. I was a forward who relied on speed. Another of my friends and former colleagues is Shaka Hislop, the Reading goalkeeper. My football career came to an end at around this time because it became clear that cricket was what I was destined for. My father was delighted because cricket had always been his passion.

CHAPTER TWO

CAPTAINCY

GIVEN THE JOB OF LEADING WHICHEVER CRICKET TEAM I WAS A member of meant a lot to me. From a very young age at school I found myself assuming the role of captaincy. The decision about who was chosen to lead the side was based purely on ability. Are you the best batsman? Are you the best bowler? If either of these questions fitted you then you would be in line for the top position. It had nothing to do with your knowledge of the game or your ability to motivate a group of individuals. Leading teams at school level was easier for me. Because of your ability you become more popular with your team-mates; they respect you more than other members of the team. There is no pressure at this level, maybe because the role I had as a captain was mainly to perform as the best batsman of the team by scoring most of the runs, and the bowlers were left to take care of the rest. Captaincy at this level was sheer enjoyment.

My first real opportunity to prove to myself and to others that I could become a future captain came in 1987. I was chosen as my country's national Under-19 team captain. Of course, there was some luck in that. Ian Bishop was also eligible for selection. He was a more experienced player than I was at this level, and I suppose if he hadn't opted to go to England to play league cricket he most probably would have been made captain.

I had one year's experience in the Northern Telecom Youth Tournament in 1986 and Trinidad and Tobago won the tournament. This meant we arrived in Jamaica as defending champions. Northern Telecom have been sponsoring this tournament for many years and thanks to them players such as myself were given an opportunity to match our skills against our counterparts from other Caribbean Islands. From this tournament a lot of the players immediately moved straight into their senior national teams. So this youth tournament was used as a stepping-stone for enhancing our careers.

We defended our crown admirably, winning the first three games against Barbados, Leeward Islands and Guyana convincingly to give us 48 points after the third round. At this same stage the host country Jamaica had 34 points, two wins and a loss on first innings. This meant the next game, Jamaica versus Trinidad and Tobago, was a virtual final.

Trinidad and Tobago batted first. I got 36 and with some useful contributions from the other players we managed 234. Jamaica had among them their captain Jimmy Adams, a present West Indies player. Jimmy is a player I have a lot of respect and admiration for. I think he's the most dependable batsman in the current West

Indies team. Yes, another Larry Gomes and his record at present is a lot better. Jamaica fell short of our total by 25 runs, scoring 209, so we got the first innings points needed to win the Championship. All we needed now was to bat ourselves out of a possible outright defeat. Soon we were in severe difficulties at 25–5 and Jamaica were staging a bold fightback.

I think this is the first time I can say the responsibility of captaincy played an important part in my batting. At 25–5 I was still there, and the desire to keep out the Jamaica bowlers kept me going. I had already visualized myself raising the Northern Telecom trophy in my first year as captain. I knew I could not disappoint myself but also my team-mates and the many people back in my country who were tied to their transistor radios. All of this was on my mind while I was at the wicket. I and a young player Darryl Roopchand held the innings together long enough to secure a draw. My 116 had something to do with those expectations and goals, Roopchand also got 50 and Trinidad and Tobago retained the Northern Telecom Cup. That year Trinidad and Tobago won every award at the prize-giving ceremony. Along with the championship trophy, the Most Disciplined Team trophy was presented to us. I won the Most Runs and the Most Valuable Player trophies and Rajendra Dhanraj received the Most Wickets trophy. Both Dhanraj's and my achievements were new records. Carl Hooper, whose ability I was in awe of, had held the batting record with 480 runs in a series, but I eclipsed that with 498. Dhanraj had equalled the bowling record, held by Carl Hooper again, with 33 wickets in 1986, and now he was on his own with 44 wickets in five matches. In all, he took 120 wickets in the Northern Telecom at an average of 12.86.

From this tournament the West Indies Under-19 team

was going to be selected for the first ever youth World Cup, which was to be held in Australia to commemorate the Australians' bicentenary. Sadly it was the first and last such competition. The visit to Australia in February and March was one of the most enjoyable trips of my cricketing career and it brought me into contact with a number of players who went on to become Test players, including the England captain Mike Atherton, Mark Ramprakash, Nasser Hussain, Martin Bicknell, Basit Ali, Inzaman-ul-Haq, Aqib Javed, Mushtaq Ahmed, Wayne Holdsworth, Shane Thomson, Chris Cairns, Venkat Raju, Narendra Hirwani and Jimmy Adams. The fact that so many players went on to reach Test standard proved the value of the tournament and the relevant authorities should make every effort to revive it.

I led the Trinidad and Tobago youth team to success, but to remain captain of the West Indies youth team to tour Australia was a big surprise. Players such as Jimmy Adams and Roland Holder had more experience at this level and even at our senior regional level. I thought one of them would be given this great honour. The camaraderie among the players was excellent and the experience was invaluable. Atherton impressed me then as a potential Test captain. He skippered the side without fuss and appeared to have the necessary temperament for the job. Sam Skeete, our fastest bowler, dismissed him for 1 in the match at Renmark which England won by 63 runs.

The West Indies lost to Pakistan in the semi-final by 2 wickets, and Australia beat Pakistan in the final by 5 wickets with Alan Mullaly, now with Leicestershire, taking 2–53. Jimmy Adams was top run-scorer for the West Indies with 272, at an average of 54.40, and I scored 222 with an average of 37.75. I thought this was a good

24

performance by everyone considering our players weren't accustomed to playing one-day cricket. Our experience up until then was restricted to the longer version of the game.

On my return home the West Indies Cricket Board and their selectors' confidence in me went one step further. The Pakistanis were touring and I was named captain in their upcoming match against the West Indies Under-23 team. Captaincy at this stage started becoming a very serious part of my cricket. The possibility of captaining the West Indies cricket team one day was developing in front of me. I saw Keith Arthurton for the first time in the Under-23 match. He scored a brilliant 124 against the likes of Abdul Qadir and others in a drawn match.

I must have been pleasing everyone with my ability to lead teams, but even I was surprised at my rapid progress. Trinidad and Tobago youth team captain 1987, and in 1989 I was captaining the West Indies B team on their tour to Zimbabwe. There were a few Test players in the touring party. I was a bit apprehensive not knowing how players such as Carl Hooper, Patrick Patterson, Tony Gray and others would react to my inexperience. Actually I expected the most problems from Patrick Patterson, but it did not materialize since he sustained an ankle injury in the first warm-up game and was side-lined for the rest of the tour.

I don't think I've ever gone into a tour lacking so much confidence in my batting. I spent extra hours practising and even that and a few warm-up games did not help me leading up to the first four-day international. Zimbabwe scored 344, David Houghton, Zimbabwe's top batsman at the time, making 165. West Indies replied with 396 and I scored 145. Carl Hooper still maintains that is the worst 100 he has seen, and for once I could not disagree with him. I played and missed on numerous occasions. Sometimes I would cover-drive and the ball would take the inside edge and go through mid-wicket for 4. Now what could I say was responsible for my getting 100? Of course a great deal of luck, but I think most importantly was the responsibility of captaincy together with the desire to lead from the front. From then on the myth that the responsibility of captaincy adversely affects an individual's performance never got backing from me.

My first international match was drawn and I came in for a bit of criticism of my tactics during the Zimbabweans' first innings. West Indies went on to win the remaining two four-day matches, and I must say things went more smoothly than I had expected. I think that was the beginning of the great friendship I now have with Carl Hooper. As a cricketer I think he had the potential to be the most elegant batsman in the world today. He seems to have too much time to play the ball and his cover drive, as Curtly Ambrose will tell you, is a joy to watch.

It may seem a 'fairy tale' story but on my return home I was named captain of the Trinidad and Tobago senior team at the age of twenty. If there is something that I would like to erase from my cricketing career it is the 1990 Red Stripe Cup. I think my selection as captain was seen by some players as taking things a little too far. There were many reasons for our lack of success in my first year as captain. The most notable one was my own bad run with the bat which came at the worst possible time. Also, many of the older players resented the fact that a 'little boy' (I must say I was really quite small) was made captain ahead of them and they never gave me 100 per cent support.

The campaign started badly with a 58-run defeat in Jamaica on a pitch of low bounce which made shot-playing difficult against the high-quality fast bowlers on view. Ian Bishop took 11 wickets for us and Patrick Patterson responded with 9 for Jamaica. We led by 2 runs on the first innings but had the match wrested away from us when Jimmy Adams scored 109 in 402 minutes. When he was on 27 Ken Williams appeared to catch him in the gully off the bowling of Bishop but umpire Glenroy Johnson ruled that Williams had touched the ground with the ball before completing the catch. At tea on the final day the outcome was still in doubt, with Trinidad 174–5, but when Gus Logie was bowled for 75 the rest of the batting collapsed.

Our second match resulted in another defeat, by 4 wickets against the Windward Islands, but it was not a rout. Needing 83 to win on the last day the Windward side were 61–6 with Joey Pierre in hospital needing stitches to a wound above the eye after being hit by Bishop. The confidence of our players was slowly draining away and we reached the lowest point in the next match against the Leeward Islands in Port of Spain when we were bowled out for 88 and lost by 8 wickets. By this time I was being blamed. People were saying the pressure of captaincy had affected my batting and it was a mistake to give me the job. That was not so; I was just having a bad run at a bad time, like everyone else in the side with the notable exception of Ian Bishop. These things happen; it didn't mean I lacked the qualities needed to be the captain.

The argument to take the captaincy away from me was strengthened in the fourth match in Barbados when we were outplayed by an innings and 87 runs. Roland Holder, who made 124 in Barbados' total of 441, was let off when I missed a stumping off Dhanraj. I was deputizing for the injured David Williams. I have kept in matches before and quite like the job. After scoring 45 in the first innings I was out in dubious circumstances for 33 second time round, caught by wicket-keeper Ricky Hoyte, son of former West Indies wicket-keeper David Murray, off a bouncer from Victor Walcott.

Luckily for me I was not put through the agony of losing all five matches – the last one against Guyana was entirely washed out by rain. I averaged only 22.25 from 178 runs, Phil Simmons 17.62 from 141, and only Gus Logie with 39.00 from 156 could have been said to have played near to his usual form. No one scored a century and there was only one total over 200. Most of the critics overlooked the fact that a couple of the matches had been played on unsatisfactory pitches. The West Indies *Cricket Annual* summed it up as 'a disastrous, shocking and distressing season'.

The fact that we recovered to win the one-day tournament, the Geddes Grant Shield, beating Barbados by five wickets in the final, did not save me from being sacked. I was very upset. I did not feel it was right to take the job away from me after only one season. Gus Logie took over the following year, the fifth captain in as many seasons.

Coming to the end of the Red Stripe Cup I was starting to feel that I would get some runs very soon. It happened as soon as I did not have the responsibility as captain. I remember telling Bryan Davis, one of the local selectors, that I felt I was going to score 100 against England. I had been selected for the President's XI against them in Trinidad, and after they were bowled out for 252 I scored 134 off 180 balls in our first innings total of 294. In the same match Robin Smith was robbed of a deserved century in the second innings and I felt sorry for him. He was on 79 when the last man Devon Malcolm joined him. After hitting Robert Haynes for successive sixes Smith drove to the boundary for what he thought was going to be a single but Delroy Morgan let the ball go through for four, so that Malcolm had to face the next over. That took Smith to 99 and he stayed one short of his hundred because Malcolm was bowled by Patrick Patterson with the fifth ball of the next over.

After the disappointment of 1990 I concentrated more on my game, and getting in to the West Indies team and establishing myself. By the time the 1994 Red Stripe Cup season came around I had already played a few Test matches and was somewhat established as a regular member on the West Indies team. This was the year that I was reappointed captain of the Trinidad and Tobago team, a job I felt I should never have had taken away from me. The experience of being sacked after only one season had scarred me deeply. I was determined to prove my critics wrong, but the prospects were not good. Ian Bishop was still out injured, Gus Logie had retired and the Trinidad side was a relatively inexperienced one.

The team was picked after trials but I maintained that was not the best way to do it. A player who performed well in a trial might not be the best person to succeed in a competitive match. I wanted the best sixteen players in the country called up, and that was what happened. Another key player, the pace bowler Eugene Antoine, was also injured and we had at the start to rely on nineteen-year-old leg-spinner Dinanath Ramnarine as one of the key bowlers in our attack. He went on to take 15 wickets. He is a very dedicated young cricketer who in my opinion has a bright future in the game.

In the opening match we scraped through against the Windward Islands in St Lucia, pace bowler Marlon Black hitting the six needed to win with the last pair at the wicket. The next game saw us lose to the champions, the Leeward Islands, at Sturge Park, Plymouth, Montserrat by

110 runs, with Curtly Ambrose, Kenneth Benjamin and Winston Benjamin knocking us aside. The pressure was on my inexperienced team in the third match, at home to Jamaica, and when I came in we were 38–2 in reply to Jamaica's 206. By the close we had taken that to 103–6, with me unbeaten on 49. Next day I played one of my most satisfying innings in the Red Stripe with 180 out of the 219 runs scored while I was at the crease, or 82.19% of the runs.

I was out caught at long on going for a second successive six off Robert Haynes, the former West Indies leg-spin bowler. We won that match by 3 wickets and followed up by beating Guyana by 78 runs in Port of Spain. I scored 169 to enable us to recover from a deficit of 104 on the first innings. If we had beaten Barbados in our final match we would have won the title rather than the Leeward Islands, but after my 206 helped us enforce the follow on, Roland Holder's unbeaten 116 in the Barbados second innings meant we had to settle for 8 points instead of 16 and we finished runners-up. It had been a great Red Stripe series for me, and my total of 715 runs for an average of 79.44 was a record.

What a way to respond! I was proud of the guys and they showed a lot of team spirit, and hopefully the success that we had in 1994 would serve them well in the future. Personally it was nice to rub off the disappointment of the 1990 Red Stripe season with an effort such as this.

In the absence of Richie Richardson and Desmond Haynes, in 1994–5 I held my position as vice-captain of the West Indies team since the last Test match against England in Antigua in April 1994. I would be lying if I said that captaining the West Indies Test team one day is not one of my goals. Since my schooldays I've dreamt about that moment and if ever it comes I'd grasp it with both hands and do the best job that I can.

CHAPTER THREE

A FRUSTRATING START TO
MY TEST CAREER

I TOOK PART IN FOUR NORTHERN TELECOM COMPETITIONS IN ALL, scoring 1,140 runs at an average of 51.81. The outstanding bowler at that time was my Trinidadian colleague Rajendra Dhanraj, who toured India with the West Indies late in 1994. Others who took part at that time were Stuart Williams, the Leeward Island bastman, and Jimmy Adams, the Jamaica and Nottinghamshire player whose career has run parallel to mine in many ways. These young players had one thing in common, they wanted to play for the West Indies. It was my first experience of inter-island competitive cricket and it gave me an insight into the strength of character, as well as cricketing ability, that was required to reach the top. I am not sure that the present-day young cricketers have the same burning desire and ambition.

There was a clamour for me to be picked for

Trinidad and Tobago and it was answered in 1988 when I was selected to play against the Leeward Islands, whose opening bowler Curtly Ambrose was in his first full season. I was more successful this time, scoring 14 in the first innings and 22 in the second. Ambrose took a record 35 wickets that season but mine was not among them. There was some controversy when he was no-balled for allegedly throwing the fourth ball of his ninth over. It never occurred to us that there was any doubt about the legality of his action and it was a mystery why he was called by umpire Cumberbatch. With players like Viv Richards, Richie Richardson, Keith Arthurton, Eldine Baptiste and Winston Benjamin, the Leeward Islands had probably the strongest squad in the competition at the time.

I kept my place for the following match, against Barbados at the Queen's Park Oval, and in between played in a Geddes Grant one-day match against them. The boys at Fatima College were given a day off to watch me. It turned out to be a chastening experience. I was dismissed second ball by Malcolm Marshall, whose figures were 2–12 in eight overs, and felt like going underground. Next day I had to face the ribbing of my schoolmates. Two days later, in the Red Stripe encounter, I scored 92 before falling lbw to Joel Garner. I batted 349 minutes and hit just four boundaries, a contrast to my later form but understandable in view of my inexperience and fierce desire to do well. I managed to survive against Marshall, the leading West Indies bowler of the day, and those runs helped me finish top of the batting averages in my first season, with an average of 46.66, although I must confess I only played two matches because of my commitment to the West Indies Youth Team tour of Australia for the Youth World Cup.

My second season in Red Stripe cricket could not have begun better. I made my maiden first-class century against Guyana in Guaracara Park, Pointe-à-Pierre, sharing a stand of 85 with Michael Carew. My 127 took just over five hours. Nearly all of my hundreds have been totals well over 100 because I firmly believe that, having reached the milestone, it is essential to go on to the next one and the one after that. Subconsciously, the temptation is there to relax a little once the 100 goes up, which I believe is the reason why so many players are out shortly afterwards.

My euphoria was cut short in the second innings of a low-scoring game when I was lbw to Linden Joseph, the former Hampshire bowler, and Trinidad were bowled out for 86, losing by 5 wickets. Under the captaincy of Phil Simmons, Trinidad lost their opening three matches in the competition before beating the champions Jamaica, with Ian Bishop taking 9–90. That was before Bishop started having trouble with his back. At the time he was one of the fastest bowlers in the world and a natural successor to Michael Holding in the West Indies side.

I finished up that season playing for the West Indies Under-23 side against the touring Indians at Warner Park, Basseterre. On a flat pitch I scored 182 in just six hours before being caught by Kris Srikkanth on the long on boundary off the bowling of Hirwani. It was a high-scoring draw – West Indies making 405 in reply to the Indians 411 and 39–0. I was selected for the Board XI against the Indians two weeks later but there was only one day's play through rain and I didn't get in.

My first Test match call-up came in April 1989 when I was picked for the West Indies squad on the eve of the Third Test against India. I was two weeks short of my twentieth birthday. The West Indies had such a strong batting side – the top six were Gordon Greenidge, Desmond Haynes, Richie Richardson, Gus Logie, Viv Richards (who missed the first Test after an operation) and Keith Arthurton – that I knew I had little chance of making the final XI. I was appointed twelfth man and was thrilled to be so close to fulfilling my ambition. Just being there was part of a learning process which would help me when I was finally chosen. Everyone in my family, all my friends, were delighted for me, particularly my father Bunty. He had been forced to retire through ill-health seven years earlier and had already had two heart attacks. On 15 April, after the end of the first day of the Test at the Queen's Park Oval, he died at the age of sixty-two. It was the saddest time of my life. My father had done so much for me. He gave me every possible support in my career and in his latter years had devoted his life to helping me reach my goals. It was a tragedy that he died when I was so close to attaining them. He always said to me that if you wanted to achieve anything in life you must have dedication, discipline and determination. I have tried to be faithful to that creed, and when I scored my 375 in Antigua I dedicated it to him and his memory. When the funeral took place, the whole of the West Indies team attended.

Though the pitch in my first Test was a slow turner which helped the Indian spin bowlers, the West Indies won the series with their first victory over the Indians at the Queen's Park Oval since 1962. The Indians had done so well there because the pitches are traditionally helpful to spin. There was not one spin bowler in Viv Richards' side in that match but Malcolm Marshall took 11 wickets and Courtney Walsh, Ian Bishop and Viv Richards shared the others.

A year on, my innings of 134 for the President's XI

against England got me back in the Test 13 at the Queen's Park Oval but it was Gus Logie, back after injury, who was preferred to me for the last batting position and he justified his pick with an innings of 98 in the West Indies first innings 199. I was serving a long apprenticeship and it was becoming very frustrating. I wondered when I was ever going to make my début but it was one of the problems being associated with the leading side in world cricket. It was not easy to break in. The West Indies selectors were not renowned for making too many changes.

I felt my best opportunity would probably come on the next tour. No tour was scheduled later that year but when Pakistan's planned visit to India at the end of 1990 fell through after the countries failed to agree terms, the West Indies were invited to make their third visit to Pakistan in ten years, and I was chosen in the party. We journeyed to Pakistan via Toronto where we played a one-day fixture, and the day after our arrival, with no time to acclimatize, we played the first one-day international in the National Stadium, Karachi. Up to then I had appeared in front of comparatively small crowds. Now we were playing in our 200th one-day international in front of a volatile capacity crowd of 25,000 and it was very intimidating.

Pakistan batted first and Imran, reappointed captain the day before in preference to Javed Miandad after almost six months out of the game, helped them reach 211 in their 40 overs with an unbeaten 53. Imran came straight out and opened the bowling, dismissing Carlisle Best for a duck. Desmond Haynes, 67, and Richie Richardson, 69, put on 137 for the second wicket to quieten the crowd a little, and though I was down at number four in the order, Haynes, who skippered the side because Viv Richards had stayed at home in Antigua to recover from surgery, signalled to Gus Logie to come in ahead of me when Richardson was caught on the boundary off the bowling of Waqar Younis.

Waqar's early overs had gone for a lot of runs and he had to retire to the outfield while Haynes and Richardson were going so well. Now he was a different bowler. He bowled Logie first ball and I went in at 137–3 facing a hat-trick. The crowd were screeching 'Waqar, Waqar, Waqar', and as I took guard I looked round to see where wicket-keeper Salim Yousuf was standing. He seemed a long, long way back. Somehow I managed to survive the first ball. Then the second. Until that moment I had never faced a bowler who could bowl as fast as this and I had batted against all the West Indian fast bowlers and England's Devon Malcolm. None of them approached Waqar in speed and hostility. I made only 11. In seven balls he took 3 wickets for 6 runs, finishing with 5–52. We lost that match and we also lost the remaining two one-day matches, which I didn't play in.

My next game was against the Combined XI at Sargodha, and going in at 3 I made my fifth first-class century, 139 off 270 balls in our total of 367. I knew I had to take every opportunity to impress. Perhaps if Viv Richards had not declared his unavailability I would have been back working as a clerk for Angostura Bitters. Carlisle Best and Gus Logie, experienced players I looked up to, had given me bats when I was much younger and were now ahead of me as contenders for a place in the middle order.

I missed out on the first two Tests, the first in Karachi won by Pakistan by 8 wickets and the second by the West Indies in Faisalabad, but was chosen for the third and last Test in the Gaddafi Stadium in Lahore after Carlisle Best damaged the webbing of his right hand in a fielding practice.

Once again, I found myself going in at a time when

the Pakistanis were right on top and the batting side was under great pressure. Gordon Greenidge, who had a miserable tour averaging 9.66, went early and so did Richie Richardson, who was surprised to be given out lbw. There were twenty-five lbw decisions in the three-match series, only four of them against Pakistan. The score was 24–2 when I reached the crease and I was caught at the wicket off a no-ball and nearly popped a catch to short leg off the bowling of Wasim Akram before I succeeded in getting off the mark twenty minutes later. Akram, with 9 wickets in the match, was a more effective bowler than Younis who by this time was beginning to look tired.

There had been talk among the players about the way those bowlers managed to swing the old ball but there were no protests. I couldn't remember either umpire Khizar Hayat and Riazuddin, at twenty-six the youngest umpire ever in Test cricket, spending too much time examining the ball. As a newcomer in Test cricket I didn't feel it was my place to get involved. I played and missed a few times and was dropped by Salim Malik at slip off Younis when I had reached 42, but I still rated my 44 as one of my most disciplined innings. I was quite pleased with myself even though my two-hour innings was ended by a catch at short leg by Aamer Malik off the bowling of Abdul Qadir.

Carl Hooper and I added 95 for the third wicket on a slow, low pitch full of cracks and it dug us out of trouble. We were all highly delighted for Carl after he reached 134, his second Test hundred, which came three years and thirty-seven innings after his first. He showed in that match what a great temperament he has. Test cricket is about mental strength as much as ability. With the number of overs reduced to sixty a day because of the shortage of light in Pakistan at that time of year, and other diversions such as a presentation ceremony with the State President, we were forced to go for quick runs in the second innings and I was one of several who went cheaply, caught at mid on by Salim Malik off Imran for 5 in 24 balls. Wasim, who shared 37 wickets in the series with Waqar, took 4 wickets in 5 balls at the end of the innings. He would have had a hat-trick if Imran had held a reasonably easy catch off Bishop at mid on.

Pakistan's target was 346, a near impossible one in the conditions, and Imran, unbeaten on 58 in 292 minutes, saved them from defeat. It was tense as Haynes crowded the bat with fielders who appealed constantly. Play was held up for five minutes when Courtney Walsh, fielding at third man, was struck a painful blow on the back by a missile thrown from the crowd. Courtney was very upset about it and had to go off for treatment. Some other players were hit by apples.

Pakistan is a dangerous place to play cricket. The behaviour of many of the spectators there resembled the worst excesses of hooligans at English football matches in the recent past. Firecrackers were going off all the time, hampering visibility. However, I was glad to have the chance to tour there and was naturally very pleased to have made my Test début at long last.

My next Test appearance did not happen until seventeen months later, in April 1992 against South Africa at the Kensington Oval, Barbados. And that can be considered the most frustrating time in my cricket career, especially as I had had a record-breaking season in the 1991 Red Stripe Cup competition, setting a new record aggregate of 627 runs in ten innings, seven of which yielded me scores of over 60. I averaged 69.66 and the only person in the competition who beat that was Desmond Haynes, who took my record away from me a week later when he finished the season with 654 runs, average 109. I scored an unbeaten 122 in the drawn match against Jamaica at Sabina Park, and when I received a call to go there at the end of February to join the West Indies squad I thought I had a good chance of making my home début in the First Test against the Australians. That was despite not being chosen for the President's XI that drew with the Australians earlier in the month. To my dismay, I was named as twelfth man. That killed my spirits. I didn't know what I had to do to impress the selectors. I had outscored all the Test players in the Red Stripe with the exception of Desmond Haynes. I would have loved to have continued my Test career against the Australians.

My only appearances against the tourists were for the West Indies Board XI at Kensington Oval, where I scored 56 and 36, and for the West Indies Under-23 XI at Arnos Vale, St Vincent, when I scored 22 and 4. I was captain of the Under-23 side and an indication of my state of mind at the time was that I dropped three catches and held two in a drawn match.

The series against Australia produced a lot of bad feeling with the umpires making reports about bad language in the middle and Viv Richards criticizing the Australian coach Bob Simpson. The West Indies won 2–1 to keep their world crown, and they did it with the same eleven players, perhaps the only occasion a side has gone through a series without making changes. They lost Ian Bishop before the series started with a stress fracture of the back which was to keep him out of cricket for nearly two years. Ian played in our first match for Trinidad and Tobago and bowled 29 overs before it was discovered that he had the injury and needed a long rest.

The Trinidadian public were upset about losing such

a fine cricketer and they were also unhappy about my exclusion from the Test side. But no-one was more upset than me.

CHAPTER FOUR

PLEASE LET ME GO HOME!

ALL MY FRUSTRATIONS ABOUT HAVING MY TEST CAREER delayed for so long came out at Edgbaston the day before the Fourth Test between England and the West Indies started there in 1991. A few weeks earlier Viv Richards told me: 'Don't worry about your pick for England. You'll be in the sixteen.' I wondered why I hadn't played in the home series against the Australians if I was that much of a certainty. I had been in the best form of my life and some of the players who played in all five matches hadn't established themselves.

The 1991 tour of England was the most miserable period of my life and everything boiled up that day at Edgbaston. I was bowling to Viv Richards in the indoor nets when he drove the ball back to me and, trying to jump out of the way, I came down awkwardly on my ankle. It hurt a lot and I had to be helped back to the dressing-room. By this time tears were welling in my eyes and when I got there I burst into tears and said to Lance Gibbs, the manager: 'I want my air ticket to go home. I've had enough!'

'Calm down,' he said. 'Tell me what happened.' It wasn't the incident in the nets. It was an accumulation of all the slights I felt I had endured on the tour. I was twenty-two, eager to advance my career, and I hadn't been given a chance. When Gordon Greenidge was injured early on the tour, Clayton Lambert, the 29-year-old left-hander who was playing for Blackhall, the North Yorkshire and Durham League club, was called in and played in the last Test at the Oval. That was the solitary Test of his career.

I felt I tried to have as much respect as I could for the senior players but didn't think some of them showed the younger ones much respect back. One of them had made a remark at practice which implied I got into the side because Joey Carew was a selector. This was a senior player whom I idolized and it disturbed me greatly. I was thoroughly dismayed at the atmosphere around this time.

In practice, I was usually the last person to bat which often meant that the manager or some of the non-bowlers were the only ones left to bowl at me. I am happy now that that has changed. An incident in an Indian restaurant after our defeat in the First Test at Headingley hadn't helped my relations with Lance Gibbs. We were bowled out for 173 and 162 and England owed their first victory over a West Indies side since 1969 to a magnificent unbeaten 154 by Graham Gooch, their captain. Gooch showed the application and high level of concentration needed to combat the conditions and during dinner I said to David Williams, the reserve wicket-keeper, that I didn't think we had batted too well.

Gibbs heard me and said: 'A player like you wouldn't

have scored many anyway at Leeds. You would have been a failure.' I resented the way he said it, as if he wanted to do me down. He may have been a great bowler for the West Indies but I don't think he was a good manager. His handling of certain players, me included, could have been much better. 'You think you can bat like Gary Sobers,' he said.

'I don't know yet if I can bat like Gary Sobers,' I said. 'But I would like to achieve what he has achieved.' For the rest of the summer I tried to stay out of his way.

Now we were face to face in the visitors' dressing-room at Edgbaston and I had to explain why I wanted to go home. He said he would speak to Viv Richards about it. As I was unlikely to be fit in time for the Oval Test in just over a week's time, he saw no reason why I ought not to be released. I went to hospital for treatment and finished up having a plaster cast put on my foot.

I had to accept that the only way I would get into the side was to wait for someone to retire. I had been seen as a one-day cricketer. I played in the third Texaco Trophy international in front of a 24,871 crowd at Lord's but only because Greenidge was injured. I made 23 before being caught and bowled by Richard Illingworth in a high-scoring game. The West Indies lost all three one-day games and that gave a little more confidence to Gooch's side, who went on to draw the Cornhill series 2–2.

After that I seemed to have travelled all round the world playing one-day matches – in Sharjah, Karachi, Lahore, Faisalabad, Perth, Melbourne, Adelaide, Sydney, Brisbane, Christchurch, Auckland, Wellington, Berri and Kingston before I finally became a regular in the Test side. Too much one-day cricket is not good for a young player. It doesn't help his development especially if he is a batsman.

I learned a lot from my unhappy experiences in England. It made me stronger mentally. I resolved that I would score so many runs that the selectors wouldn't be able to ignore me. I would force my selection on them and give them no alternative but to choose me. It also gave me more understanding of how young players should be treated. Some of the senior men in the 1991 side may have been great cricketers who contributed a lot to West Indies cricket, but their attitude towards newcomers could have been different. Now I would like to encourage youngsters rather than show them indifference. If I ever become captain, I will make a point of that.

I played at Bristol and Worcester in the two opening matches of the tour, scoring 30 against Gloucestershire in a one-day game and 26 against Worcestershire. Phil Newport bowled me at New Road, the first of several occasions when he has dismissed me. Viv Richards scored a typical 131 from 153 balls in a drawn game and his great friend Ian Botham upstaged him with 161 in 139 balls.

Two weeks later I thought I had helped my chances of a pick in the Test side by scoring 93 against Somerset at Taunton, but after scoring 3 and 26 in the next match against Leicestershire, falling victim to the Australian John Maguire in both innings, I learned that Phil Simmons was going to open in the First Test at Headingley with Dessie Haynes. I could understand that they wanted a specialist opener and Phil Simmons, who is someone I think very highly of, fitted the bill. Unfortunately he didn't have a very successful series, but later on he made a number of important contributions to the success of the West Indies side. He's a strong, very positive player but his record would be much better if he had been tighter.

I failed at Derby and Northampton but was more hopeful after an innings of 75 against Hampshire at

Southampton before the Nottingham Test. I scored 82 against the Minor Counties at Darlington and the same against Wales at Brecon but by this time I had given up hope, and when I damaged the ligaments of my ankle at Edgbaston that was my tour finished. I appreciate that with an average of 24.57 from 344 first-class runs (the matches against the Minor Counties and Wales were not first-class) I hadn't exactly forced my way into the reckoning with a good tally of runs, but I still think that with more encouragement and help I would have contributed more to that tour.

Because of the World Series and the World Cup in Australia and New Zealand, I was only able to take part in three matches for Trinidad and Tobago in the 1992 Red Stripe Cup competition, scoring 135 in the opening game against Barbados, and averaging 47, but we won the Grant Geddes Shield by beating Barbados by 8 wickets. Viv Richards retired, Gus Logie was about to retire – and I found myself playing my second Test in seventeen months against South Africa in April. Since then I have made sure I stayed in the side.

CHAPTER FIVE

ONE-DAY CRICKET

I AM NOT AN ADMIRER OF ONE-DAY CRICKET BECAUSE IT IS not a true test of ability, but I do see the need for it because it brings in much-needed revenue and attracts large crowds. The introduction of night cricket, the wearing of coloured clothing and the use of a white ball have contributed to the popularization of the sport. I think these ideas add to the excitement of one-day matches. They are good for the heartbeat. There is room for all this in cricket as a money-making aside to real cricket. But when it starts to take over and Test cricket is cut back to accommodate it, then the time has come for the authorities to act. The International Cricket Council should in my view be tackling this problem in the interests of the game.

In limited-overs cricket the batsman has to take risks to score quickly from the start. It is easier to be tempted into playing loose shots. When you are out doing that there is no blame attached to you because risk-taking is demanded. The batsmen can easily pick up bad habits. In England, for example, you often see batsmen backing away to leg trying to force the ball through the offside when bowlers are bowling on a line of leg stump with a legside field. Batsmen will be trying to reverse sweep off the spin bowlers. Warwickshire have a number of players who are particularly skilled at playing the shot. I never play it myself because it has too high a risk attached to it. It has come into vogue because of the growth of one-day cricket. Like the hook shot, it often gets batsmen out. Its disadvantages outweigh the advantages.

In the 1994 season Warwickshire won 22 of their 26 one-day matches to prove they were the outstanding one-day side in the country. My contribution, however, was not great. I scored only 364 runs off 462 deliveries in the Sunday League. That was a much slower rate than I scored my runs in first-class cricket. I tried to play the same way as I did in normal cricket except that I had to force the pace more. Technically, I batted the same way which is the West Indian approach. We do not adjust because it is a limited-overs game.

Spectators go in their thousands to one-day matches because they think they are more exciting than other forms of cricket. But that is not so. One-day cricket is in the main a boring game. Once the side batting second falls well behind the necessary run-rate everyone knows the result. Or if a side is asked to bat first when conditions favour the bowlers, the game is over as a contest if they make a low total and the opposition are able to bat in much better conditions. That happened in both the Benson and Hedges Final and the NatWest Trophy Final in 1994. There is no draw to play for once the side batting second is unable to win.

In the field the emphasis is on limiting runs so the fielders are pushed back and the bowlers tend to bowl defensively. After the early overs, the close fielders are taken out and it becomes a defensive strategy. In Test cricket fortunes swing one way then the other, but that does not happen so much in one-day cricket.

Australia was the venue of my first World Cup in February and March 1992. It was a successful tournament for me but not for the team. I opened with Desmond Haynes in the eight matches we played and was our highest scorer with 333 runs, average 47.57, and a strike rate of 81.61 per 100 balls. The eventual winners were Pakistan who faced elimination after their disastrous early-round results, including a 10-wicket defeat by the West Indies in their opening match. It was a painful start for me. I was on 88 off 101 balls when Wasim Akram caught me on the foot with a yorker and I had to be helped off by Phil Simmons, whose place I had taken. Wasim, who is up with Waqar, Ian Bishop and Curtly Ambrose as one of the fastest bowlers in the world, bowls the yorker as well as anyone.

At this pace, well above 80 mph, there is little to choose between these bowlers in pace. Just how quick they are on a certain day will depend on the state of the pitch, the ball, the conditions and the state of the game. That World Cup was the first opportunity many of the world's batsmen had to see South Africa's Allan Donald. He is similar in pace to the others and deserved his 13 wickets in the competition. Akram, who didn't have Waqar to support him because of a stress fracture in a bone in his back, finished the leading wicket-taker with 18 wickets at 18.77. Wasim is more dangerous because of his extra variety. He bowls both sides of the wicket and moves the ball both ways. He also bowls an extremely testing bouncer as well as a bruising yorker.

My right foot was still very sore when our next match took place against England at Melbourne four days later and it was no surprise that I went early for a duck, caught behind by Alec Stewart off the bowling of Chris Lewis. I had a hole cut in the toe of the boot to help ease the pain. The first ball I received hit me a painful blow in the box and the second got me. I was one of seven batsmen who failed to reach double figures, and though the conditions favoured England's swing bowlers our total of 157 was far too short of the target, and in front of a crowd of 18,170 England won comfortably by six wickets.

Desmond and Curtly were rested for the next match against Zimbabwe in Brisbane two days later and Richie Richardson was unhappy with our total of 264. He thought we should have been more ruthless in our approach. With the bruise on my right big toe giving me less trouble I was able to score a run-a-ball 72. Zimbabwe could only reach 189–7 in their 50 overs.

The tournament was partly staged in New Zealand and our next match was in Christchurch against the South Africans. It was our first official match against the South Africans and it proved a disaster, especially in the field. Richie Richardson sent the opposition in on a well-grassed pitch and they owed their 200–8 to a gritty 56 from the experienced Peter Kirsten. I was out for 9 and again there was a dreadful collapse with Richardson, Hooper and Arthurton making only one run between them. Haynes came back after two painful blows on the index finger to score 30 and Gus Logie made a brilliant 61 from 69 balls. We were all out for 136 in 38.4 overs.

Our decline continued three days later at Auckland when a crowd of 28,999 wildly excited Kiwis cheered the home side to a 5-wicket victory. Martin Crowe won the toss and put us in and opened the bowling with Dipak Patel, the off-spin bowler who used to play for Worcestershire. On a slow pitch, Patel was so accurate that his ten overs cost only 19 runs and put us well behind the necessary run rate. I made 52 in our total of 203–7 but it was hard going against defensive bowling and well-set fields. The left-hander Mark Greatbatch, who was on a great run at the time, won it for his side with a rapid half-century off the same number of balls. He hit sixes, off Malcolm Marshall over extra cover, Anderson Cummins over square leg, and Curtly Ambrose over third man. When he was caught on the cover boundary for 63, Crowe took over with an unbeaten 81 from as many balls. Play was stopped when Winston Benjamin was hit by missiles thrown from the crowd. While police moved in, Richie Richardson called the players together for a brief talk but it proved to be in vain.

We kept our chances of reaching the semi-finals alive by beating India by 5 runs in Wellington two days later after the rain reduced our target to 195 off 46 overs. We reached it with 5.3 overs to spare after I hit 41 off 37 balls and Keith Arthurton made an unbeaten 54. Malcolm Marshall was dropped for that match and it was sadly the end of a great career. Phil Simmons took over and bowled a full complement of nine overs. In one-day cricket he is a useful medium-pace bowler.

Simmons was the key man in our 91-run victory over Sri Lanka, scoring 110 off 123 balls and justifying his selection. In 40° heat, the Sri Lankans appeared exhausted after a schedule that was even more hectic than the one we had undergone. Facing our total of 268–8, they were 177–9 at the end of their 50 overs. The organizers wanted to take the tournament to as many places as possible and Berri, a small fruit-growing town by the Murray River in South Australia, was definitely the smallest place used. Only 2,650 people turned up and it was almost like playing in a club game.

The West Indies had to win the final qualifying game against Australia in Melbourne on 18 March to reach the semi-finals but it was to be another disappointment in front of a noisy crowd of 47,572 spectators. Facing Australia's total of 216–6, we lost half the side for 99 runs, and any chance I had of turning things round ended on 70 when I called for a sharp single and Winston Benjamin refused to run.

Pakistan, roused by Imran's call 'to fight like cornered tigers', surprised everyone by going on to beat England in the final by 22 runs. Most of us agreed with Richardson's view that 'all the other teams have improved a helluva lot and are no longer afraid of us'. But we should have performed better than we did.

The South Africans had shown their quality in the World Cup when they lost to England in the semi-final in a farcical match ruined by rain. Their target at the end was 22 from 13 deliveries, but after another stoppage it was revised to 22 off one delivery. Everyone sympathized with them about that. It should never have been allowed to happen.

Just over two weeks later, Kepler Wessels and his players arrived in Kingston for the first of the three one-day matches against the West Indies, and with only 72 hours to acclimatize found themselves under-prepared. The nets in Kingston were poor and they were further handicapped by not having a white ball, which tended to swing more in the World Cup than the red ball normally used in one-day internationals.

The match was one-sided, South Africa scoring 180 in 42.2 overs in reply to the West Indies 287–6, their highest one-day total on the ground. The South Africans couldn't contain the hitting of Phil Simmons, who struck five sixes in his 122 off 113 balls. One, off the slow left-arm bowler Omar Henry, sailed out of the ground and there was a five-minute delay while police retrieved the ball from a souvenir hunter. A foretaste of the insularity that was to be found later in Barbados was the way the home crowd in Jamaica booed Richie Richardson in protest against the omission of the local hero Jeff Dujon from the World Cup party.

The second game in Port of Spain was even more one-sided. The South Africans contributed to their own downfall in their innings of 152 in 43.4 overs and we passed it in only 25.5 overs without losing a wicket. Dessie Haynes and myself were both unbeaten on 59 and 86 respectively. Simmons scored his third one-day hundred in four matches in the third and final game, also at Port of Spain, and the West Indies won easily by 7 wickets.

There is a tremendous atmosphere at day–night one day internationals in Australia and the players respond to it. I have been critical of one-day cricket but I am the first to agree there are good games in this form of cricket, matches that spectators can appreciate. One of the most exciting I have played in was the Australia v. West Indies second final match in the Benson and Hedges World Series Cup in the 1992–3 season at Melbourne. The crowd was 72,492 and the noise was electrifying. It was such a stimulating match because it was low-scoring and so tight.

Australia batted first and finished with 147 off 47.3 overs, with Curtly Ambrose taking 3–26 to claim the man of the match award. Three Australian batsmen were run out by direct throws, which is one of the most thrilling parts of the game, especially when there is a call for the off-field umpire to make a decision. The West Indies made a poor start losing Desmond Haynes, run out for a duck, Phil Simmons for a duck and Richie Richardson for 5. At 23–3 we were in trouble and the crowd was baying for more wickets. I opened the innings as I often do for the West Indies in one-day cricket. I do not like opening because it means you are facing the new ball and the chances of being dismissed are greater, but I will do it if asked in limited-overs cricket to help the team. Carl Hooper, who was 59 not out at the end, helped me add 86 for the fourth wicket before I was caught in the gully off the 100th ball I faced for 60. It was one of my best one-day innings. Ian Bishop joined Hooper, and in an extremely tense finish the West Indies just made it with 6 wickets down.

It gave us our sixth victory in eight World Series competitions in Australia. The first final in Sydney was also won by us, by a margin of 25 runs in front of a crowd of 37,581. I opened in that match, too, and my innings of 67 helped us on our way to a total of 239–8. Ambrose, fired up when Dean Jones insisted he remove his white wrist bands, had remarkable figures of 5–32 in Australia's 214. Each country, Australia, West Indies and Pakistan, played eight matches before the two final games so it meant we took part in ten one-day internationals.

These matches make so much money that the danger now is that more and more countries are switching their schedules to accommodate more one-day games. When I toured India at the end of that year we were scheduled to play only three Tests but ten one-day internationals. In fact, that was later halved because of an outbreak of the plague. In Pakistan the trend is similar. In the West Indies, we usually play a five-match one-day series alongside the Tests, which are either five or three in number. South Africa, now they are back in world cricket, have also gone for the one-day option, packing their schedule with these matches.

I think the pendulum has swung too far and cricket will suffer as a result. There needs to be a reduction in one-day matches and an increase in five-day Test matches which represent all the best values of the game. The highest form of cricket is Test cricket and that needs to be preserved at all costs. Only England, in my view, has the balance right. The Test and County Cricket Board believes that three one-day internationals is enough when a tour takes place and it insists that five, or six Tests when the West Indies or Australia tour, is the right number. When two countries tour England playing three Tests each, there are four one-day games, two against each country. The temptation is there to play more one-day internationals but so far the TCCB seems to have resisted it. Sponsored competitions are springing up all over the cricket-playing world to accommodate this craving to add more one-day matches to the already overcrowded programme. Only England and the West Indies remain traditionalists.

In the 1991–2 season I played in 25 one-day internationals; the year after the total was 22. In the 1993–4 season it was 19 in ten different cities or towns. In late October and early November 1993 the West Indies won the Pepsi Champions Trophy in Sharjah, beating Pakistan in the final by 6 wickets, and it was the fourth one-day series involving the countries in less than a year. Basit Ali played an exceptional innings of 127 in only 79 balls to confirm that he is one of the rising stars of world cricket. My 153 in 142 balls proved to be the third-highest one-day score by a West Indian and we passed Pakistan's 284 with 4.3 overs to spare.

Four days after the final, the West Indies were taking on Sri Lanka in the second match of the Hero Cup competition, staged to celebrate the sixtieth anniversary of the Bengal Cricket Association. The venue was the Wankhede Stadium in Bombay and we won by 48 runs in an uneventful match. Only five countries took part. Pakistan were ordered to withdraw by their government after threats from militant Hindu groups.

India, the hosts, were in danger of not reaching the final after the West Indies bowled them out for 99, but they hung on to force a tie against Zimbabwe, each side making 248 runs in exactly 50 overs, and beat South Africa by 43 runs. In the semi-finals India just beat South Africa by 2 runs and we beat Sri Lanka by 6 wickets. The tournament was dogged by bad behaviour from spectators. At Ahmedabad, during the first match against India, our players were pelted with fruit, bottles and any kind of rubbish the locals could lay their hands on. The game was held up and we spent forty minutes in the middle of the pitch while police restored order. Later, Keith Arthurton had to leave the field for treatment to his eyes after a firecracker exploded near him. There was also a dispute about television coverage.

The final, India v. West Indies, was played in front of a volatile 100,000 crowd at Eden Gardens in Calcutta, the world's largest cricket ground, and with the semi-finals having been played on the same pitch it was not a high-scoring match. India's 225-7 ought not to have presented too many problems but on a pitch of uneven bounce Anil Kumble took the last 6 wickets for 26 runs to record figures of 6.1–2–12–6, the best by an Indian bowler in one-day internationals. I was top scorer with 33 in our total of 123. It was a disappointing finale.

There was a peculiar incident when Roland Holder played defensively to a delivery from Kumble and the bails fell off. Neither umpire Ian Robinson nor Carl Liebenberg of South Africa saw how it happened and sought assistance from the third umpire, Dr Sekhar Chodhuri. After rerunning the video, Dr Chodhuri pressed the out button and Holder was given out bowled. But as Richie Richardson pointed out, the third umpire had no jurisdiction over whether a batsman was bowled or not and it seemed odd that this particular official came from one of the two competing countries in the final.

CHAPTER SIX

MEMORABLE TEST MATCHES

THE NIGHT BEFORE THE FINAL DAY OF THE INAUGURAL FIRST TEST between the West Indies and South Africa on 22 April 1992, I was having a drink or two in a bar in Bridgetown called 'Harbour Lights' when I spotted some of the South African players.

'Don't drink too much,' I said. 'You'll be batting early in the morning.' One of them said: 'I don't think so.' Needing 201 to win, the South Africans were 122–2 and the West Indies record of not having lost in Barbados since 1935 was in dire danger. We especially did not want to lose to South Africa as this was their first Test match since sporting links with that country had been cut. We did not like the implication of losing to them, of all nations, as we had always felt supported by many black Africans. So it meant a lot to us to preserve our record in Barbados.

One of the players chided me about whether I would be wide enough awake to take a catch if it came my way. He was off target with that jibe because I took five catches in the match and my effort to dismiss the South African captain Kepler Wessels the next morning was one of the best catches I have ever made.

The South Africans were giving the impression that they would win the match and I think that hardened our resolve to make sure they didn't. Next morning I saw Richard Snell, who took 8 wickets in the match, and said: 'You remember what I told you last night? You've got it coming.' He laughed.

Snell was soon at the crease. And soon back in the pavilion. He was one of five players who made ducks as his side's last 8 wickets went down for 26 runs. The match was over twenty minutes before lunch with the West Indies victors by 52 runs. It was one of the most amazing turnarounds in the history of Test cricket.

One-day cricket bears little relation to Test cricket, and we had known that the South Africans would be much stronger opponents in this solitary Test in Barbados than they had been in the three one-day matches. We were suffering from the disadvantage of not having played in a Test since the one at the Oval in August 1991, and since that time we had played 26 one-day internationals. Wessels won the toss and, following the example of the winning captains in the previous ten Test matches at the ground, asked the opposition to bat. At 219–3 we were in a reasonable position but the last 7 wickets fell for the addition of only 43 more runs.

Hudson, a solid, phlegmatic player, was immovable in the South African innings of 345 which gave them a useful lead of 83. But he was fortunate to reach 163. Walsh dropped him at long leg on 22 and wicket-keeper

David Williams missed him on 66. This was the first match played by the West Indies fast bowlers when the new ICC restriction of one bouncer per over was in force. I think it inhibited the bowlers, none of whom looked particularly penetrating. Jimmy Adams, with his slow left-hand spin, was the most successful bowler with 4–43. Jimmy is a very underrated bowler. When conditions suit him, he is a very useful all-rounder to have in your side. He is also a top-class wicket-keeper.

The third day was full of controversy. Dessie Haynes, who made 23, saw the second ball of the innings from Allan Donald roll back on to the stumps and fail to dislodge the bails. When I reached my maiden Test fifty I tried to work a delivery from Tertius Bosch down to fine leg and set off for a run. I felt my back foot may have touched something but when Hansie Cronje, fielding in the gully, said: 'Hey, the bail is off!' I felt confident that I wasn't out under Law 35, as my interpretation of it was that I completed my shot. The umpires, David Archer and Steve Bucknor, conferred, and not having seen the incident decided I was not out. There was some murmuring from the South Africans but I didn't feel like walking because it was so confusing.

If a third umpire had been watching a TV monitor he might well have been able to clear the matter up and I would have accepted his decision. I tend to move my back foot quite a way back but this was the first time it happened to me. Fourteen runs were added to my score before I was given out by Archer, caught by wicket-keeper David Richardson. I was sure the ball hit my pad, not the bat, and Allan Donald, the bowler, later said he thought I hadn't touched the ball. These things happen at the highest level and you just have to hope they are balanced out. I was very annoyed because I felt my first Test hundred was coming up.

We were 164–6 at one stage, only 81 ahead, but Jimmy Adams bailed us out with an authoritative 79 not out in 221 minutes. It was his Test début and he made sure it was a memorable one. The last wicket stand of 62 with Patrick Patterson was a real match-saver. Without it the West Indies would have lost.

Curtly Ambrose took out both openers, Mark Rushmere and Hudson, one of my five victims at slip, and at 27–2 we were back in the game. That changed, however, when Wessels and Peter Kirsten, the most experienced batsmen in the South African side, added 95 in the remaining 42 overs that day.

Before play resumed on the final day we had a team meeting at which Richie Richardson emphasized how important it was not to lose. We had to be convinced we could do it and show mental strength. Courtney Walsh was the bowler who inspired the victory with a dynamic spell of 4–8 in 11 overs. Once he removed Wessels for 74 and Kirsten for 52 the other batsmen went quietly, Curtly Ambrose picking up 6 wickets for 34 runs in 24.4 overs.

Afterwards Clyde Walcott, the then President of the West Indies Board of Control, now Chairman of the ICC, said to me: 'I hear you are the person who should be man of the match.' I had scored 17 and 64 and held five catches but that hadn't compared with the maiden Test hundred, 153 in eight hours forty minutes, of the South African opener Andrew Hudson and the 8 wickets for 81 runs of Curtly Ambrose. Hudson and Ambrose shared the man of the match award.

'Why?' I asked Mr Walcott.

'Because you had the South Africans out until four in the morning,' he said.

I was embarrassed that he had found out. Actually it was two o'clock, not four. It was not something I did every night, especially in my second Test, but my philosophy has always been that I have to feel comfortable and relaxed. And if that means going out for a drink I will do it. Some of my team-mates relax by going to their rooms early, having a meal from room service and watching videos. They might feel that suits them but sometimes I have the urge to meet my friends and listen to a little music.

Now I am vice-captain I won't be staying out too late. That would set a bad example to the younger players. It is part of the West Indian way of life to have a drink and talk and listen to music and I don't think anything will ever change that. It is what suits the individual best. If I had to sit in my room I know I would be miserable. That would not help me get into the right frame of mind for the next day's play. I might still go out occasionally but I would never do anything which would jeopardize my career. The West Indies players are left to make their own decision about when to go to bed and they are very professional about that. They know how much success on the cricket field means to them and the people they represent. The only time in my experience a curfew was imposed was in the World Cup in 1992. It was the idea of the manager, Deryck Murray. Personally I do not think curfews work because there is always the temptation to break them. Each individual will know what is best for him.

I would never stay out until 2 a.m. in a Test match now, but one bonus from that incident at the 'Harbour Lights' was that I was able to tell my colleagues that the South Africans were celebrating victory in advance, and that fired up Courtney Walsh and Curtly Ambrose, who bowled them out.

That Test match was one of the most extraordinary of recent times. Hardly anyone watched it because of a boycott by the Barbados public, who were upset at the exclusion of Anderson Cummins from the side and other imagined slights, like the failure to make a Bajan, Desmond Haynes, captain in succession to Viv Richards, and the way Malcolm Marshall's career ended. I thought it was terrible that such a campaign could be mounted because it threatened the future of West Indies cricket which is one of the few unifying forces in the West Indies. I couldn't see the point of the protest and it was sad that some commentators backed it.

On the final morning only 500 people were present but they made plenty of noise. The attendance was given as 6,500 for the five days and there was hardly any atmosphere. Some of the attendances at county games in England are as low as this but you do not expect it for the first-ever match in the Caribbean between the West Indies and South Africa. Fortunately for the West Indies Board, who find it hard to cover the expenses of Test series, BP paid for the expenses of the South African team so the tour did not make a loss. The Board actually made a profit for the first time in fifteen years.

At the end of the game all eleven West Indian players linked hands as they went on a lap of honour around the near deserted ground, 'to show the people of the Caribbean how united we are' in the words of Richie Richardson. It was his first Test as captain after the ending of the Richards–Greenidge–Marshall–Dujon era. He was relieved at the outcome and so were all the players.

In the next Test series, we went down to Australia for five Test matches and the World series. This was the best series I have ever played in and fortunately for me contained two memorable Test matches. For the first time since 1972–3 there were no Viv Richards or Gordon Greenidge in our side. Also missing were Jeffrey Dujon and Malcolm Marshall, our highest wicket-taker in Tests. I had played in only a few Tests and was not certain to be picked. My anxiety increased after I was asked to open in the match against New South Wales in November and was dismissed for 16 and 3, caught by wicket-keeper Phil Emery off the bowling of Wayne Holdsworth on each occasion. I was not happy about opening and never have been in first-class cricket, but when Richie Richardson told me I was starting with Phil Simmons I had to make the best of it. When you open, you have to play in front of the wicket more and I find that restricting. If you open the face of the bat you stand more chance of being caught.

As Gus Logie, the vice-captain, was one short of a century when he was run out I thought he might be preferred to me for the First Test in Brisbane. Fortunately for me he wasn't, and going in 4 in the first innings I made 58, after we were 58–3, helping Keith Arthurton, who made a magnificent 157 not out, put on 122 for the fourth wicket in our first innings 371, which gave us a lead of 78. There was a lot of appealing by the Australians, particularly at the end of the match when Ian Bishop and Courtney Walsh blocked out the final six overs. We were set to score 231 from a minimum of 65 overs and with Richie Richardson going well we had a chance of winning. But when he was out for 66 he called a halt to the run-chase which I had failed to support. I was caught at slip by Mark Taylor off Craig McDermott for nought.

The Australians were particularly aggrieved that they won so few lbw decisions. There were only eleven in the whole series. With every decision they make being analysed in great depth on television, umpires have to be very sure they do not make a mistake and many err on the side of caution. There was criticism of the umpires at the time and it was felt Australia ought to have independent umpires. If the International Cricket Council could afford to pay for neutral umpires at every Test series I think the players would welcome that, but at the moment there is a compromise with National Grid sponsoring the expenses of one umpire from a different country in each series.

Both Allan Border, Australia's captain, and Merv Hughes were in trouble in that game with the ICC match referee Raman Subba Row for comments about the pitch and Border was fined 2,000 Australian dollars, or half of his match fee, and Hughes 400 Australian dollars. Border failed to show up for his hearing. The tall West Australian Bruce Reid had figures of 7–151 off 53 overs and was likely to be a key performer for Australia. But he broke down with a bad back before the Second Test in Melbourne and it was left to the wholehearted Merv Hughes to carry out most of the pace bowling along with Craig McDermott. Merv, immensely popular with the crowds, took 20 wickets in the series at 21 apiece.

After shading it over four days we had come close to defeat and knew we had to improve in the next Test at Melbourne. Border won the toss again and with the pitch expected to wear, it was a blow to us. Mark Waugh upset Ambrose by the way he kept backing away to hit over the slips and Curtly was not amused when chances were missed off Waugh on 20 and 72. Curtly rarely says much on the field but his body language says it all. Eventually he had Waugh caught by wicket-keeper David Williams for 112. Border made a characteristic 110 and Australia's 395 was a potentially match-winning innings.

Our first innings 233 was a poor effort, with Keith Arthurton again playing well for his 71. I managed 52 and it was a sign of the slowness of the huge Melbourne outfield that we ran two fours and eleven threes in our stand of 105. If Peter Burge had been the ICC match referee I might have found myself being called in to explain myself because when I was given out lbw by umpire Steve Randell off the left-arm over the wicket bowling of Mark Whitney I raised my bat indicating I thought I had hit it. I felt sure I had made contact but when the umpire signalled I was out, I left the wicket without saying anything. A similar thing happened in the NatWest Final when I showed my bat to Tom Moody to indicate I had hit the ball. On that occasion I was given not out. I do not see anything wrong in that. It is not blatant dissent. It would be different if a batsman knew he hadn't hit the ball and was trying to con the umpire.

There is a lot of agitation now to have more electronic aids to help umpires. A device could probably be fitted to the bat which would confirm whether the ball was hit but I do not think such aids are a good thing for the game. We must leave decisions to the umpires wherever possible.

The crowd at Melbourne topped 50,000 on one of the days, the biggest crowds I have ever played in front of outside India. The Australians enjoy themselves at games and make a lot of noise, much more than their counterparts in England. There is a carnival atmosphere; no-one sleeps there like they do at Lord's. It is very stimulating to play in Australia and the noise helps inspire the players.

Phil Simmons scored his maiden Test hundred in his twentieth Test innings in our second innings but it was not enough to prevent us losing by 139 runs. The last 9 wickets went down for 76 runs, with the recalled Shane Warne, playing in his fifth Test, taking 7–52, a fine piece of spin bowling. I was out to Whitney again, superbly caught close up at short leg by David Boon off a firmly struck shot. Boon is as good a short leg fielder as there is in the world. He is completely fearless and though he has been struck a few times he still stands there.

Following the draw at Sydney where I scored my 277 (see next chapter) we expected the pitch at Adelaide for the fourth Test to be the usual flat one favouring batsmen. But it had more grass on than usual which delighted our quartet of fast bowlers, Curtly Ambrose, Ian Bishop, Courtney Walsh and Kenneth Benjamin. They all played a part in our amazing victory by the closest ever margin in a Test, by just one run. It was crucial for us to win that Test or otherwise we would have ended our run of being unbeaten in a Test series since 1980. It was so close at the end that I remember wanting to cry, but until Craig McDermott was caught behind by Junior Murray I did not know whether to cry through disappointment or joy. McDermott couldn't withdraw his bat in time and it was the faintest of touches off the glove. The umpire Daryl Hair, my favourite talisman of an umpire, raised his finger and we embraced each other in our sheer delight. Mr Hair officiated at Sydney when I scored my 277 and he was also the neutral umpire at Antigua when I made 375.

Six of the previous seven Tests at the Adelaide Oval had been drawn producing three totals of over 500, three over 400, two individual double centuries and 21 single centuries. Usually wet weather meant the pitch had to be covered more than was customary and as Ambrose said: 'It was really good for fast bowling. You could have done almost anything and got away with it on that kind of track. It had a bit of bounce and a bit of movement.' Merv Hughes with 5–64 bowled particularly well in our first innings 252 in 67.3 overs and I top-scored with 52 before becoming McDermott's only victim of the innings. Bishop, bowling really fast, dismissed Mark Taylor in the second over and forced Justin Langer, a 22-year-old left-hander from Perth who was making his début, to go off for repairs when he split his helmet. David Boon was hit a painful blow on the forearm by Ambrose and also went off. He returned on the third day and was 39 not out when Ambrose, with 6–74, ended the innings at 213.

A remarkable 17 wickets fell for 259 runs on the third day, with the West Indies being bowled out for only 146 in their second innings. Only a courageous innings of 72 from Richie Richardson gave it any respectability. The last 6 wickets went down for 22 in nine overs with Tim May, who gives the ball a lot of spin, taking 5–5 in 32 deliveries on his home ground. It has to be said we didn't perform particularly well, Richardson excluded. The skipper passed his 5,000 runs in Test cricket during his innings. He was out to a sharply turning leg break from Shane Warne which he edged to Ian Healy.

Australia had two days to score the 186 runs they needed to regain the Worrell Trophy. Ambrose made a breakthrough in the fifth over, having Boon lbw for 0. Taylor, 7, failed again and when Ambrose removed both Steve and Mark Waugh and Allan Border, caught by Desmond Haynes at short leg fending off a shoulder-high delivery from Ambrose, the Australians were 72–5 and in serious trouble.

But Langer, appearing in a new helmet, batted with great courage and in partnership with Warne, and then May, gradually edged his side closer to the target. It was Australia Day and the ground started filling up as people realized that the home side might be capable of winning a Test they looked to have lost. The ratings on Channel 9, who were showing the match live, rose to 42 which is apparently a record for cricket. Langer who was brought in as a late replacement when Damien Martyn was injured in a pre-match practice, added 28 with Warne, who was dropped off successive balls, and a further 42 with May before his 4¼-hour innings of 54 ended with a catch to Junior Murray off Courtney Walsh's bowling. With Australia 144–9 we thought we had won again, but the last pair of May, who finished 42 not out, and McDermott took their stand to 39, three runs short of victory, when Walsh started the 79th over in murky light.

May got a single off the third ball and Haynes prevented what might have been the winning runs when he stopped a pull from McDermott from close range. The tension on the field was the tautest I can remember. The fielders were urging Courtney on and the last ball of the over was a testing one, short and rising. McDermott pulled back from it. We all went up in the slips, confident that his glove had made contact. Our celebrations afterwards were so boisterous that the management was later presented with a bill for 1,000 Australian dollars for what was described as 'incidental damage'. Richie Richardson said he knew Courtney would get a wicket with that ball. 'I never lost hope,' he said. That was one of the secrets of our success on that tour. We were never ready to accept defeat. Curtly claimed 10 wickets for 120 in 54 overs, a magnificent piece of sustained fast bowling.

He surpassed that in the final Test in Perth when his spell of 7–1 in 32 balls saw Australia collapse from 85–2 to 119 all out, and they lost the match by an innings and 25 runs and, with it, the series. Curtly's first innings figures of 18–9–25–7 were amazing. That was the best I had seen him bowl until his performance against England in Trinidad in 1993 when he bowled Mike Atherton's team out for 46. Six of those victims were caught by Junior Murray or the slip fielders. The pitch at the WACA is normally quicker than almost any other Test pitch in the world, and with the wind, known as 'the Fremantle Doctor', behind him, Curtly was awesome and he never bowled a bad ball. Almost every delivery was fast and rising and the batsman was forced to play it. Australia's first innings of 119 was their sixth-lowest total in 77 Tests against the West Indies and it had a demoralizing effect on Border's side. Border himself went to a first-ball duck, caught by Junior Murray off Ambrose, and failed to score second time round when Bishop bowled him. It was his first pair in 138 Tests.

Our batsmen made a quick start and we were 135–1 at the end of the first day with Phil Simmons unbeaten on 34 and me on 16. Dessie Haynes, who had one of his least successful series, had more bad luck when he was hit above the right eye hooking the new Australian fast bowler Jo Angel. Next day, 4 wickets went down rapidly, including mine without addition to my score, but Simmons, 80, Richardson, 47, Keith Arthurton, 77, and Murray, 37, saw us through to a commanding 322 which proved to be enough.

In Australia's second innings of 178 it was Ian Bishop's turn to do the damage with 6–40 from a fine, sustained burst of genuinely fast bowling, and his final figures for the series showed a total of 23 wickets at 20.87 apiece, proving that he was fully recovered from his stress fracture of the back. Curtly took just 2 wickets in Australia's second innings of 178 but finished the series with 33 wickets at 16.42 apiece.

Like many of the West Indian fast bowlers, Curtly was never coached. He was born in a small village, Swetes, in Antigua, where he still lives, and played cricket at his school, All Saints Secondary, until he was fourteen. He also played a lot of windball and tennis-ball cricket which encourages you to bowl pretty fast. The boys of the village played on a pasture near the school. Basketball was Curtly's favourite sport and he played for Swetes which had its own club. But to get anywhere in basketball you have to join a club in the USA and that didn't happen, so at the age of 21 he took up cricket again, and within two years was representing Antigua. Two years later he made his Test début. Ever since I have known him he has bowled the same way; his consistency is remarkable. As a person he is an extremely nice guy but he can be moody, and you have to be careful how you approach him. Success hasn't changed him. When he goes home he still plays cards and dominoes with the same people he knew when he was unknown. He is a regular attender at the Moravian Church in Swetes. Most of the players are religious and during that tour we would have a brief period saying prayers before our daily team meetings. Richie Richardson encouraged that and it became a regular feature.

Curtly also taught himself to play the guitar, and when he shared a room with Richie, who also plays a guitar, they would sing duets. He is also a lover of calypso and reggae music and when he goes home plays with a local band called the LA Crew, one of whose members is Kenneth Benjamin's brother who plays the bass guitar. A private person who shuns the spotlight, Curtly doesn't like giving press interviews but he had to in Perth after his match-winning performance.

After the victory in Perth, all sixteen members of the squad climbed aboard the four-wheel drive station wagon Curtly won for being voted Man of the Series and did a lap of honour with Richie playing a guitar borrowed from a spectator. We sang 'Rally round the West Indies' and Curtly's voice was one of the loudest.

Curtly's greatest asset as a bowler is his control. He can always hit a spot and deliver the ball at a height which unsettles the batsman. Earlier in his career he used to get a lot of wickets with yorkers but these days he uses it more sparingly. On his first tour in 1988 Malcolm Marshall told him that with his height no batsman should ever be able to drive him, and not many have since then. His great ambition is to become the third West Indian behind Marshall, 376, and Lance Gibbs, 309, to pass 300 wickets in Tests. If his fitness holds up he should do it, but he was forced to miss the 1994 trip to India because of a shoulder problem caused by wear and tear and that must concern him.

Richie Richardson's handling of his bowlers was first-class and he showed great tactical skill throughout a fiercely competitive series. As a motivator, he ranked very high, always getting the best out of his players with his positive thinking. Our team meetings, at which everyone was encouraged to contribute, helped create a feeling of unity.

On to the Queen's Park Oval, and the West Indies versus England. We had already taken a 2–0 lead in the series. The opening Test had proved to be an easy win in the end even though England held the advantage early on after Atherton and Alec Stewart put on 121 for the first wicket. Kenny Benjamin bowled magnificently and stopped them going on to a big first innings total with 5–66 off 24 overs, including the wickets of both Atherton and Stewart. The West Indies slumped to 23–3 against Malcolm and Andy Caddick at the start of their innings and Keith Arthurton's second Test century, 126, along with my 83 helped us recover to 407, a lead of 173.

Devon Malcolm, who is as quick as any bowler in the world when he is in the right frame of mind and bowling on a pitch which has some pace in it, bowled a number of short deliveries to me early on, giving rise to claims that I was suspect against bowling directed at my body. He may have seen Geoffrey Boycott make that assertion on television. The real reason I appeared to be struggling at the start of that innings was that my eyes were giving me trouble and I had difficulty in focusing on the ball. I saw an eye specialist later who told me I was suffering from tyrigium, the growth of a thin film across the eye which can be treated with drops. Viv Richards had the same problem and had it cured by a minor operation on the 1984–5 tour of Australia. It is a common complaint in hot countries. So far, I have delayed having the operation, but if I am advised it is necessary I will have it.

Jimmy Adams, who made 95 not out, ran out of partners, otherwise he was a certainty for a hundred. He showed his versatility in England's second innings by adding three more catches at short leg to the three he took in the first innings to equal the Test record.

Sabina Park is always a good pitch for the fast bowlers to bowl on and there was plenty of action when England batted again, with Atherton being struck several times by Winston Benjamin and Courtney Walsh before Walsh, bowling round the wicket, had him caught by Adams off another intimidating delivery. Graeme Hick held us up with a stout innings of 96 before edging Kenny Benjamin to substitute fielder Roger Harper at slip. The West Indies victory would have been completed on the third day but for a last wicket stand of 39 in 45 minutes from Caddick and, surprisingly, Devon Malcolm.

When Courtney Walsh pitched the ball up to Malcolm he found himself being driven, so he dropped a few deliveries short. This led to the first controversy of the tour because Malcolm, who has never been able to handle bowling of this kind, turned his back on several occasions and was struck a few blows. The umpires, the

Zimbabwean neutral umpire Ian Robinson and the West Indies Board of Control official Steve Bucknor, made no attempt to intervene and there was a storm of protest in the English press. It caused a little bad feeling. Malcolm, who was born in Kingston, was eventually bowled by Walsh and the West Indies duly won the next morning by 8 wickets. Malcolm injured a knee and went home after the Kingston Test, and though he returned for the last two was not considered fit enough to play. English supporters claimed the outcome of the series might have been different had he been fit for the whole series but I do not believe there was much validity to that argument.

The pitch at Georgetown, where the Second Test took place, was slow as usual, and the one in Port of Spain was equally unhelpful. Mike Atherton's 144 at Georgetown was a worthy study in concentration before Curtly Ambrose dismissed him. Atherton proved to be the most reliable of England's batsmen in the series and his 510 runs was the second highest behind my 798. Two hundreds and two fifties in nine innings represents a high degree of consistency. It is said that West Indian fast bowlers always 'target' the opposing captain on the grounds that, if he goes, the others will lose heart and follow. I do not really think that is true, although when Ambrose got Atherton again in the second innings for 0, the rest of the batsmen, except for Alec Stewart who made 79, seemed discouraged at losing their leader so soon. England never recovered from that setback and the West Indies won easily by an innings and 44 runs.

The West Indies selectors had made a bold change in the batting line-up, replacing Phil Simmons with nineteen-year-old Shivnarine Chanderpaul, the first Indian to represent the West Indies for a decade and the first teen-ager for two decades. Chanderpaul, the leading scorer on the 1993 West Indies youth side tour of England, showed he had the temperament for Test cricket by scoring 62 in our first innings total of 556. He indicated very quickly that his selection wasn't because the selectors wanted to include a Guyana player on his home ground. He was in on merit and has stayed in.

It was also a good Test for me. My 167 off 210 balls was my second Test hundred and my first in the West Indies. It gave me a lot of pleasure. Ian Salisbury was England's most successful bowler on a pitch taking some spin with 4–163 but he was too expensive; among the good balls were far too many bad ones. Ambrose's dismissal of Atherton took him past 200 wickets; he had 8 wickets in the match in all, one more than Kenny Benjamin.

The third Test was at Trinidad and it was there that Curtly surpassed his Georgetown figures with two of his greatest performances, 5–60 in the first innings and 6–24 in the second. His spell of 7.5–1–22–6 in the final 80 minutes of the fourth day's play saw England dismissed for 46, their second lowest Test score of all time, just one run more than their lowest ever total against Australia in 1886–7. Some experts including Michael Holding said it was Curtly's finest hour and I agree.

England only needed 194 to win in their second innings but their coach Keith Fletcher was correct when he described it as 'an awkward total to get, especially against these boys'. Atherton went to the first delivery of the innings from Curtly, lbw, and once more the after-effects were felt right through the side. Mark Ramprakash was run out off the fifth ball and the second ball of Ambrose's next over nipped back to remove Robin Smith's leg stump. Smith, who plays quick bowling well, looked totally at sea. Curtly's strengths are unerring accuracy, great pace and a subtle variation in that pace, and it is easy to see why he is such a lethal bowler. Despite England's dominance earlier in the Test match, Curtly demonstrated his amazing ability to turn things around and obliterate an entire team.

Alec Stewart and Graeme Hick survived for five overs before Hick snicked a leg cutter to Junior Murray. Stewart, the only batsman to reach double figures, had his off stump sent cartwheeling at 26–5. Courtney Walsh gained his first wicket when the promoted Ian Salisbury edged the ball to me at slip, and in front of a swelling, excited crowd, Ambrose removed both left-handers, Jack Russell and Graham Thorpe, to leave England 40–8 at the close. 'The worst hour of my life,' said Atherton. Curtly explained afterwards that he was fired up by the guilt he felt at throwing away his wicket at the end of our second innings.

Next morning, only 26 balls were needed to remove the last two wickets, with Caddick providing me with my fifth catch of the Test. Not that five catches made up for the disappointment of being given out lbw in the first innings by the ICC umpire Srinivasaraghavan Venkataraghavan, the former Indian and Derbyshire off-spin bowler whom I believe to be a good umpire. I had made 44 in 104 deliveries, patiently building up what I was hoping would be my first century on my home ground, when Chris Lewis, bowling round the wicket, pitched the ball about a foot outside the off stump. I was struck above the thigh and it was such a painful blow that I didn't bother to look at the umpire. I was more concerned about the pain. The first indication I had that Venkat had raised the finger was when I heard the England players shouting jubilantly as they rushed to embrace Lewis. I saw the replay several times afterwards and felt the TV evidence backed my judgement that I was extremely unlucky. The other players were very sympathetic. These things happen in cricket but I am yet to be convinced they balance out. I seem to be particularly unlucky at Port of Spain. In the second innings I was out for 12 to a spectacular catch at mid off by Salisbury off the bowling of Caddick. The New Zealand-born bowler irritated some of us with the loudness of his appeals and his general behaviour; he was always making a lot of noise. I was not happy with that second innings failure; my mental approach wasn't right. It was a loose shot at a time when the situation called for a more disciplined approach. Still, the main thing was that we had won the match and the series and we began to think a whitewash might be on. Even though we did not quite manage it in the end, the series was a successful one for the team and for me in particular.

CHAPTER SEVEN

277

'This is your day, son. Just keep on batting.'

Sir Gary Sobers

THE BEST INNINGS I HAVE PLAYED IN MY CAREER SO FAR WAS MY 277 for the West Indies at the Sydney cricket ground at the beginning of January 1993. Some people will be wondering how it could not be bettered by the world-record innings of 375 or even my 501 against Durham in the county championship. World records are things to be cherished, and I must say I would not give up my 375 or my 501 for anything. But as a batsman you do certain things and they leave a bigger mark on you. Such as my 277. The context of the innings, my stroke-play and the eventual role played in the outcome of the series make the 277 the innings I would most like to replay. Personally I don't like describing my batting but I think I have to convince you that this innings at the Sydney cricket ground was a gem.

A drawn Test match in Brisbane and the loss in Melbourne gave Australia a 1–0 lead going into the Third Test match. The Australians have a superior record over the West Indies at the Sydney Cricket Ground and another customary victory would put them two up in the series with two matches left.

Australia won the toss and batted first. From the end of the first day on a very placid pitch we were behind and under a bit of pressure. Our bowlers seemed ineffective on this non-responsive pitch and Australia were able to bat through the first day and most of the second before they declared on 503–9, giving us some batting late on the second day. Phil Simmons went early, caught by Taylor off McDermott for 3, and we ended the day on 24–1. We knew at this stage that we had to battle very hard to save this game. Early on the third morning we lost Desmond Haynes bowled by Greg Matthews for 22. I was next in, the score was 32–2 and the Australian tail was up. I had just watched two days of batting and to me the Australians seemed pretty comfortable with the pitch. I didn't want to put myself under any undue pressure, and I decided to go out and bat as confidently as I could regardless of the position we were in.

Why this innings is so special is because I'm sitting here trying to recall something that stood out more than the rest and I find it very difficult because there was hardly a false shot. I was amazed at my timing and stroke-play from the very start. When I was on 35 the rain came and interrupted play for a short while. The telephone in the dressing-room rang and I was told someone was on the line for me. It was Sir Gary Sobers, who was in Australia at the time promoting Barbados tourism. 'This is your day, son,' he said. 'Just keep on batting.' This was a great confidence-booster for me because I have so much respect for this man and it was a great feeling to know that he believed in me. My 50 came up in 43 balls and I found myself scoring at a rate slightly faster than my captain, Richie Richardson. This was my fifth Test match and my ninth Test innings. I had three half-centuries in Test cricket but no hundreds. I thought this was the right opportunity to score my maiden Test century. Again there were no hiccups between 50 and 100 when finally I turned Greg Matthews to short fine leg for a single to complete my first Test hundred.

Of course that's another high point in every batsman's career, to score his first Test hundred, and I was very happy to get over that first hurdle. What stuck with me most was when Richie Richardson (who also made a century) came to congratulate me. He said to keep going, get a big one and make up for the times when you don't get any. That was my intention, to continue batting for as long as possible. We were still in a bit of danger and the team needed me to stay out there. There were a few anxious moments after I got my hundred but nothing too alarming. I must say I remember one particular shot, a square drive off Greg Matthews again, to bring up my 150. My first and only chance came when I was on 172. Allan Border had just taken the second new ball. Merv Hughes ran in and bowled one just short outside the off stump. I tried to square drive it off the back foot but only succeeded in offering Steve Waugh a difficult catch at gully. To my amazement he dropped it. Steve Waugh normally has very safe hands and I counted myself very lucky to be still there.

Inch by inch I got closer to my first-ever double century. I mean first-ever, because I had never scored a double century at any standard of cricket I played. I got close at school level. I also got 193 against the Jamaican Under-19 team in 1988, followed by 182 against the touring Indian team playing for the West Indies Under-23. On 199 Shane Warne was bowling and I had a look around the field. I settled in my stance waiting impatiently for him to deliver the ball. It was a leg break pitched on leg stump and I flicked it down fine for 3. I felt elated being out there defying the Australians and coming up with my best-ever performance at such a much-needed time. The entire match was played in very overcast conditions with a few interruptions for rain. This meant that there were not many people there to watch the game but those that were appreciated my innings.

After my double century I was helped by the electronic scoreboard, which would display any records I was approaching; this made me focus a lot more and it seemed that between 200 and 250 I had broken a few records. I had never felt so much in control of an innings, and when I passed 250 I started counting down to Sir Gary's record of 365. At 277 I played the ball towards cover and called for a run. I was half-way down the pitch when Carl Hooper called 'No' and I knew I had no chance of beating Damien Martyn's throw. It was one of the few occasions when I have been run out. Normally I consider myself a good judge of a run and I believe there was a run to be taken there that day. I was not angry or resentful about being dismissed. I was excited and delighted to have scored my maiden Test hundred and broken a few records on the way. My 277 came off 372 balls and contained 38 boundaries and it was the fourth-highest maiden century in Test history behind Sir Gary's 365, Bobby Simpson's 311 and R.E. Foster's 287 against Australia in 1903. It was also the highest score by a West Indian against

LEFT: With my nephew Marvin (left) outside our house in Cantaro, Santa Cruz, Trinidad.

BELOW: Holding two of my early trophies, the Harvard Coaching School trophies for most runs and for the outstanding player of the year. With me are (left to right) my nephews Ronnie and Marvin and my sister Karen.

With my father Bunty, after being named the Schools Cricketer of the Year.

FAR LEFT: Here I am at home holding one of my bigger trophies!

LEFT: India, 1983. My first experience of international cricket as a member of Trinidad and Tobago schoolboys versus India schoolboys.

MAIN PHOTOGRAPH: (Sitting, 3rd left). Captain of the Trinidad youth team in the Northern Telecom Youth Championship in 1988. GORDON BROOKS

LEFT: My first senior overseas tour, to Pakistan in 1990.

RIGHT: Playing without headgear – rare these days – for the West Indies against the Combined Universities at Oxford in 1991.
CHRIS COLE/ALLSPORT

FAR RIGHT: Début at Lord's. Batting in a Texaco Trophy match for the West Indies in May, 1991. GRAHAM MORRIS

At Leicestershire, with the West Indies team that toured England in 1991.

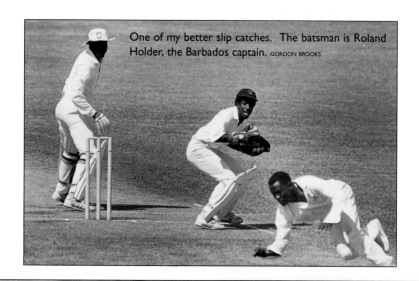

One of my better slip catches. The batsman is Roland Holder, the Barbados captain. GORDON BROOKS

Helped off after being struck on the foot by Wasim Akram in a one-day international in Melbourne, 1992.

ADRIAN MURRELL/ALLSPORT

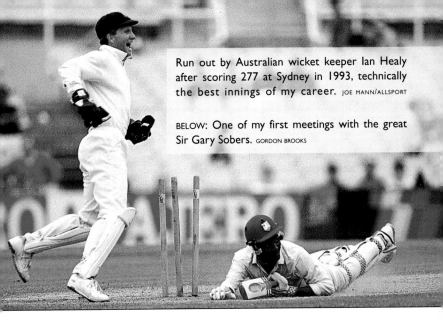

Run out by Australian wicket keeper Ian Healy after scoring 277 at Sydney in 1993, technically the best innings of my career. JOE MANN/ALLSPORT

BELOW: One of my first meetings with the great Sir Gary Sobers. GORDON BROOKS

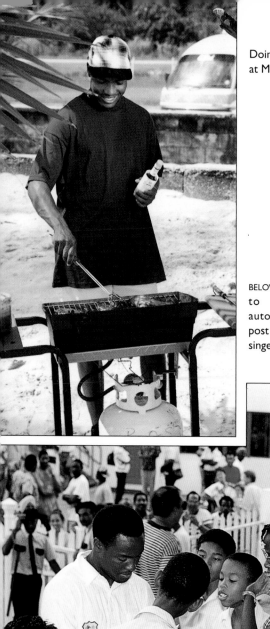

Doing an ad for Angostura Bitters at Maracas beach, Trinidad.

BELOW: Something I will always try to find time for, signing autographs. On the left of the post is David Rudder, the calypso singer.

Australia, beating Gordon Greenidge's 226 two years previously.

Gordon was present at Sydney, and so was Doug Walters whose 242 on the same ground in 1968–9 was the previous best score between the teams. The critics and former players were very kind and Rohan Kanhai, the team manager, said it was one of the greatest innings he had ever seen. Mike Coward, writing in *The Australian*, said: 'This was more than an innings. This was more Lara's theme. This was the cricketing equivalent of a grand opera, a performance which took the art of batting to a higher plane. Such was the power, beauty and refinement of Lara's innings that everyone at the ground was compelled to ask whether they had ever seen the like.'

There are moments in any sportsman's life when he realizes he has reached new heights and it happened for me on that overcast day in Sydney. Richie Richardson, who helped me add 293 for the third wicket, scored a top-class century, 109, but said: 'I can hardly remember my innings. I remember more the shots Brian was playing. It was kind of difficult playing and being a spectator at the same time.' The electronic scoreboard flashing up new records added to the excitement. One record I just missed out on was Bob Cowper's 307 against England in Melbourne in 1966, which remains the highest Test score in Australia.

The importance of the innings went further than helping the West Indies draw the Third Test. The team spirit and our performance sky-rocketed after the Sydney Test. Everyone seemed very focused and was not just looking forward to levelling the series but winning it. After the Third Test we went back into the World Series, winning the trophy with two straight victories at Sydney and

Melbourne, followed by our one-run victory in Adelaide and complete dominance at Perth. It was my first full series in Australia and the atmosphere at cricket there is second to none. It is a place I suppose all the cricket-playing countries look forward to touring and I am looking forward to my return visit.

CHAPTER EIGHT

DISAPPOINTMENT AT THE QUEEN'S PARK OVAL

THE QUEEN'S PARK OVAL WAS FULL, WE WERE IN THE LAST OVER of the second day of the West Indies v. Pakistan first Test in April 1993, and I was 96 not out. The crowd was humming with excitement, the drums were beating and the carnival atmosphere was everywhere. Everyone was expecting me to fulfil one of my major ambitions, to score a Test century on my own ground.

I intended to achieve the landmark before the day's play ended, but when the occasional left-arm spin bowler Asif Mujaba bowled a delivery into the rough outside my off stump I advanced my right foot well down the pitch to pad the ball away. It turned more than I expected, caught me on the back of my left leg and ran back on to the stumps. Everyone commiserated with me afterwards and I was acutely disappointed. It was a desperately unlucky way to be dismissed, especially as it was Mujaba's only wicket of the series. Richie Richardson did his best to cheer me up. 'Don't worry,' he said. 'I've had a 99 here. You weren't the first.'

The series had been billed the unofficial world championship of Test cricket, with the West Indies, victors in Australia a short time before, against the holders of the World Cup. I made a good start to the five one-day internationals with innings of 114 and 95 not out in the opening successes for the West Indies in Kingston and Port of Spain, but the Pakistan team, captained by Wasim Akram, came back to make it 2–2. The decisive match was in Georgetown and it resulted in one of the few ties in the history of one-day cricket.

Two runs were needed off the last ball with Carl Hooper and Ian Bishop batting and Bishop drove towards deep mid on. The batsmen completed the first run and were going back for the second when hundreds of jubilant spectators ran on to the field. The substitute fielder Zahid Fazal threw the ball in to the bowler, Wasim, who promptly dropped it. The scores were level when the second run was completed, and as we had lost 5 wickets to Pakistan's 6 we believed we were the winners of the match and the series. But Raman Subba Row, the English ICC Referee, ruled that the result should be recorded as a tie on the grounds that the crowd had impeded the fielders. The West Indies Board accepted this verdict as 'absolutely fair'.

If that was controversial it was nothing compared to what followed when the Pakistan party flew to Grenada to play a friendly against theWest Indian Under-23 XI. Thirty-six hours before the match was due to start Wasim Akram, Waqar Younis, Mushtaq Ahmed and Aqib Javed were arrested and charged with 'constructive possession of marijuana'. They were released on bail and, with all of them pleading their innocence, Pakistan manager Khalid Mahmood threatened to call off the rest of the tour. I do not know the facts and I do not believe anyone will ever discover the truth of the matter. The players said they were drinking with two English women on the Grand Anse beach next to their hotel when someone identified himself as a policeman and told them they were going to be arrested for a drugs offence. If found guilty, they could have been fined up to £62,000. Mahmood told the Press: 'The charges are utterly ridiculous. If I thought there was anything in them I would help to bring about justice but there is not a scrap of evidence.'

The players were bailed at £250 each, with Walter St John, President of the Grenada Cricket Association, standing surety. Wasim, Waqar and Mushtaq all played against the Under-23 side and played a prominent part in their team's 111-run victory. Until the final day, the threat of the tour ending with that match remained. A short time after the conclusion of play, a police officer arrived at the team's hotel with letters to each of the four players saying they would be allowed to leave the island and in the end, the charges were dropped.

That did not pacify Khalid Mahmood or the Pakistan Board. 'There is a feeling of shock, frustration, rejection and annoyance among the team and it is no way to prepare for a Test match,' he said. He insisted that security would have to be improved if the First Test in Trinidad was to start. The problem was resolved when the West Indies Board agreed to postpone the start of the Test for twenty-four hours and apologized 'for any embarrassment the Pakistan team may have been subjected to arising out of this incident'.

The West Indies players were not too happy about the

delay. When the game finally started on the Friday the pitch was cracked and dry, and with the ball swinging the indications were it would be a low-scoring contest. The ball normally tends to keep low at Queen's Park but this time it occasionally scuttled along the ground. Umpires Dickie Bird, the independent umpire from England, and Steve Bucknor gave seventeen lbws, a world record beating the previous record of fourteen in the Pakistan v. Sri Lanka Test at Faisalabad fifteen months previously.

Bird, who celebrated his sixtieth birthday during the match, gave six of them and said: 'They call me a not outer at home but I've been in a world record here.' The West Indies made only 127 in their first innings and some of the batting was none too good. Pakistan fared little better, collapsing from 100–2 to 140 all out against Ambrose and Bishop, who shared 9 wickets between them.

The next day it became a very different game as the West Indies ran up 333–3, with Desmond Haynes helping me add 169 for the fourth wicket. Haynes batted through the innings for a record third time for 143 not out in our total of 382. Richie Richardson made 68 off 72 balls and was involved in an incident when the teenage bowler Ata-ur-Rehman stuck out a foot and appeared to be trying to trip him up while going for a run. Mr Subba Row saw it and called Mudassar Nazar, the Pakistan coach in to ask him to warn Rehman about his conduct.

Pakistan needed 370 to win, which was virtually impossible in the conditions. They lost their first three batsmen, Aamir Sohail, Ramiz Raja and Inzaman-ul-Haq, to lbw decisions and ended on 165. Basit Ali, a small, compact young player making his début, created a good impression with his 37. That victory by 204 gave us a 1–0 lead.

The Pakistanis had little time to recover morale before

the Second Test started in Bridgetown five days later. Wasim, recovering from flu, won the toss and, with some green on the pitch and a couple of early showers to aid swing bowlers, decided to ask us to bat. The outcome was another huge setback for his team. By the end of the first day's play the West Indies were 351–4. Haynes made 125 and he averaged 134 in the series from 402 runs. Waqar took 4 wickets but at a high cost, almost 6 an over. He is such an attacking bowler that he often goes for more runs than any rival fast bowler; he is always striving to take a wicket. Reserve wicket-keeper Moin Khan dropped Phil Simmons twice in one over which proved costly, because Phil scored 87 off 90 balls to set us on our way. In the end we made 455.

Basit Ali again showed he had the technique and temperament for Test cricket with his unbeaten 92 in Pakistan's 221. Following on, they did marginally better, reaching 262 which left us to score 29 to win. There was no doubt the arrests in Grenada had undermined the confidence of the Pakistanis and that contributed to the one-sidedness of the series.

The West Indies would doubtless have won the Third Test but for rain which cut short play on three of the days at Antigua. Wasim had no luck with the toss and our 344–9 on the opening day put the match out of the reach of his side. Carl Hooper's 178 off 247 balls was the highlight of our first innings 438, and such was his mastery that, when he and Courtney Walsh put on a record 106 against any country for the 10th wicket, Walsh, who made 30, faced only 30 balls in 23 overs. I was going well on 44 when I tried to drive the left-arm spinner Nadeem Khan, making his début, and was given out stumped by Rashid Latif. I thought I had grounded my bat and the TV replay seemed to support that.

Inzaman-ul-Haq, a powerful driver, made his maiden Test century, 123, after he was dropped at long on by Winston Benjamin. Our second innings 153–4 was enlivened by the bowling of Waqar, who suddenly discovered his most hostile pace and swing after coming on in the 13th over. He got all 4 wickets, mine among them. Three of them were lbw; with that fast in-swinging yorker of his, he must get more lbws than almost any other top-class bowler.

Our 2–0 win in the series proved Imran Khan wrong. He said that Pakistan were the next world champions and would prove it in the Caribbean. Even if the drugs affair hadn't happened I do not believe the result would have been any different. The previous Pakistan tour under Imran in 1987–8 had ended in a 1–1 draw but we were a more confident side this time, and confidence plays such an important part.

CHAPTER NINE

375

WHEN I WAS VOTED TRINIDAD'S SPORTSMAN OF THE YEAR IN January 1994 I made a short speech in which I said: 'I would like to be a little more consistent and maybe score a few double hundreds and even a triple.'

Within three months I achieved that improbable target with 206 against Barbados and 375 against England. The 375 was overwhelming, unbelievable. It changed my life. I became the standard-bearer for cricket, the cricketer that boys around the cricket-playing world look up to and aspire to. Many years previously I had fantasized as a small boy about beating the records of the great players and now it had happened. Since then my life has been like a whirl but I know I can cope with it. My aim now is to make big scores regularly so I can confirm myself as a great player over a period of some years, not just a few months. I am confident I can do it.

The Recreation Ground in St John's, Antigua, was the venue for the final Test match between the West Indies and England. Even though we had secured the series with an unassailable 3–1 lead, the guys, and I'm sure the whole of the West Indian public, were totally disappointed at our shock defeat in the Fourth Test in Barbados.

The mental approach of the whole side had not been right in the lead-up to that Test. We were over-confident and thought that a 5–0 win over England was still on. England, though, put up a fine performance, in particular Alec Stewart who scored a century in each innings and Angus Fraser who reached new heights during our first innings with figures of 8–75. Neither of these statistics had been achieved before by an Englishman against the West Indies. I have always had great admiration for Angus Fraser. He is a slower, less menacing version of Curtly Ambrose, but brings the ball down from a considerable height and pitches it on a line and length that batsmen are not happy with. I was surprised when he was later left out of the touring party to Australia, even though he did eventually join the team out there.

The 7,000 English supporters in Barbados were ecstatic over their team's victory, and afterwards Richie Richardson refused to admit that lack of crowd support had been a factor in the result. 'We won here against South Africa and there was hardly anyone in the ground,' he said. 'We just played badly.'

Yes, we really wanted to win this final Test in Antigua to regain the dominance over our English counterparts. Personally, before the series started I'd set my sights on scoring at least two centuries and I was determined to get that second one in this Test match.

Courtney Walsh, replacing the injured Richie Richardson as captain, had won the toss and on a flat, almost marble-like pitch decided to bat. The Recreation Ground at St John's is one of my favourite batting pitches and I felt conditions were right for me to get my second hundred of the series. I was not looking beyond that. I was at the crease earlier than I had expected. Stuart Williams went early, caught by Caddick off Fraser for 3, and it was 12–1 when I walked out to a carnival-like reception. The Antigua Recreation Ground has one of the most animated crowds and some of the Caribbean's best-known characters, including Chickie, whose instruments blast out non-stop and the acrobatic Gravy and Mayfield who entertained all day with their antics and comments. There is never a dull moment in the West Indies Oil Stand during a Test match. And on the other side of the ground, the All Saints Iron Band was beating out its message.

I was wearing a helmet at the start of my innings but the pitch was benign, and with the bowling not express pace I soon discarded it. For most of my time in the middle I wore the maroon West Indies cap. I did not intend to take any risks that morning. I wanted to settle in and build the foundation for a long innings. I struggled early on and it took me 51 deliveries before I reached double figures and my fifty took 121 balls. There were seven fours in that half-century. The second fifty was twice as quick, 59 balls, taking me to my century in 232 minutes. I was overjoyed to get my second century in the series, but I wanted to be still there at the close, and as long as possible after. Jimmy Adams helped me add 179 for the third wicket before he was caught by the substitute fielder Nasser Hussain off the bowling of Fraser for 59, and when play ended the West Indies were 274–3 with my score 164. That total might have been higher but for the long, coarse grass over much of the outfield. I hit twenty-four boundaries and the other batsmen managed six, including two sixes by Jimmy Adams. I was quite happy with my first day's performance, especially with the added responsibility of being vice-captain.

That night I went to bed earlier than usual. I was sharing a room at the Royal Ramada Hotel with Junior Murray, and Junior is the sort of quiet person who fits in with anything you want to do. I was grateful to him for not keeping me awake. Our pockets were quite empty after the Test match in Barbados where we were fined a huge amount for slow over-rate. So the guys were looking forward to the £50,000 available for the first batsman to record a 200 in the series. Just the thought of scoring my second double century was enough inspiration for me.

I woke up around 5.30 a.m. and immediately headed out to the golf course. I felt a lot of tension and I thought I needed to relax. For me there is no better way of clearing my mind and focusing on the day ahead. When I got to the Recreation Ground everyone urged me on and wished me luck. I got a distinct feeling that to them this was not just another innings, something special was going to happen. Angus Fraser bowled two successive maidens to me before I pulled the 14th ball I faced, from Andy Caddick, for four. My partner Keith Arthurton was suffering from a damaged hand which restricted his stroke play so the bulk of the run-making was left up to me. Keith contributed 47 to our stand of 185.

Midway through the morning I passed 200, my fourth fifty coming off 71 balls. Like Curtly's prize, the money went into the pool for the players to share. Keith Arthurton was caught by Jack Russell off Caddick at

374–5, which brought to the crease Shivnarine Chanderpaul, the fourth successive left-hander to come in. Shivnarine batted beautifully, matching me almost shot for shot against bowlers who were losing their enthusiasm for the task.

On 286, between two interruptions for rain, I played my first false stroke. A delivery from Caddick bounced more than I expected, and trying to steer it to third man I edged the ball close to Jack Russell's left glove. It was not a chance, Russell did not touch it, but Caddick let out a roar of frustration for which he could be forgiven. Chanderpaul was constantly speaking to me, urging me to keep my concentration and not give it away. For a nineteen-year-old he showed amazing maturity, and I shall always be grateful to him for the part he played in my success.

A total of 23 overs were lost due to rain interruptions. I cannot say if those overs hadn't been lost whether I would have broken the record by the end of the second day. Looking back on it, I would have liked the opportunity to do so just to forgo the amount of pressure and nervousness I encountered on the third morning. I ended the day on 320, and the minute the umpire removed the bails at the end of play one thing was flashing in my mind – the figure 365. I spent an hour after the day's play in the dressing-room, trying to come to terms with the events that had taken place and those that were hopefully still to come.

Cricket-watchers in Antigua do not necessarily need events such as this to maintain their carnival spirit, but somehow this time it seemed like the party would go on all night, through to morning and until the record was broken. Back at the hotel faxed messages were already piling up. Some urging me on to the record, some already congratulating me. I tried reading as many as I could, using them as a means of motivation. My room-mate Junior Murray and I entered our room together; he immediately rushed and took my bedspread off and asked me what I wanted for dinner. He was acting like his life depended on my well-being. He answered all the phone calls, saying 'Sorry, he's asleep'. I thought that was very nice of him.

I was wide awake at four the following morning and couldn't get back to sleep. I was thinking about all the people who had told me I could do it, some of them years before, and I felt I owed it to them to set a new mark in the cricket books. I ruled out nipping out to play golf again. I thought of the targets in front of me – Graham Gooch's 333, Don Bradman's 334, Wally Hammond's 336, Hanif Mohammad's 337, Len Hutton's 364, and the big one, Sir Gary Sobers' 365. I played a few shots in my mind. My palms were sweaty. I had not been this nervous before.

Despite being awake for so long I almost missed the team bus. When I arrived at the ground, people slapped me on the back and wished me well. The gates had been open since eight and the ground was full. I wondered if these people had spent the entire night there. Sir Gary was there. So was Desmond Haynes, who flew in from Barbados especially. And so was Mrs Jean Pierre, the Trinidad and Tobago Minister of Sport who was a sporting great as a netballer.

I sat in the dressing-room fighting to hold back the tears. There was one person missing, and if I could have emptied the entire Antigua Recreation Ground just to have my father back watching me break the world record, I would have been the happiest person in the world. My mind went back to all the many sacrifices he made for me, not for me to go on to break world records, but to see me happy and also to see his favourite son make full use of his life. By now I was anxious to get out there, and I know he was willing me on to this historic landmark.

Inevitably the tension got to me, and when play got going my strokeplay suffered. Mike Atherton claimed the third new ball after two overs and my first stroke off it, from a delivery from Caddick, went over cover's head for my fortieth boundary. Caddick expressed his annoyance and Chanderpaul came down the pitch to tell me to be careful. I edged another delivery to third man, another sign of nervousness, before square-cutting Chris Lewis off the middle of the bat for four. That shot, a much better one, took me past Gooch's 333, and Bradman's 334 against England at Leeds in 1930.

Chanderpaul was dropped by Hick – who had lost his touch as a catcher – just after he reached his fifty. When I played and missed at Fraser, the bowler smiled ruefully and said: 'I don't suppose I can call you a lucky bugger when you are 340.' I like him. He's a nice guy. An extra cover drive off Fraser soon afterwards took me past Hammond and Hanif. In the West Indies Oil Stand, Gravy, dressed up as Santa Claus, was whipping up the crowd. The noise was very loud and incessant. Three times in an over from Lewis I decided to go for two runs to deep-set fielders. The first time there was an appeal when Russell broke the stumps from Mark Ramprakash's throw from square leg but I knew I was in and so did the umpires. I struck the ball in Ramprakash's direction a second time and again called for two. Chanderpaul is a good runner. I was happy to be batting with him. The third two, which took me to 357, was the easiest of the lot, to Fraser at third man. I tried to drive Lewis in the next over but missed, the ball passing centimetres from the off stump. Chanderpaul came down the pitch to give some much-needed support. 'Don't throw it all away,' he said. 'Make sure you get there.'

An extra cover drive off Caddick took me past Sir Len Hutton and level with Sir Gary Sobers. The crowd was on their feet, hundreds of them seemed to be massing on the boundary line. Lewis was bowling from the factory end. Atherton had the field set to stop a single. It was 11.46 and of course I would never forget that time. Lewis prepared to bowl his third ball of that over. I knew from the way he was running up that it would be short and I found myself moving into the hook shot before the ball was bowled. Yes, the ball was short, and I pulled it away through mid wicket in the direction of the Cathedral for four. I punched the air in celebration. The moment for me, the way I felt, was indescribable, a moment in my lifetime maybe never to be repeated – elation, wonderment, pure joy – the ultimate pinnacle of my career. Everything that was happening was like a dream. My bat held high, cap in hand, and in the distance hundreds of spectators racing in my direction. Suddenly I felt a hug. It was Chanderpaul, and before I knew it we were surrounded by numerous police trying their best to keep the spectators away. A path was cleared for Sir Gary to come to the middle and congratulate me. He clasped me and said how very proud he was. 'I'm very happy for you. I knew you could do it, son. You were always the one.' Now I don't know how to describe this moment. The man considered the best ever all-rounder to grace the cricket field and now the previous holder of the world record of 365, the highest score in Test cricket, was offering me his congratulations for eclipsing his record. When he left the playing area the police eventually cleared a space and quite instinctively I bent down and kissed the pitch.

After a few minutes play resumed. I wanted to bat

on. I wanted to become the first player to pass 400 runs in a Test match. But I found it difficult to concentrate at the same level. Maybe if we could have gone off for an interval I might have been able to recharge and get going again. That was not to happen. I got two more singles and a boundary before Caddick bowled one outside the off stump, the ball swung further away from me, and I got an outside edge to wicket-keeper Russell. I was not too disappointed. This could have happened a long time ago. Caddick shook me by the hand as I departed. The English players had congratulated me at the time I broke the record and they seemed quite happy for me. Earlier, I had asked Mike Atherton why he hadn't made it easier for me by relieving the pressure. I told him we had played together in the Youth World Cup in 1988 so I expected a little ease. He said: 'You wouldn't enjoy it so much if it got easy, so work for it!'

As soon as I was out Courtney Walsh declared at 593–5, with Chanderpaul 75 not out. I had batted 766 minutes for my 375 off 538 balls and hit 45 fours and no sixes. And I felt very, very tired. Viv Richards was in the dressing-room to congratulate me. So was Desmond Haynes and dozens of others. I sat down and someone took my pads off for me. I had used the same trousers, the same shirt, the same socks, the same jockstrap right the way through those 766 minutes and I must have been very smelly. I did that because of superstition. I didn't want to change a thing. I had all my kit washed later at the hotel and have kept it ever since. I haven't used any of it. It remains part of my cricketing treasure. All of the items were signed by my team-mates.

I had to go back out on the field for England's innings. Two sessions and two days remained but the pitch played so well, too well really, that a result was never in prospect even though Kenny Benjamin removed Alec Stewart and Mark Ramprakash and England were 70–2. Atherton, 135, and Robin Smith, 175, put on 303 for the third wicket, a record for England against the West Indies. That night I received many more faxes from all over the world congratulating me on my achievement. It was hectic at the hotel and it was around 2 a.m. before I was able to get to bed. Junior Murray was laughing and joking. I found it hard to sleep; I kept replaying my innings shot by shot.

England went on to get 593, the same total as the West Indies. I spent part of the final day off the field complaining of weariness. The match was drawn. I received the Man of the Match award and Curtly Ambrose was judged the Man of the Series.

Three days of celebrations were about to start in Trinidad and Tobago and when I arrived at Piarco Airport late on the night of 21 April, there was pandemonium. The Prime Minister, Patrick Manning, was there to greet me and so too were thousands of my fellow countrymen. The night went satisfactorily – a few speeches and then I was rushed off to my village where my friends and members of my family were waiting.

The next day the schools were given a day off to enable the children to watch the motorcade tour of the island. It started in Arima, in east Trinidad, and the journey to the City Hall in Port of Spain took more than two hours. At the City Hall I was presented with the keys of the city. The tour ended at the Queen's Park Oval where thousands of schoolchildren had waited three hours to see me. In the evening the Prime Minister gave a reception for me at his residence. The next day I was presented with the Trinity Cross, Trinidad and Tobago's highest award, by the President, Noor Hassanali. Sir Gary Sobers received a similar award at the same time. The

Prime Minister announced that a street off Independence Square would now be renamed 'Brian Lara Promenade'. I was very thankful for all this but what remained with me the most was the joy and the proud look on the faces of the people of my country.

CHAPTER TEN

ARRIVAL IN ENGLAND

NINE DAYS AFTER SCORING 375 I LANDED AT HEATHROW AIRPORT to start my county cricket career with Warwickshire. The scenes in Port of Spain had been chaotic and I was apprehensive about what welcome I might receive on my arrival. There were fewer people to meet me but it was frightening all the same.

Camera crews and photographers were at the airport and journalists were pulling and tugging to interview me. I was a cricketer here to play cricket but I was being treated like some kind of world-famous celebrity. I found the hype rather frightening. One of my best friends, Dwight Yorke, the Aston Villa and Trinidad and Tobago footballer, was with me to give support, and so was my agent Jonathan Barnett.

Jonathan and his partner David Manasseh have signed

up a number of the world's leading cricketers. Also on their list are golfers, footballers, and other sportsmen. They were the ones responsible for negotiating my contract with Warwickshire. Waqar Younis and Wasim Akram, two of their most famous clients, who play for Surrey and Lancashire respectively, are the highest-paid players in English county cricket. According to Jonathan, several counties had been interested in retaining my services besides Warwickshire. Nottinghamshire, who needed someone to take over from the New Zealander Chris Cairns, made an offer but I suppose negotiations fell through, for they signed my friend and colleague in the West Indies side Jimmy Adams instead.

Worcestershire was another county contacted as they wanted someone to take over from Kenny Benjamin. They settled on Tom Moody, their Australian signing who was unavailable in 1993. There were talks, too, with Middlesex but their committee wanted a bowler. The other offer came from the Lee Lancashire League club Denton who had tried to sign Viv Richards. Denton's offer was similar to Warwickshire's and I had to give it careful consideration. So many great West Indian cricketers from Learie Constantine onwards have played League cricket and I would be joining a long list.

I turned down Denton's offer because I was not really interested in playing League cricket. The money was good and the workload was light but money has never been all that important to me. I had to be sure it was the right career move. At the time I was not sure whether Warwickshire would be able to sign me. They had not had the final medical report on the Indian all-rounder Manoj Prabhakar, who was their first choice. Dermot Reeve wanted Prabhakar, a cricketer who opened both batting and bowling for his country. I met Warwickshire's wicket-keeper Keith Piper while playing in the Total Cup in South Africa in 1992 and on that trip he said Warwickshire were seeking an overseas player. I knew Allan Donald would not be available because of the South African tour of England during the 1994 season. It was the first inkling I had that Warwickshire might fancy me and it raised my hopes of fulfilling one of my major goals in my cricketing career.

I had played against Dermot Reeve and maybe what he saw did not fit in with what he wanted as his overseas player for 1994. He was adamant about having Prabhakar, presumably because he wanted a bowler as much as a batsman. I think that Warwickshire first approached my fellow Trinidadian Phil Simmons, who asked for a two-year contract which they were not prepared to give him because Allan Donald was contracted for 1995. Phil, who is managed by Jonathan Barnett, signed for Leicestershire instead and I was delighted when he started his county cricket career with a record-breaking double century.

Apparently the club also had talks with the Australian batsman David Boon during the Fifth Cornhill Test at Edgbaston. Boon had an outstanding tour of England that summer; he is a very solid and reliable player and I felt sure he would be a success in county cricket. Shane Warne was also contacted but Bobby Simpson and the Australian Board of Control were reluctant to allow him to be exposed to English cricket. The talks with David Boon were brought to an end when, again, Reeve compared the two players and preferred Prabhakar and the Indian all-rounder duly visited Edgbaston and signed a one-year contract. But in February 1994 Prabhakar strained an ankle during India's tour of New Zealand and had to return home. Dennis Amiss, the recently-appointed Warwickshire chief executive, was asked to find out the facts about Prabhakar's fitness and the Indian was told he would have to present himself at Edgbaston for checks. He did so and the club's doctors decided that his ankle might not stand up to the rigours of the English season and the contract was cancelled after compensation was agreed. Warwickshire's committee then agreed to pursue their interest in me.

Prabhakar, whom I had played against in the past, must have been acutely disappointed. During the West Indies v. England Test in Barbados, Rohan Kanhai said to me that Warwickshire, the county he played for himself with such distinction, were bidding for me. He said he gave them the highest possible recommendation. I spoke to Mike Smith, the Warwickshire chairman of cricket who was manager of the England side, and he confirmed that negotiations with my agent were well advanced. I suppose the fact that Mike Smith was in the West Indies and saw my cricket first-hand must have helped. He told me that Tony Cross, the club's vice-chairman, was on the way to see me. When I saw Tony, the talks did not last very long. My agent and I were very happy with their offer and I agreed to sign for one season. I knew Rohan Kanhai, Alvin Kallicharran and Lance Gibbs had all played for Warwickshire with great success. If I was able to match their contributions over the years I would be delighted. They were three of the greatest cricketers ever produced by the West Indies.

Prabhakar was reported as saying: 'My good wishes are always with Warwickshire and also Brian Lara. He has done a great deal for cricket and I wish him every success.' The signing in Barbados took place only a few days before my innings of 375 in Antigua. I think Warwickshire were very happy with the timing. They might well have had to pay considerably more had it happened after my record-breaking innings.

The flight from Port of Spain to Heathrow on 27 April gave me time to reflect on my new career. I was excited at the prospect. English county cricket has always been considered by many great players of the past a test for young pretenders. My drive to Birmingham was slightly fraught because Jonathan had arranged for me to call in at Pebble Mill on the way to do a interview, which meant we arrived late at Edgbaston for the press conference organized by the club. On my arrival, I received the keys for my sponsored Peugeot 405, silver in colour and bearing the number plate L375 ARA. I discovered later that was a gimmick for the photographers, who took countless shots of me with my new car. The real number was L289 URW and once the cameramen had gone it replaced the bogus one.

I was ushered into a large room which was crammed with TV crews, photographers and newsmen. I joined Mike Smith, Mr Cross, Dennis Amiss and Dermot Reeve, on a dais. It was all rather intimidating and I would rather have been walking out to play my first county innings. Dermot Reeve presented me with my county cricket cap and said it was the first time in the club's history that a player had been capped before he faced a single ball. Mike Smith also presented me with a silver salver commemorating my innings of 375.

I answered questions, most of which seemed to be geared towards my breaking more records. Would I beat Graeme Hick's 405 at Taunton or Archie MacLaren's 424 at the same ground? I found it all rather far-fetched. When I last toured England with the West Indies side I scored a disappointing 341 runs for an average of 28.41. I tried my best to smile and be as polite as possible, and afterwards the Warwickshire officials said they thought I had handled myself extremely well and had made a good first impression.

That pleased me because it is so easy to make a slip. 'I know people are expecting more records from me,' I said at the press conference. 'I am sure that people will be expecting a lot of good performances from me from now on and I hope I don't disappoint them. I'll try to take things stride by stride and hopefully we will all have a summer to remember. You have to realize that I have still to fulfil my goal of establishing myself in Test cricket and I am still aware that one innings cannot do that for me. I can tell you now that I was very scared to find out what was going to happen to me next. I actually went home and begged God to guide me.'

More interviews followed with a variety of people and there was an amusing incident when two representatives of the *Daily Mirror* tried to present me with a cake which had the words *Daily Mirror* on. I was contracted to write an exclusive column for the *Daily Mail* and one of the *Mail* representatives was worried that it might infringe his newspaper's agreement. There was some ducking and diving before someone rang the *Daily Mail* sports editor to give his permission for the *Mirror* to take their picture. It duly appeared next day on the back page. The coverage, I thought, was quite remarkable. I realized the pressure would now be on me all the time.

Writing about famous sportsmen whose lives are conducted at this high level of public scrutiny, the England football coach Terry Venables once wrote in the *Observer*: 'Few of us can comprehend the pressures and expectations these people live with daily. The public do not understand, nor do managers or the press. Even team-mates don't appreciate what it is like living in that mainstream where life becomes magnified and distorted. It is the same with Gazza, whom I managed at Spurs. None of the good things get noticed, only the negatives. I am sure they think the whole world is against them.'

I did not think that was the case then, but later in the season, when the critical stories started appearing, I felt a lot of sympathy with that view.

After more pictures taken against the background of the main scoreboard, which was displaying the score 375, I visited the dressing-room where I saw a cheeky message from Roger Twose, Warwickshire's left-handed batsman. 'Welcome to Edgbaston, from the best left-hander in the club,' it said. I was introduced to a few of the players who were at the ground and other members of the staff.

The club had provided me with a house at Harborne just outside Birmingham City Centre but I was delayed because I couldn't find the keys of my new car or the keys of the house. I suspect I might have been the victim of a practical joke. When I eventually arrived at the house along with Dwight Yorke and David Manasseh I was very surprised to find it was extremely small. I am not suggesting that I came from a house with a lot of space but I thought that, with the workload ahead of me, confinement in a small space was the last thing I wanted. David made some calls and suggested the club might want to find something more spacious. I flopped down on a settee in front of the TV set and was so tired after all the excitement that I went to sleep. When I woke early next morning the TV set was still on, my neck was hurting and my body felt very stiff.

In the hours that followed, David Manasseh persuaded the club to find more comfortable quarters and later in the week I was taken round a much larger, more convenient flat on the Hagley Road. More than fifty writers, broadcasters and photographers were at Edgbaston for my first

game, against Glamorgan the next day. To the disappointment of the media men, and myself, Glamorgan
captain Hugh Morris won the toss and decided to bat.
Still jet-lagged, it was not what I wanted. The pitch was
greener than I thought it might be but played innocuously
and we had a long, tiring day in the field. One of the
colour supplement writers wrote that it was twenty
minutes before I touched the ball.

There was not much for them to write about. The
game was conducted without the passion and enthusiasm
which was common in Red Stripe cricket at home, where
the season is much shorter and players are trying hard to
impress the selectors. I had the impression that some of
the players, realizing they were at the start of a five-month
haul, were coasting a little. Anxious to avoid being fined
for not bowling our overs at the required rate of 110 before
the close of play, we were tending to rush things and not
enough time was being spent on working out how we
were going to get batsmen out. It was as though the
theme was 'keep plugging away, they're going to get
out eventually'. This does not tend to make for exciting
watching and I could understand why so few spectators
now watch county cricket.

Warwickshire were the most inventive and imaginative
of sides in the field in that season but I still thought they
could have done more to work on the faults of opponents.
Cricket is a thinking game after all. Later in the season my
fears about county cricket were confirmed. Too many
sides were treating it like a marathon race with their
players pacing themselves. Most of the players were
more concerned about performing just enough to retain
their contract for the following season than trying to make
themselves into Test players. There was a distinct lack of
ambition around the clubs, I felt.

Glamorgan were 158–5 at one stage with Tim Munton, who impressed me on that opening day and never stopped impressing me throughout the summer, taking four of the wickets. Tim is one of the most reliable opening bowlers in county cricket and I was surprised he was not picked again for England during the summer.

We were held up on that opening day by the left-hander David Hemp, whose patient 127 was his maiden first-class hundred. He went on to have such a good season that he was picked for the England A team tour of India ahead of Warwickshire's Roger Twose and Dominic Ostler. I thought Twose and Ostler were harshly treated by the selectors. Both played excellent cricket throughout the county season and deserved more, possibly an England A tour. Dominic is a fine striker of the ball who just needs to be a little more single-minded to become a contender for England's Test team; I feel sure his time will come. Roger is a very adaptable cricketer who scored 277 against Glamorgan, his highest score and almost as many runs as he had scored in the whole of the previous season. He batted for 606 minutes which was the longest innings ever played by a Warwickshire batsman.

Ostler and Twose put on 50 for the first wicket, in reply to Glamorgan's 365 which took 132.4 overs to compile, before Ostler was bowled by the Barbados bowler Otis Gibson, who had succeeded Viv Richards as the club's overseas player. It was four minutes past two and I had just had my usual light lunch. I was using a new bat which I had not previously used because my 375 bat, autographed by most of the players who played in Antigua, was propped up against the fireplace at my flat. I had decided not to use it again.

I felt quite nervous returning to bat in English conditions after my disappointing tour in 1991. That was understandable. Even though only about 3,000 people were in the ground everyone was expecting me to get runs. I immediately became the prize wicket amongst the opposing bowlers. Otis Gibson suddenly found a few extra yards of pace. I was to discover this at every ground I played that summer: the other side's fast bowlers were determined to bowl their fastest at me, particularly the overseas players. I found this helped me to concentrate more on not getting out and yet still remain the exciting stroke-maker the public came to see. I suppose you can say I relished the challenge.

I made a cautious start, none of the first six balls really connecting with the middle of the bat. The first few deliveries are always the most important. If a batsman survives them he should be on his way to making a good score. The seventh delivery I faced, from Glamorgan's England A team off-spin bowler Robert Croft, was up to the bat and wide of off stump and I struck it for the first of my 23 boundaries. Those making charts of my innings said afterwards that fourteen of my fours were hit square on the off side. This gave rise to talk on the county circuit that it was suicide to give me any width on the off side. Bowlers said they would have to tuck me up by bowling straighter. Neal Radford, the Worcestershire bowler, was reported as saying that he had worked me out and could not wait for the opportunity to expose my faults.

I finished up with 147 off 160 deliveries which meant that Warwickshire gained extra time to press for a result. I think I may have shown that, even in a four-day match, the quicker runs are scored the better chance there is of achieving a result. I have always looked to dominate the bowling and dictate the terms. I was pleased I had passed my first test but had to admit I was very annoyed at being dismissed three short of 150 when I was so well set. Croft bowled into the rough outside the off stump and I played a loose shot which gave Matthew Maynard an easy catch at slip. Maynard, whom I got to know in the winter tour by England, had been chiding me about what he should bowl to me if he came on. 'I'm fed up with seeing you make all these runs,' he joked.

I remembered what Richie Richardson had told me when I was last in Sydney. 'If you get a hundred make sure you go on and make sure it is a big hundred,' he said. 'Go on as long as you can, make up for the bad times when you don't score any.'

Those words remained with me and may explain why most of my hundreds are big ones. Of those 147 runs, 104 came in boundaries, which meant that I didn't have to do much running.

Dermot Reeve told the press: 'That was the best session of batting I've seen since I came here and I just feel sorry for the Birmingham public that they are going to watch me after he gets out.'

Hugh Morris, who was obviously not thinking straight at the time, was kind enough to compare me with Viv Richards. 'I never thought I would see anyone better than Viv but now I am not too sure,' he said. That night I celebrated with some friends over a Chinese meal, which I love to eat as often as possible.

CHAPTER ELEVEN

A CENTURY IN EACH INNINGS

IT WAS A VERY SATISFACTORY START BUT WE CAME CLOSE TO being beaten in our next Championship match, home to Leicestershire, the unrated side who ran us closest to the title. I have to say it was the best match for me of the summer.

Nigel Briers, the Leicestershire captain, decided to bat first and his 154 was the mainstay of his side's 403 off 123.2 overs. Briers is a patient batsman, the kind of player who excels in county cricket because of his temperament and high degree of concentration. I managed to score my first-ever hundred in each innings, 106 off 136 balls and an unbeaten 120 off 163 in the second which saved the game. It took my tally of centuries to four in a row and there was talk of my beating the world record of six in a row jointly held by Sir

Donald Bradman, Mike Procter and Charles Burgess Fry.

After Roger Twose went for 51 in the first innings the rest of the batsmen collapsed against the off-spin bowling of Adrian Pierson, who had left the Warwickshire staff in 1991 because his opportunities were becoming limited. His 8–42 was his best analysis of his career and all 8 wickets came in a spell of 58 balls during which he conceded only 11 runs. I was one of his victims. 'He bats as though no one can get him out,' he said. 'But he takes chances and that's how I got him out.' I think I proved him wrong in the second innings.

During the break Dermot Reeve, our captain, said he wanted 254 to save the follow-on, and once we had done that they would have to set us a target to chase for victory. This was going to be my first experience of this type of cricket. I did not agree but kept my mouth shut. I know one day was lost to rain but I still didn't see the need for us to start manufacturing results so early in the season. Well, we got 254 exactly before Pierson spun his web around our batsmen. The feeling in the dressing-room was one of optimism. I could not understand why. Leicestershire were leading us by 149 runs and somehow our guys thought that their captain would instruct his players to play attacking cricket so as to set Warwickshire a reachable total. Quite rightly he did not, and Warwickshire were left to score 285 in 57 overs. Leicestershire were able to apply the pressure throughout our second innings but Gladstone Small and myself were able to survive until the end, with Warwickshire scoring 206–7.

There was just one more match left, a Benson and Hedges tie against Middlesex at Lord's, before I took the opportunity to return home to Port of Spain to do a little promotional work for one of my first sponsors, Angostura Bitters, and collect a few clothes. When I first arrived in London I did not have much clothing with me. Warwickshire were quite happy for me to use up some of my free air miles. It meant I missed the friendly game at Oxford, a ground where many first-class players score hundreds and enhance their averages. The fact that I might be missing out on one when a world record was looming did not bother me. I have never consciously thought about going for records and I did not intend to start now.

The B and H tie was only my second match at Lord's and it was preceded by another car incident when Dwight Yorke, who drove me to the ground the day before, lost his car keys and we had to leave the car there for a couple of days. I made 34 in 47 balls and we won a low-scoring game by 3 wickets. On a slow pitch I hit seven boundaries, one less than Middlesex achieved in their innings. Richard Johnson, the nineteen-year-old Middlesex pace bowler, dismissed me with his second delivery. He looked an exceptionally good prospect and I was not surprised he was selected for the England A tour of India. Johnson needed knee surgery later in the season and was out of the game for several weeks. I hope the demands of county cricket do not blight his career.

By now the publicity was building up about my chances of equalling the world record of six successive hundreds. Mike Procter, coach to the South African side at the time, was interviewed on the subject and was reported as saying he thought I could do it or even break it. Taunton was the venue of Warwickshire's next Britannic Assurance Championship match and that was the ground where many of the leading records in English cricket, like the 424 of Archie MacLaren and the 405 of Graeme Hick, were set. It was smaller than many grounds, with short boundaries behind the wicket at each end. But the square boundaries, where the majority of my runs are scored, were longer. The pitch was usually a good one for batting depending on the weather.

With Dermot Reeve playing for England at the time, Tim Munton captained the side for the first time that season, and when he lost the toss to Somerset captain Andy Hayhurst it condemned us to almost two days in the field watching the Somerset batsmen, Hayhurst in particular, bore a sizeable crowd. When Hayhurst eventually declared after 147.2 overs Somerset had only made 355 at just over 2 an over. The young opener Mark Lathwell was the liveliest of Somerset's batsmen with 13 boundaries in his 86 but Hayhurst needed 322 deliveries for his 111. It may have been effective for his side but it made tedious watching. Four-day cricket encourages batsmen to play that way, but if a player adopts those tactics those at the other end should try and score quicker. The object should be to try and win the game and obtain maximum points, not just occupy the crease and see what happens.

Warwickshire's openers Dominic Ostler and Roger Twose were still there on 57 when play ended on the second day and that helped my chances of scoring another hundred, because if one of them had been out and I had batted Tim Munton would have had to declare in the morning to try and get a result. That was the first of several pieces of luck I had in that amazing match at Taunton.

It has taken me some time to understand the manoeuvring that goes on behind the scenes to fix declarations in English cricket which decide matches and, often, the outcome of the whole championship season. Personally I am strongly opposed to one side having to bowl badly to enable the other team to score quickly enough to make a declaration that the first team feels it can go for. I think that devalues the game and cheats the spectators. The duty of the players should be to try as hard as they can to advance their own careers and improve the chances of their team winning. To switch into reverse and toss the ball high into the air to invite the opposing batsmen to hit it out of the ground seems to me to be a denial of that. It would be much better if the points system could be rearranged so that obtaining a lead in the first innings could be more substantially rewarded. In the Red Stripe competition this has always been the case and it makes the cricket competitive right the way through the match. It would be interesting to work out how many points are gained in a season in England through rigging declarations. In Warwickshire's case last season it was not many though the Taunton match was a leading example.

Tim Munton, who impressed me as a very shrewd and knowledgeable captain, talked with Hayhurst before play began and discussed a number of equations before finally agreeing on a target of 321 in a minimum of 95 overs. That meant Tim had to declare Warwickshire's first innings at the overnight score of 57–0 in 21 overs, with Ostler 41 not out.

Somerset's openers went in for a token 3 overs to score the 22 runs which would complete the equation. It was then that the first of the negative incidents which happened over the summer took place. I had just been presented with a mobile phone to use for the rest of the summer and some of my team-mates thought it would be funny if I took it out on to the field and received a phone call. Dermot Reeve, who was no longer on England duty, decided to make the call. During the second over the phone rang so I had no choice but to answer it. On the line was Dermot Reeve, obviously having a joke at my expense. One of the *Daily Mail* photographers noticed me with my phone to my ear and took a picture which was used in next day's paper. There was no interruption to play because immediately I realized it was Dermot, I rang off. It was meant to be amusing but the umpires, Kevin Lyons and Ray Julian, were not too happy and reprimanded me.

I gather Ian Botham and Allan Lamb had used mobile phones on the field as a joke in the past, but I could understand the umpires being annoyed and I apologized to them. I would not like anyone to think I was acting like a prima donna and that, even though we were involved in a period of joke cricket at the time, I was flouting the customs of the game. The rest of the players thought it was extremely funny. Many times during a day's play they were hearing my mobile telephone ringing in the dressing-room but this was something different.

Fortunately none of the other newspapers picked up on the incident and it received minimal publicity. The view in the Warwickshire dressing-room about Hayhurst's declaration was that it was an extremely favourable one. He was missing three of his leading pace bowlers, Adrianus Van Troost, the Dutchman who for two or three overs could be as fast as any bowler in the country, England opening bowler Andy Caddick, a New Zealander who qualified by residence, and the reliable Neil Mallender. But we supposed Hayhurst had taken the weather forecast, which was for occasional showers, into account. He was right to be on the generous side because 35 overs were eventually lost to the weather in our second innings after Saturday's play had been washed out. I went in just before lunch and at the interval was 5 not out in a total of 87–1. It rained heavily during and after lunch and prospects of a resumption were remote. The players were discussing an early departure to Birmingham before the Benson and Hedges quarter-final against Kent at Edgbaston the next day. I was so tired I spent most of the early part of the afternoon asleep. Just before 4 p.m. I was wakened to be told that the rain had stopped and the match was restarting. Warwickshire now needed 234 from 31 overs. The outfield was soggy and the light poor. The prospect of a victory was equally poor.

Alec Davis, Warwickshire's amiable scorer, asked me what the tactics were going to be as he left the dressing-room to return to the scorer's box on the other side of the ground. 'Some crash, some bang and definitely plenty of wallop,' I said. 7 an over was a tough target in the conditions but I was determined to try and win the game for my side. I was not thinking of equalling the record of the great West Indian batsman Everton Weekes, who had scored five consecutive hundreds. I knew about the record; it was in the back of my mind. But my main aim was to see my side come out of the match with maximum points.

I did not make a good start. Dominic Ostler and I had been running extremely well, both playing shots at fielders and trusting each other to run. But at 96–2 with Dominic on 51 I called him for a tight run and, realizing I would not make it, sent him back. I was the one who should have gone but my instinct was to stay because I felt confident that I could win the game. It was not something I would normally do. I apologized to Dominic afterwards and he accepted my apology. It made me all the more determined to play a match-winning innings.

Several times the light faded and in a normal game the batsmen would have wanted to come off. Graham Rose, Somerset's medium-fast bowler, twice bowled beamers at me. One was so close when I ducked that I ricked my neck and needed treatment which might have cost us another over. 'It slipped,' said Rose. I had to accept his word. The outfield was wet and the bowlers were using towels to dry the ball. I was rather sceptical though when he bowled a second one.

I do not believe any bowler deliberately bowls a beamer, the head-high full toss, because it is such a lethal delivery. It can cause serious injury, much more so than the bouncer which tends to rise, whereas the beamer comes straight at the batsman from an awkward height. But if an umpire is satisfied that the bowler has deliberately bowled this frightening type of delivery he should act accordingly.

After Dominic Ostler's exit, I must have played my most attacking first-class innings. Paul Smith joined me and scored 38 off 31 balls, and when he was out at 170–3 we still needed 151 from 21 overs. I was on 37 and remained confident we would reach the target. Asif Din, who scored a century to help Warwickshire win the NatWest Trophy the year before, joined me to add support at the other end. My fifty came off 51 balls and soon the fourth-wicket stand with Asif added a further 50 runs in 32 balls. Asif's share was 7; he provided valuable back-up. Mushtaq Ahmed, the Pakistan leg-break bowler whom I rate a better all-round bowler than Australia's Shane Warne because of his greater subtlety and range of spin, found difficulty in bowling because of the conditions. Hayhurst had to use him because his medium pacers, Rose particularly, were proving so expensive.

Rose's final analysis was 0–117 off 18.4 overs. One of the shots which pleased me most that extraordinary day was the six I took off him over square leg, the longest boundary, to go from 93 to 99. A fast-run two took me past the hundred in 72 deliveries and it was the fastest century of the season, beating the 76-ball century of the New Zealand batsman Martin Crowe on the same ground two weeks previously. Crowe took some time to reach his best form in the Cornhill series against England but I have never doubted he is one of the best strokemakers in the world. But for his knee problems which keep him in and out of the New Zealand team I feel he would be achieving much more than he already is. Watching him bat later during the Lord's Test when he performed so magnificently on one leg I wondered just how much more he could contribute to New Zealand cricket. Nowadays the top players are expected to play almost all the year round and it is not easy for them to protect their fitness. But that is something I intend to do myself. I do not want to end up on crutches.

In my Taunton innings, exactly 50 per cent of the runs were scored in boundaries, fourteen fours and two sixes or 68 out of the 136 runs which were scored off 94 balls. I managed to keep the strike during most of the final period and when the 100 stand came up with Asif, his share, a vital one, was 22 off 21 deliveries. When Mushtaq at last bowled me only 25 runs were needed off the final six overs with 6 wickets left. Asif, 41 not out, ensured that we achieved the target. Our partnership had added 126 in 13 overs with Asif scoring 27 of them.

The statisticians worked out that my aggregate of runs since the Antigua Test was 884 in five innings with one not out and they were talking about all kinds of records being at my mercy, including the 4,952 runs of Denis Compton in a calendar year. I wasn't too sure about that. I knew my current vein of runs could not continue. The law of averages meant I was due to fail.

So much cricket is played in England there is no time to reflect on the last innings or recover from the last minor injury. I needed treatment on my neck but felt sure I would be fit for the Benson and Hedges tie against Kent the next day. The game proved to be one of the most controversial of the summer. Edgbaston was shrouded in low cloud when I arrived and in normal circumstances there might have been a start when the light rain stopped. However, the pitch was damp after apparently being left uncovered the previous weekend. Mark Benson, the Kent captain, was not happy about it and nor were his players. Dennis Amiss thought it was playable and the umpires, realizing that one of the captains was opposed to starting on such a pitch, ruled that no play could be possible before lunch. Various alternatives were discussed, like taking the match to another ground. Derby was mentioned.

Finally it was decided that under the rules of the competition there would have to be a shoot-out in the indoor nets, with five nominated players of each side bowling at the unprotected stumps. Every player involved was against the idea. It is a cruel way to go out of a competition if you lose. There are spare dates in the programme when these matches can be rearranged and our view was that there should have been a postponement. It would have been the only fair way to resolve the matter.

I had no wish to take part in the shoot-out even if I had been asked. I watched from the back as the bowlers took their turn. Tim Munton was first to go and, as everyone would expect of him, hit the target. His second delivery missed. That was the pattern all the way through. Munton, Gladstone Small, Paul Smith, Dermot Reeve and Richard Davis all succeeded with one of their two chances. Likewise Carl Hooper, Mark Ealham, Duncan Spencer and Min Patel for Kent. The tension heightened when Nigel Llong, one of Kent's younger and less experienced players, stepped up to bowl the last ball. If he had succeeded, the process would have started again until someone missed. Nigel was narrowly wide with his second effort and everyone felt desperately sorry for him, even the Warwickshire players. We all believed a better system should be used to decide qualification for the next round. Kent later protested to the TCCB and their protest was rejected. One of their players, Matthew Fleming, was reprimanded by the Board for writing a critical article about the affair in *The Cricketer*.

CHAPTER TWELVE

SIX OUT OF SIX

BY THE END OF MAY THERE WAS INCREASING SPECULATION about whether I could break the record of six consecutive centuries. Christopher Martin-Jenkins worked out that my aggregate of 884 runs in my previous six innings was only 30 behind Bradman's. If conditions were ideal for batting I might have had a reasonable chance but when Warwickshire arrived in London for their next Britannic Assurance Championship match, against champions Middlesex at Lord's starting on 26 May, the weather was indifferent and prospects of play virtually nil. The first day's play was washed out and, after hearing that the chances of a prompt start the following morning were slim, I accepted an invitation to go to Tramp's in Jermyn Street for dinner. Robert Sangster invited me to join his table and we had a convivial evening.

I drink, but not excessively, and on that occasion I restricted myself to mineral water. It was the early hours of the morning before I returned to the team hotel. I do not normally go out to night clubs before important innings but because of the likely late start I did not feel I had acted unprofessionally. One or two newspapers heard that I had been in Tramp's and wrote about it. One Sunday newspaper came up with the story two weeks later and implied that I was indulging myself. That was simply not true.

I was surprised to find when I arrived at Lord's that the game was going to start on time. Mike Gatting, the Middlesex captain, won the toss and predictably asked Warwickshire to bat. It was not an ideal day or time to be pursuing a world record. Martin-Jenkins wrote in the *Daily Telegraph*: 'Conditions could not have been more inimical for anyone attempting a batting record, let alone a hard-wicket player still coming to terms with the problems of batting in damp and cold. It was the sort of morning in which the moisture creeps insidiously up the legs through the soles of one's boots.'

I agreed with every word. I was soon walking out to the middle, to warm applause from a sparse crowd after Roger Twose lost his off stump to a swinging delivery from Neil Williams, one of county cricket's most accurate and underrated bowlers. The ball was moving both ways in the air and off the pitch and I knew I would need a lot of luck to survive long enough to make another century. Lord's has peculiar problems anyway with the slope, and bowlers like Williams and Angus Fraser knew just how to exploit the conditions. There were three lbw appeals in the first ten balls I faced, one a particularly loud one from Gus Fraser which umpire David Constant turned down. Most English umpires are of an extremely high standard and rarely give a batsman out lbw unless they are convinced he is out. That was one of the features which impressed me most about county cricket. The umpiring is consistently the best in the world, mainly I suppose because nearly all the officials were top-class players themselves. That does not happen so much in other countries.

I reached 26 from 49 balls – the number of balls was indicative of just how much I was made to struggle for my runs – when Richard Johnson bowled a ball down the leg side, away from the pad, and I got a faint nick to wicket-keeper Keith Brown. I didn't wait for the decision. I was very annoyed to be out to what I would term a 'nothing' ball.

It was a very frustrating way to be dismissed when a world record was 74 runs away. It wasn't as if it was a good ball. I was just trying to work it on the leg side and could so easily have left it. If I remember right, that was the only time in the whole of the summer of 1994 that I was out in that fashion. It is a shot where the batsman does not have so much control. When I leg-glance I like to do it close to the body so that if I misjudge the shot and edge the ball it hits the thigh pad or top of the pad. That was definitely too wide a ball to try to score from at that stage of the innings.

The Middlesex players embraced Johnson and deservedly so. It was the second time he had dismissed me in seventeen days. He has an equable temperament, like Gus Fraser, and I believe he has a fine career ahead of him. When he arrived at the ground he did not think he was playing; his name was not on the scorecard. Kevin Shine, a faster bowler recruited from Hampshire, was down at number 11 but when Mike Gatting saw the conditions he made the right decision to promote Johnson, which was unfortunate for me. Interviewed afterwards, Johnson said: 'It's a great wicket to have but all I was trying to do was keep it tight and not give him anything to hit.' Warwickshire scored only 211 in 89 overs and Middlesex bettered that by 38 in their first innings with Mike Roseberry scoring 119.

We had to score quickly in the second innings to make up for the lost first day and that was my intention on the Monday, the final day, when I went in to bat again to another pleasing reception. Conditions were easier but the ball was still swinging. The day before I recorded a first-ball duck in a Sunday League game against Middlesex, lbw to the medium-pace bowler Mark Feltham. The *Sun* newspaper had offered £1,000 to the first bowler to do it and Feltham, a cricketer who has spent most of his career in and out of the Surrey and Middlesex sides, was delighted to be presented with the cheque the next day. I was out trying to work the ball to leg. It did not upset me; these things happen. The best of players are eligible for membership of The Primary Club, an organization based in Beckenham, Kent, which collects charity money for the blind from its members, who have been out first ball.

On the Monday, in much better light, everything seemed to go right for me and I reached my hundred off 111 balls. One of my drives split the thumb of my West Indian team-mate Desmond Haynes who had to go off for repairs. In many ways this innings was the highlight of my first month in England. Eventually I reached 140 off 147 deliveries with twenty-two fours and one six. I am not a big six-hitter. I prefer not to take chances and keep the ball on the ground if possible. But that particular six pleased me a lot because it was about the furthest I can remember hitting the ball. John Emburey was the bowler and earlier, just before lunch, I mistimed one of his quicker deliveries and provided him with the chance of a comparatively easy catch. To his intense annoyance he dropped it.

He had been having trouble with one of his eyes and next day was due to see an eye surgeon. After lunch he bowled an off break on the off stump and I swung through the line with some power without it being one of the hardest shots I have played. But to my amazement the ball sailed away towards the top of the Lord's pavilion, striking the guttering on the roof of the South Turret and breaking some slates as it bounced down. A few more feet and it might have cleared the pavilion, a feat which I understand has only once been achieved at Lord's. The experts said it rivalled a shot by Glamorgan's Mike Llewellyn in the 1977 Gillette Cup, when the bowler was also John Emburey.

When I was finally out the Long Room rose to me and it brought goose pimples to my arms. It was one of the highlights of my career. Scoring six centuries in seven innings had apparently been done by only seven other batsmen – Fry, Bradman, Procter, G.E. Tyldesley, V.M. Merchant, W.R. Hammond and P.J. Kirsten. I was pleased and proud to join the club.

The match was to end less auspiciously for me when Dermot Reeve asked me to bowl later in the afternoon. His declaration at 306–5 after negotiations with Mike Gatting set Middlesex a target of 269 in 50 overs. Earlier on, when Roseberry was striking the ball well, Middlesex went for the runs, giving us a chance of bowling them out. But when two quick wickets fell they stopped going for their shots and Dermot felt something was needed to rekindle their interest in the target. He proceeded to set an attacking field, which I was unhappy about because it meant he wanted me to give them some runs.

I bowled three overs, one of which consisted mainly of full tosses, which cost 31 runs. I had not warmed up and the whole business was unsatisfactory. At the end of my third over I felt some pain in my shoulder and asked permission to leave the field, which was granted. In my absence, Middlesex revived their run chase, only to lose more wickets, and with nine down Fraser had to block out the last over from Tim Munton to avoid defeat.

CHAPTER THIRTEEN

501

JUNE 6 1994 WAS THE FIFTIETH ANNIVERSARY OF THE LAUNCHING of the Anglo–American invasion of France in the Second World War. It was also a very special day for me, the day I beat Hanif Mohammad's world-record first-class score of 499 for Karachi against Bahawalpur in 1959. My innings of 501 not out against Durham at Edgbaston broke so many other records that even now I am not sure of the exact number.

To have broken this record forty-nine days after beating the Test score of 365 was simply unbelievable. I am asked countless times which was the better innings and I say it is impossible to make a comparison. I am just happy to cherish both records. Obviously beating a record in a Test match is the peak of anyone's career but it was a paradise of a batting pitch in Antigua. It was a good one, too, at

Edgbaston and Durham's bowling, though committed and accurate right up to the final overs, could not be compared with England's.

I did not use the same bat in both innings. At Edgbaston I had a fairly new Gray-Nicholls scoop bat weighing 2lb. 7oz. with a blue handle and sponge under the grip. I have not used it since. These two bats are so special to me that I keep them in a special place. It would have to be an abnormally high offer from a collector even to make me think of selling them. I don't think I ever would whatever the future holds for me.

The odds against anyone breaking a world record, particularly from Warwickshire's side, must have been extremely high, especially after Phil Bainbridge, the Durham captain, won the toss and decided to bat. His decision left us spending the better part of two days in the field while Durham set a number of county records. Their 556–8 declared was their largest total since joining the championship in 1992, and John Morris's 204 was the highest individual total for them.

The way I started my innings gave no indication that I was going to make history. Anderson Cummins, my West Indian team-mate from Barbados, was the bowler I faced when I went in midway through the afternoon, and I knew from previous meetings with him that he would bowl the first ball short. I also knew that it would be a quick one. I was preparing to move on to the back foot as he delivered and played the shot a little too early. The ball went past his outstretched hand and he may well have got a finger on it. It did not worry me that I could have been out first ball.

Like Viv Richards used to, I want to dominate the bowler from the first ball. It is a mental thing. You have to show him who is in charge. It was said of the late George Headley, one of the first of the great West Indian batsmen, that he always wanted to hit the first ball he faced for a boundary. I have never tried to follow that course, but if there is a chance of scoring a boundary at the start of the innings I will try to take it. It is a part of the West Indian way of playing cricket.

The period before tea at Edgbaston was one of my sketchiest at the crease in my year with Warwickshire. My feet simply would not go to the right places. Having quick feet is essential to a top-class batsman, but like a dancer they have to be in time to the music, or in this case the bowling.

When I had reached 10 I tried to force a yorker from Anderson pitched on leg stump, and having got my right foot in the wrong place missed it and was bowled. I was relieved when Peter Wight, the longest-serving of the umpires on the panel, shouted 'No ball!' Anderson was not looking too happy. Next ball was a little bit quicker . . . and shorter. Luck continued to go my way. When I was on 18 Simon Brown, Durham's medium-fast left-arm over-the-wicket bowler, had me playing down the wrong line and I edged an easy chance straight to the wicket-keeper Chris Scott. Thinking I was out, I walked a couple of steps towards the pavilion only to realize he had dropped it. If he had been quick-thinking, he might have been able to run me out. But like Anderson a few minutes earlier, he was horrified. 'Jesus Christ,' he said, 'I hope he doesn't get a hundred!' Bainbridge added a third slip and I promptly edged a four past the new man.

At tea I declined any refreshment and asked Keith Piper if he could go to the Indoor School with me to sort out my problems. When I am batting badly I believe I can put things right with some co-ordinated practice. Bob Woolmer believes videos are the answer;

he has the players filmed regularly so they can look at their mistakes. That is not a method I prefer. After ten minutes or so of Keith throwing balls at me I felt happier.

The final session saw me go on to reach my seventh hundred in eight innings, a feat which apparently no-one else has done although a dozen players, including Bradman who has done it four times, have recorded seven in nine innings. I was unbeaten on 111 at the close of play, and though I might have been out on a number of occasions I felt it was an innings to cherish. The ones you have to work hard at are usually more rewarding than the ones that come easy. I had been hitting the ball at fielders, something I usually manage to avoid. I have this mental note of where they are, and when I play the shot I open the face of the bat to make sure it finds the gap, or alternatively close the face depending on the location of the fielders.

The next day's play was washed out, and when I arrived on Monday morning I wondered what the tactics would be. With so little time remaining, just three sessions, Dermot Reeve would be expecting to declare and be set a target by Bainbridge. But the Durham captain wasn't prepared to negotiate. He said one of his bowlers, David Graveney, was unfit to bowl and he wasn't 100 per cent himself. Dermot was upset that no deal could be arranged and now only bonus points could be played for. He said he might want to declare later and bowl a few quick overs to improve Warwickshire's over rate. That often happens when there is no chance of a result because the players do not like being fined fairly large amounts at the end of the season. County cricketers earn such a comparatively low salary; why do the authorities want to take it way from them?

I had a fifteen-minute net before the start and I wasn't moving well. Roger Twose said jokingly: 'You're just a glam fast-century flashpot. Why don't you set out your stall for the really big jobs like I do? Bet you can't beat my 277 today then?'

Right from the first ball, a delivery from Simon Brown which I worked away for 2, I felt very comfortable; the ball was hitting the middle of the bat. My timing was good. Brown and Cummins didn't bowl badly; they compared favourably with many opening pairs around the counties. Bainbridge wasn't a front-line bowler, however, and in the absence of Graveney the 22-year-old left-arm spinner David Cox, who was making his début, had to bowl 30 overs. Cox managed to find the edge on one occasion. Graveney, sitting in the dressing-room, said: 'The more runs he scores, the more ice I'm going to put on my leg!'

Trevor Penney, my partner, let me have the strike as much as possible. He is a very unselfish, uncomplicated player. 'Batting with Lara gives you an inferiority complex,' he said. His share of what was to be a third-wicket stand of 314, 13 short of the county record, was a valuable 44.

My intention had been to bat as long as I could, but the runs were coming so freely that it occurred to me I might be able to beat a few records, even MacLaren's 424. In those two hours before lunch I scored 174; Trevor's share was 27. Exactly a hundred of my runs came in fours, with a further five sixes. My score at lunch was 285 and the only half chance I had given, to Cummins at 238, went through for a boundary. I did not really think he would catch it. Batsmen need luck and I believe they make their own luck. The better your form, the more luck you get. The worse your form, the worse your luck becomes.

Keith Piper helped me take off my pads and I sat for

a while thinking about how well it had gone and what might lie ahead. I had the lightest of lunches, just some mashed potato and some blackcurrant juice. Alec Davis, our scorer, came in and I asked him whether 174 was any kind of record. 'I'll try and check it,' he said. I learned later that Ranjitsinhji scored 180 before lunch for Sussex against Surrey in 1902 but that session lasted 150 minutes to the 120 in the current championship. When I reached 278 just before the interval, I bettered Roger's 277 which had been the highest score by a Warwickshire batsman at Edgbaston. He ribbed me about it.

I asked Dermot if he could let me continue. 'You're not going to declare, are you?' I asked. 'I might be able to beat MacLaren's record.' He said: 'As long as you're there, I won't declare.' I did not feel too tired. For the first time that extraordinary day I started to think about Hanif's 499. I realized it was attainable if I kept scoring at this rate.

After lunch Bainbridge tried to keep me away from the strike by putting the field out, which didn't bother me unduly as I was happy for Keith Piper, who had come in after Penney and Paul Smith had departed at 437 and 488, to be given a chance of making a big score. When we met in the middle of the wicket I kept saying to him: 'Make sure you get a big one.'

Keith is a bubbly, enthusiastic cricketer and when he straight-drove through mid on and it was clearly going to reach the rope, he still kept running to my end. 'Why run?' I said. 'Don't you know when you've played a good shot?' By this time I was beginning to feel tired, especially after one all-run four to deep extra cover.

When I reached 300, I became the first player to score 300 at Edgbaston, which when I was told later I found rather surprising. At 307 I set a new individual record for the county, beating Frank Foster's 306 against Worcestershire at Dudley in 1914. I was determined to pass 375 and when I did so, that gave me some more satisfaction.

Durham's bowlers were wilting and I knew if I could keep my concentration the world record was a possibility. Graeme Hick's 405, the highest score in England this century, came and went but I was slightly concerned I was playing the odd indifferent shot. At 413 came the worst of the lot. I tried to pull a delivery from Brown to leg, played too early and the ball speared up into the air towards mid wicket. The nearest fielder was the Warwickshire player Michael Burns, who was substituting for one of the Durham players. One or two other fielders might have gone for it but they all hesitated. Burns, who also hesitated, just failed to get to it. I made a mental note not to play that shot again. Two runs earlier I had become the nineteenth player in history to score 300 runs in a day, or so I was told in the newspapers the next day.

As in Antigua, I was telling myself to keep going, it's getting close. MacLaren's record of 424 went. Then Bradman's 452. Keith Piper kept saying: 'Please, please, don't get out.' I was delighted when he reached his maiden hundred. No one deserved a century more and I was even more delighted for him in September when he was picked for the England A tour of India. England have to look for a younger keeper to succeed Steve Rhodes and Jack Russell and he is the best of the younger ones.

Our fifth-wicket stand of 322 was a county record. An hour from the close of play I still needed 60 more runs but I was unconcerned. Once I passed 424 I felt I could do it. With the regular bowlers near to exhaustion, Bainbridge gave 10 overs to Wayne Larkins, the former England opening batsman, and John Morris. Both were expensive, but little more costly than his main bowlers.

I was aware that the final hour had been called at 5 p.m. with my score in the 470s and believed I had plenty of time available. The 136th over began at 5.28 with my total 497 and it was bowled by Morris, David Gower's partner when the two England players were fined on the previous tour of Australia for joy-riding in a light aircraft during a match.

Believing I still had time on my side, I blocked the first three deliveries. The fourth was a bouncer which struck me on the helmet. I had intended to glance it down to fine leg and it was just as well that I missed it because we would have run one, which would have left me on 498 with Keith facing the final two deliveries. The pressure would have been on him to get a single from the fifth ball.

Being hit by an innocuous medium-pacer provoked some mirth in the middle. 'I've found his weakness,' said Morris. Keith came down the wicket to ask if I was all right. On the way he checked with umpire Wight about the finishing time. Wight told him this was the final over. I didn't know that. 'You've only got two balls left,' said Keith. 'Are you sure?' I asked him. 'I've checked with the umpires,' he said.

In the West Indies they can bat on, but in England it is in the rules that play has to end after half an hour of the last hour if there is no chance of a result. Bainbridge said later he would not have asked the officials to give me another over. 'Rules are rules,' he said. I knew I had to hit one of those remaining deliveries for a boundary and, as Morris bowled, I came down the pitch and swung through the line towards extra cover. There was no fielder close enough to stop it and I felt relieved, happy and tired all at the same time. I had kissed the pitch in Antigua but there was no chance of doing that this time, so many people came rushing on to the field.

My Warwickshire colleagues formed a guard of honour, bats held high in the air as I came off, pursued by photographers and fans. I had no idea at the time I had broken so many records; I thought it had only been two or three. It was some time before it all sank in. The players engulfed me in the dressing-room and a bottle of champagne which was presented to me for being Warwickshire's player of the month in May was emptied over my head. I only drink champagne on special occasions and this was one. Another bottle was quickly opened. I toasted Keith, whose unbeaten 116 was just the kind of innings he needed to prove to everyone that he had a lot of ability with the bat as well as having great talent as a keeper.

Warwickshire's 810–4 off only 133.5 overs was another of the many records broken that day. I had also scored more runs in a day, 390, than anyone else, outscored every other left-hander, and recorded most boundaries in an innings, 72.

Mushtaq Mohammad, Hanif's brother who lives in the Birmingham area, had been present and he arranged for Hanif to ring me. 'I am not sad at losing the record,' said Hanif. 'Records are there to be broken and I congratulate you. It is great for cricket.'

In his many interviews the next day, Hanif made the point that I was short in stature like most of the leading batsmen – himself, Bradman, Gavaskar and Rohan Kanhai. I think he is right to suggest that short players handle fast bowling better than tall players. They are also lighter on their feet.

The Press were waiting in the players' dining-room a few yards away to interview me. I tried to be calm and rational and emphasize the point that breaking records doesn't make you invincible or a great player. That comes only after a player has been at the top in Test cricket over a long period of time. I hope I can do that.

There will be times when I fail. I know there are bad patches to come. My main aim is to be more consistent. I am only twenty-five; there are many years ahead of me.

It was some time before I managed to get my soaking clothes off and have a shower. The telephone kept ringing. Joey Carew was one of the callers which pleased me. There was no time to dwell on my success. Next day Warwickshire were due to take on Surrey in the semi-final of the Benson and Hedges Cup. I had to go home and pack. First there were the autograph hunters to oblige, literally hundreds of them. They all wanted their scorecard signing.

CHAPTER FOURTEEN

DIZZY AT THE OVAL

THE SCHEDULE IN ENGLISH CRICKET IS SO TOUGH THAT THERE is no time to rest, particularly if a team is successful. The day after my record-breaking innings Warwickshire were due to play Surrey, unbeaten in one-day cricket up to then, at The Foster's Oval in the semi-final of the Benson and Hedges Cup. I had intended to drive myself to London but I was so tired there was a danger of me falling asleep at the wheel so I went with Keith Piper as my chauffeur.

Keith was brought up in London and learned his cricket at the Haringey Cricket Club with former West Indies and Jamaican cricketer Reg Scarlett, but as we drove into London in the early hours he got lost. It was around 2 a.m. before we arrived at the Tower Hotel next to Tower Bridge. When I woke the next morning I did not feel too much like playing in a high-pressure game. My head was buzzing. There was no time for any practice by the time we arrived at the ground and I tried to take a little rest before the start. It was a hot and humid day and I could have done with Dermot winning the toss. Alec Stewart won it and decided to bat on an excellent batting pitch.

It meant a long, tiring three and a half hours out in the middle while Surrey's batsmen, particularly Graham Thorpe who scored 87 and David Ward with 61, took advantage of the conditions. Towards the end of the innings I felt I couldn't continue. I was feeling dizzy and asked permission to go off. A doctor who examined me said I was exhausted and recommended an ice-pack on the back of my neck.

Bob Woolmer was anxious to get me back on to the field. 'You can't stay off much longer, otherwise you will have to bat down the order,' he said. 'You've got to go back out there.' I told him I needed more time. I simply could not face it. I tried to sleep but it was not really possible. Altogether I was off the field for 46 minutes, and I knew that the longer I stayed off the longer I would have to wait to bat under the rules.

Surrey made 267–7 off their 55 overs and the feeling in the Warwickshire dressing-room was that we were capable of beating that. There was a lot of pressure on Surrey to win a trophy after many years without one and we knew their players were anxious. Eventually I went in at number 6 at 120–4. The game was evenly balanced after Dominic Ostler, 44, and Roger Twose, 46, had given us a good start. Tony Pigott, the 36-year-old pace bowler Surrey signed from Sussex, had taken 3 quick wickets to raise the hopes of the home supporters.

There were 30 overs left and 148 runs to make, and in the conditions 5 an over was a reasonable target. Normally in one-day matches batsmen have little time to play themselves in; they have to play shots from the beginning. But I felt it was a situation where I did not have to take too many chances. In one-day cricket the batting side knows exactly what it has to do. The batsmen have the target in their minds throughout the innings. There is often less of the unpredictability of Test cricket which unfolds in a more exciting way. Test cricket is a battle of minds. In one-day cricket it is about runs per over and keeping up the run rate.

I prefer Test cricket, as I have said, because it is the real thing, the highest level a player can perform. But I do not totally decry one-day cricket. It is a spectators' game, often spectators who would not be present if it was a normal game of cricket. Most players like it because it provides them with a buzz. In one-day knock-out competitions there is the bait of reaching the final and winning a trophy.

Nor do I criticize the use of coloured outfits and named shirts in Sunday matches. I think that brings colour and excitement to the game and creates greater interest. I have to say, though, that when you are playing so much cricket it is easy to mix things up. During one Axa and Equity League game I started to put on a pair of white pads. 'What are you doing?' said one of the players. For a moment I didn't understand what he was talking about. 'I'm putting my pads on,' I said. 'Yes but it's Sunday, you should be putting the blue pads on,' he said.

Though I felt desperately tired at the Oval I was seeing the ball well and struck nine fours in my innings of 70 off 73 deliveries. Dermot Reeve was unbeaten on 46, playing the anchor role, and following his success with the ball was presented with the Gold Award. I was bowled by Surrey's all-rounder Adam Hollioake, charging down the wicket. As Warwickshire were only 16 runs short of the target it did not matter. Hollioake is one of several very promising young cricketers to have come up through the Surrey ranks and I believe he has a good future in the game. Thorpe again impressed me. It was mystifying why the England selectors had left him out of the series against New Zealand.

I needed a rest and had taken steps to get one. The next day I was booked to fly BWIA back to Port of Spain for a few days with my family and friends. That was the great advantage of my concession of 375,000 TT dollars-worth of free air miles from the airline; it meant I was able to go home occasionally and travel first-class. But I almost missed the flight. I needed to do some last-minute shopping and went to Selfridge's. Unfortunately the traffic coming out of London was heavy and there were only a couple of minutes left before the aircraft was due to leave when David Manasseh and I sprinted down the enclosed walkway to board. To my surprise there were a couple of national newspaper correspondents in first class and around a dozen others, including photographers, back in economy. My 'private' visit home was not going to be very private.

I was relieved to see my old captain Viv Richards in first class. Viv had been in England on business and we sat and talked for an hour or two. Viv had been the greatest batsman of his generation and had been through everything I was now going through. He was able to give me some useful advice. The next day it was announced he had been awarded the OBE in the Queen's Birthday List, a well-deserved honour. David Manasseh discussed what we should do about the Press corps. I did not want them following me around the island and ruining my short break.

Viv had helped out some of the journalists with a few flattering quotes. 'It makes me so proud that this boy has become a man so quickly,' he said. 'This boy, whom I kept back a little because I knew he was so special and I wanted him to grow in his own space, in his own era, has set himself the greatest standards any cricketer has ever achieved. I am a religious man and when people told me cricket was dying, I said, man, a Moses will come to deliver us. Well, Moses has come. His name is Brian Lara. I am only surprised he has done so much, so quickly. What it tells me is that he can become the greatest batsman who has ever lived.'

Viv got off the plane at Antigua, and while we waited for the final leg of the trip to Port of Spain to start, the first-class section was invaded by the Press wanting an interview, and the Kingfisher TV crew who were filming a documentary about my year.

Realizing that the photographers would want some access I arranged to meet them the next day and take them to Cantaro to meet my mother and friends. As I was contracted to the *Daily Mail*, who had three representatives on the flight, I think the rival photographers were delighted with the access. I felt I could not deny it to them. Once you reach a certain level in sport you become a public figure and you have to behave like one, with as much dignity as you can muster. A procession of taxis followed my car through the mountains and orange groves to Santa Cruz, almost like a presidential parade except there were no bodyguards.

Cantaro has changed a bit since my childhood but it still remains one of the most beautiful villages in Trinidad and Tobago. It is essentially the home of a lot of agricultural workers, and of course my late father was a manager at the agricultural station in our village. There is always a fresh breeze and a lot of greenery. Neighbours walk in and out of each other's houses and everyone knows everyone else. Some of my brothers and sisters still live there as does my mother, which makes it very nice whenever I go back.

When we arrived in Cantaro, the enormous media contingent attracted a large number of villagers. Some of them saw it as the opportunity to make themselves famous for fifteen seconds. I don't know if my mum and I had ever had a photo session together, but we certainly did this time. My mum is not accustomed to so much media attention and she soon found herself surrounded by photographers but she handled it like a real professional. Everyone was happy and we were soon on our way to visit Fatima College, my old school. When we got there, I was given a tremendous reception by the 900 boys who were starting their lunch break. These boys represent the real future of Trinidad. The school motto is Nitendo Vinces, 'By striving, You will conquer.' They mobbed me, tearing bits out of their exercise books, thrusting them in front of me with their pens asking me to sign. Some even pushed forward banknotes to sign, which I suppose was their money to buy lunch. Mervyn Moore, the principal, greeted me and I chatted with Harry Ramdass, my coach when I was at the school. I posed for pictures in some of the classrooms which I had once occupied.

Suddenly I felt tired and asked David Manasseh to call a halt. I wanted some time with Leasel, my girlfriend, and I rang the bank where she worked to advise her to take the rest of the day off to avoid being pestered by the photographers. I had been warned that they would soon be on their way to the bank once they found out where she worked. I was grateful to the Press corps that they respected my wishes for privacy after giving them most of what they had wanted.

As Warwickshire were not playing in the championship until the following week I would have liked to stay on, but the club wanted me to play in a country house game for John Paul Getty's team against Mr E.W. Swanton's Arabs on the following Sunday.

It meant me flying back to London on the Saturday night to arrive in time the next morning. Minutes before the BWIA flight was scheduled to depart from Piarco Airport, an anonymous caller rang to say there was a bomb on board the aircraft. It was one of the first times BWIA had received such a warning, I was told. Security officers were sent on board and all the passengers had to disembark.

As there were no sniffer dogs immediately available, the flight was delayed for three hours until some were brought in to examine the plane. The delay meant the pilot was running out of time and it was decided to abandon the stop in Barbados, where 126 London-bound passengers were waiting, and fly direct to Heathrow. The passengers in Barbados were flown down to Trinidad to make the connection but unfortunately for them landed at 9.52, while our flight, BW900, took off precisely two minutes earlier. It caused such a rumpus that BWIA had to issue a press statement which said: 'The captain of BW900 opted not to wait for the incoming aircraft since this would have sent him into discretionary time. This decision took into account the operating time-limit of the crew rostered for this flight.'

It led to some adverse publicity about 126 passengers being left behind because Brian Lara had to be back in London at a certain time to play in a match for John Paul Getty. BWIA offered profuse apologies and paid compensation to all those affected. But I assure them it had nothing to do with me. Blame the hoax caller!

I was rather tired when I arrived at Mr Getty's ground in Hertfordshire and made only 21. Clive Radley, the former Middlesex and England batsman, now head coach at the MCC, also played. I was introduced to Mr Getty who seemed a very nice man. He is one of cricket's major benefactors and he provided some of the money that paid for the new grandstand at Lord's.

CHAPTER FIFTEEN

INCIDENT AT NORTHAMPTON

MY MEETING WITH CURTLY AMBROSE AT NORTHAMPTON IN JUNE was billed as the confrontation between the world's greatest batsman and the world's greatest bowler. It put unnecessary pressure on me and I was not happy about it. Pride would be at stake and it was difficult enough facing a bowler of Curtly's calibre without any extra provocation. My state of mind wasn't helped when I got lost in Northampton's one-way system on the way to the ground and arrived too late for practice.

Warwickshire lost an early wicket and I was soon on my way to the middle. I wasn't wearing a helmet at the time, which I hoped hadn't given Curtly the wrong impression. I was not being arrogant; the helmet I was carrying in my hand was slightly suspect, and as you cannot afford to take any chances with this particular piece of equipment, I asked the 12th man to bring out another one.

The pitch was a good one with bounce and Curtly was bowling at his fastest, reserving his quickest deliveries for me. Fortunately I faced few deliveries from him early on. It is always easier for the batsman in these duels because he can accumulate runs and gain confidence as he does so. But the bowler has just six balls, not necessarily at the batsman he wants to bowl to, before handing over to someone else at the other end. And he also has to rely on his fielders.

The Northants players felt I should have been given out first ball. Tony Penberthy, the bowler from the other end, hit me on the pad and they all went up. But I was convinced the ball had pitched outside the leg stump. Curtly had never got me out in nine meetings and he was trying his hardest to change that. The defensive side of my game was frequently in action and several times I had to jump a foot or more in the air to get high enough to play the ball down. When the ball was off line I let it go. In that innings of 197 I recorded only one boundary off him, which indicated the quality of his bowling. I faced 45 deliveries from him and scored just 12 runs from them; his figures of 1–37 off 25 overs were remarkable in a day when the batting side totalled 448–9.

Later on in my innings, when I should have known better, I took my eye off a short delivery from him which crashed into the back of my helmet, cracking it and leaving me with a sore head. The ball came through faster and higher than I expected but it was still a bad error of judgement. When Jonty Rhodes was hit on the helmet by Devon Malcolm at the Oval in the Fifth Test he went off to hospital for treatment and was detained overnight.

My injury was not as bad as that though there was a small bump on the back of my head and I had a severe headache. I felt I was able to carry on and did so. A double century was looming and I had a bet with Keith Piper that I would record three during the season.

When I was 170 I misjudged a delivery from Curtly and edged the ball to Kevin Curran in the gully. Curtly was angry when Curran dropped it. 'These guys don't catch anything,' he moaned. I was disappointed to be out on 197 and not to pass 200 but I had equalled a record of eight centuries in eleven innings set by Sir Don Bradman. Taking into account the quality of the bowling, it had to rate as one of my best innings of the summer. Not that I had much chance to celebrate it. My head was throbbing and I had to lie down and rest.

I still felt dizzy the next day but took my place in the field as Tim Munton's 5–53 hastened the follow-on. Rob Bailey and Allan Lamb held us up in the afternoon with a third-wicket stand of 137, and near the end of it an incident occurred which was to have unfortunate repercussions for me. Bailey appeared to nick the ball and Keith Piper made a splendid catch low to his right. Umpires Barry Leadbeater and Allan Jones conferred and decided that Bailey, who was on 50, was not out. I was sure he had hit the ball and it was a fair catch and said: 'We've got him out once, let's do it again.' I was supporting my bowlers, as I always do. Jones, the square leg umpire, heard me make a remark about his eyesight and said: 'There was nothing wrong with my eyesight when I gave you not out the first ball you faced! You concentrate on your fielding and I'll concentrate on umpiring!'

Dermot Reeve intervened and said: 'Umpires in this country don't like that. You've got to keep on the right side of them.' When I tried to say something else he said: 'Don't act like a prima donna.'

I certainly wasn't doing that. It was such a minor incident. There was no attempt to abuse the umpire or dispute his decision to his face. It was the kind of incident that happens occasionally in cricket and everyone forgets by the time the next interval comes round. Bailey added 4 more runs before edging another catch to Piper and this time he walked. Keith had been off the field earlier in the day suffering from the effects of food poisoning.

At 3.25 I was feeling so dizzy I asked permission to go off, and spent the rest of the day's play in the dressing-room, lying down. This had nothing to do with the earlier incident but a few days later some of the newspapers implied that I walked off in a sulk after being reprimanded by Reeve. The day after the incident there was no mention of it in any of the newspapers but one or two writers who weren't at the match heard a second-hand account of what was supposed to have been said and it became public property. That was the start of a two-week period which was the low point of the season for me. The sniping built up and by the morning of the Benson and Hedges Final at Lord's I was being portrayed in one newspaper as 'wilful, arrogant and insubordinate'. I was now feeling the full force of the media but I had already taken the view that I was not going to let them affect my state of mind.

I was off the field all day on the Saturday of the BAC game at Northampton and by this time my left knee was sore. It has shown signs of wear and tear in the past, and when I need to rest it I rest it. I don't need scans or X-rays to tell me it is causing discomfort. When I arrived at the ground for the Sunday League match next day I was approached by the BBC cricket correspondent

Jonathan Agnew who wanted to interview me about the game but I said my knee was playing up so I didn't think I would be playing.

Dermot Reeve and Bob Woolmer must have been told about this by Agnew and they came to see me. 'I don't think I'm fit enough to play,' I said. 'My knee is troubling me.' Woolmer said they wanted me to play. 'It's live on TV and we want to make it six wins out of six,' he said. I was offended by that. They didn't seem concerned that I was injured. I had to play because it was on TV and they wanted to win in front of a sell-out crowd. Other players missed matches, even Dermot Reeve who was standing in front of me, but for some reason they seemed to be doubting whether I was genuinely injured.

It is tough for the overseas players. They are the ones the public come to see and they are expected to play in every match even if they are not fully fit. But I believe that is imperilling their international future, and I made my mind up a long time ago I would not risk my Test career just to play in a few more games.

The discussions went on and Reeve was a few minutes late for the toss. In the end I decided to back down and play but I wasn't happy about it. We duly won the match by 114 and I scored 34 off 44 balls and held two catches. Trying to sweep the leg-spinner Andy Roberts, I edged the ball into my right eye and needed treatment. It did not break the skin but was still painful. Next ball I responded with a six before I was caught in the deep off Roberts.

Woolmer was quoted in the newspapers the next day: 'He just wanted a rest. He's sore and because of that is thinking of ways to stay off the field. He's been playing a lot of cricket.' That didn't help the situation and when I spoke to him subsequently he apologized and admitted he could have handled the matter better.

On the Monday I was again off the field, this time suffering from the effects of the blow in the eye as well as from a sore knee. I was off so long I had to go in to bat at number 7 when Warwickshire's turn came to bat again, and was soon out for 2. But Warwickshire still won by 4 wickets, to preserve their unbeaten record.

Some newspapers carried stories that I had fallen out with Warwickshire and claimed the county's officials were so concerned at what had happened that they were planning what they termed 'a showdown meeting'. I was supposed to be attending a meeting at Edgbaston with Dennis Amiss the following morning. But there was no meeting. There was nothing to resolve. I was injured and felt I needed a rest. When I agreed to play in the Sunday game Reeve and Woolmer said I could have a few days off.

I had missed only one match, the friendly against Oxford University, up to then and that was a better record than a number of the other players. I did not want to make an issue of that or anything else. But I know that a lot of sportsmen are forced to end their careers prematurely because of injuries to the joints. Sir Gary Sobers was one of them. I am determined that I will not be one of them; I do not want to finish up using a walking stick.

Dennis Amiss, who is a nice down-to-earth person, rang me and suggested a game of golf to talk things over. He knew I loved golf and we arranged to meet at the Belfry. What transpired was not a meeting over a round of golf but an exchange of views. He said he wanted to help me overcome any problems I might have. For example, he could supply a secretary to deal with the mail I was receiving; some days it ran into hundreds of letters and packages. He explained how the club helped Rohan Kanhai, Lance Gibbs and Alvin Kallicharran to acclimatize to English county cricket after an odd problem or two. He asked me whether I was willing to return in 1996 or any time afterwards and I said I would like to but my mind was not made up. The idea of playing more county cricket still had an appeal but it had to be on the right terms.

The next day I had some business commitments in London and while there visited a Harley Street surgeon to get an opinion about my knee. After a detailed examination, he told me the ligaments were slightly damaged and I needed a short rest from cricket. He gave me a certificate to that effect. It wasn't a serious injury but it was one that could degenerate into something more serious.

Warwickshire were scheduled to play Lancashire at Edgbaston the next day and Dermot Reeve and Bob Woolmer were expecting me to play. When I arrived and told them I was not fit enough to play, it was suggested to me I should see the club doctor. I produced the certificate from the Harley Street man and said: 'I've seen my own doctor and this is what he says.'

Reluctantly, they agreed I could have the match off and Jason Ratcliffe was called up from a 2nd XI match to fill the vacancy in the squad. I went away for a few days and my next match was the second-round NatWest Trophy tie at Leicester. I made only 16 in our match-winning 290, and as I came in a spectator shouted: 'You'll have enough time to rest your knee now.' I thought that was very amusing.

CHAPTER SIXTEEN

THE BENSON AND HEDGES FINAL

I WOKE TO SOME PRETTY NASTY HEADLINES IN THE BROADSHEET newspapers on the morning of the Benson and Hedges Final on 9 July. *The Times* wrote: 'Caribbean charmer feels the heat as nice guy image fades.' It continued: 'Lara has taken the fine line between the letter and spirit of the law to such an extent that Warwickshire may decline to take up an option on him in 1996.'

The *Guardian* wrote: 'Has the world's greatest batsman got it all wrong? There must be questions about whether he can last out the season.' The picture of me in *The Times*, an artist's impression, showed me with receding hair and looking at least fifteen years older. When I was signing some autographs near the Tavern during the game, I took my hat off to a reader of *The Times* to show him that I did have a full head of hair!

There had been other articles about how long I had been off the field, articles that questioned my commitment to Warwickshire. I thought all this was damaging to the team and when we had a team meeting about twenty minutes before the start of play I asked for permission to speak. I told the players that I considered myself part of the team, no different from anyone else, and assured them I was still fully committed to playing with them. 'I enjoy playing for Warwickshire and want to see us win every competition this season,' I said. It was a very short speech and I could tell they accepted it and were happy. I shook hands with every player and we left the dressing-room to take the field.

The allegations were untrue but I think they wanted me to reassure them. We were all pumped up and confident of winning after Dermot Reeve told Tim Curtis, the Worcestershire captain, 'We'll have a bowl,' when Curtis called incorrectly. The toss was the decisive feature of the day. Whoever won it had to play very badly to lose the match.

The pitch was slightly damp and the conditions were such that the ball darted around for most of Worcestershire's innings. Gladstone Small and Tim Munton bowled the first 20 overs unchanged and they were magnificent. Adam Seymour, playing in his first Lord's Final, went early, bowled by Munton. Tim Curtis went early too and it was left to Graeme Hick and Tom Moody, Worcestershire's two best batsmen, to try to retrieve the situation. Dermot Reeve kept the pressure on and Hick was lbw to Paul Smith, who was digging the ball into the slowish pitch and extracting a fair amount of pace.

Gladstone felt his hamstring injury would prevent him bowling a second spell so Dermot let him bowl his 11 overs in succession. He conceded just 26 runs, 3 fewer than Tim Munton. Moody might have been able to give Worcestershire a respectable total but when he was 47 he was superbly run out by Trevor Penney at point. Though not quite in the same class as Jonty Rhodes, Trevor is a very gifted all-round fielder who is worth a lot of runs in the field to Warwickshire.

Neil Smith came on with his off breaks and turned the ball quite a lot, another sign that the pitch was a far from ideal one-day pitch. Worcestershire totalled 170 and with conditions improving we felt sure of victory. Dominic Ostler and Roger Twose started in a cavalier fashion, putting on 91 for the first wicket. Ostler's aggressive innings of 56 ended when Roger turned down a quick single and sent his partner back. It was a poor piece of cricket.

The packed crowd gave me a great ovation as they usually do at Lord's, but we had to readjust when Roger called for a run to mid on which I considered risky and was run out by Gavin Haynes for 37. I was still feeing my way on 8 when I clipped a delivery from Phil Newport straight to Graeme Hick at mid wicket. The fact that I was out in exactly the same way in the final of the NatWest Trophy, caught by Hick on the midwicket boundary, gave rise to suggestions that Worcestershire 'had worked me out'. According to some of the Worcestershire players, Tim Curtis had a hunch about how to get me out and had specifically asked his best catcher to go to midwicket. He may well have done that but it is erroneous to say that I get out regularly in that way. It doesn't happen too often. On a slow pitch I was trying to hit the ball towards mid on and changed the shot slightly, failing to keep the ball down.

Anyway, it made no difference to the result of the game. Asif Din helped Paul Smith add another 44 runs for the fourth wicket and Smith was still there on 42 when Warwickshire passed the Worcestershire total with only 4 wickets down and 10.4 overs remaining.

Paul Smith was deservedly voted Man of the Match. He had taken 3–34 in his 11 overs. He is a very determined cricketer who still plays to a high standard despite a knee condition which forces him to wear a support. He went into that match with a strain in the top of his leg and did well to contribute as much as he did.

There was plenty of champagne consumed that night but our celebrations were tempered with the thought that the toss had been so important. It is a bit of a mystery why the pitch was like that in the middle of a dry, hot summer.

Both finalists were allowed to postpone their Sunday League matches for 48 hours and when we beat Glamorgan by 4 wickets at Edgbaston three days later Paul was still on a high, taking 5–38. I was out cheaply again, bowled by the Dutchman Roland Lefebvre trying to hit the ball to leg. Roland is one of the more accurate bowlers in county cricket and is not easy to force away.

A new theory had arisen about how to get me out. David Graveney, who announced his retirement from Durham at the end of the season, was advising his fellow bowlers that it was essential in limited-overs cricket to bowl straighter to me, to tuck me up. But that theory had little to support it. The reason I got out more in one-day cricket is that you have to take more chances. It is about runs per over; you do not have time to play yourself in. The run-rate required is constantly flashing through your mind and dictates how you play.

In one-day cricket, especially one-day internationals, the concentration level required is more demanding. In any form of cricket I try to give 100 per cent concentration to every delivery, but I have to confess my mind wanders on other occasions. When the bowler is going back to his mark I might think about what is on the agenda for the evening. Once the bowler turns and comes running in I dismiss all that from my mind. I am concentrating on just one thing: the next delivery.

Warwickshire's success in the Benson and Hedges meant their odds of doing the Quadruple, winning all four competitions, were reduced to 20–1. Later that week our title challenge faced its toughest test, a four-day game at Guildford against the leaders, Surrey. When I arrived – a little late – I was surprised how much grass there was on the pitch. It was hard to distinguish it from the rest of the square. But it played on the slow side, ideal for a grafter like Andy Moles whose unbeaten 203 in our second innings was the match-winning performance.

I failed in the first innings, caught by the reliable Graham Thorpe at slip off my West Indian team-mate Cameron Cuffy. The ball moved away and I got an outside edge. I lasted longer in the second innings but was so dissatisfied with my form at lunch that I went out and practised instead of eating. I felt I was hitting the ball better after that. Tony Pigott bowled well that day and showed the large crowd there is plenty of humour in the game. When I drove one of his deliveries for a boundary he pulled out a towel from his pocket and held it aloft in mock surrender. But he had the last laugh shortly after-wards when I struck the ball straight back to him, on 44, and he managed to hold on to it.

Surrey did not bat well in either innings and our success by 256 runs was a turning point in the season for both sides. We kept winning and Surrey faltered. When they lost Alec Stewart and Graham Thorpe to England and Martin Bicknell to injury they weren't the same side. But they have a number of promising young players.

Warwickshire confirmed their leadership by beating Essex in the next match by 203 runs. Once again it was a good all-round performance. My 70 lasted 81 balls, and at Chesterfield in the following match I managed to better that with 142 off 135 balls on a very green pitch which had been obviously designed to help Derbyshire's seam bowlers. That was my eighth century of the season and one of my best. I was confident of turning it into a double hundred until I struck the ball into the air on the on side and gave a catch to Kim Barnett. Kim was hidden behind the non-striker as the bowler bowled and I didn't see him until it was too late. We won that match in convincing style, by 139 runs with Keith Piper breaking his recently acquired club record of 10 dismissals with 11.

A high-scoring draw at Worcester at the start of August yielded just one point but we remained top of the table and the odds against all four trophies coming to Edgbaston were reducing weekly.

CHAPTER SEVENTEEN

WINNING THE TITLE

AS WE WENT INTO AUGUST THE PROSPECT OF WINNING THE county championship for the first time in twenty-two years became much more of a reality. Surrey were sliding and only Leicestershire were staying with us. A lot of our success around this time was due to the captaincy of Tim Munton, who skippered the side in almost half our games because of injury to Dermot Reeve. Tim is an uncomplicated, thoughtful and nice guy and his relaxed approach got the best out of the players. He encouraged everyone to do well and I think that approach is always preferable to having someone barking out orders.

We had little meetings before each session in the field and if any points occurred to me I would speak up. As someone who had captained various sides I felt I had something to offer but I rarely offered advice on the field. When I am captain I know how irritating it can be if a player keeps coming up to you and saying you should do this or that. A number of overseas cricketers have captained county sides but I am not sure I want to do the job just yet. It would add to my experience but there are drawbacks to it.

Keith Piper kept wicket so brilliantly during our championship run-in that I often felt I was superfluous at first slip. He would dive in front of me to take catches and I found myself moving wider. His constant chat helped relax us in the slip cordon. He kept urging us on. 'Come on, let's bubble,' he kept saying.

The problem with my knee meant that, except in one-day matches, I was unable to field in the deep. I was not too happy with my catching in county cricket. In Tests I catch most of the chances that come my way. I think I have a good catching record, about two a game. With four fast bowlers there is a greater chance of being presented with catching opportunities when playing for the West Indies. But for Warwickshire I must have dropped almost as many as I caught. There was no excuse for that. Maybe it was through lack of concentration through being out on the field most days in a long, hot summer when there were few breaks.

At first slip, I watch the ball and keep the hands relaxed. The more relaxed the fingers are, the easier it is to hold on to the ball. When I am at second or third slip I watch the bat because it is more difficult to see the ball. I have safe hands and luckily so far have never had any serious finger injuries. But sometimes the ball can hit you in the wrong place and cause a bruise and one of my hands was still sore when I started the season with Warwickshire, a legacy of a catch I made in the Test series against England.

The best catch I have made up to now in my career

was the one that dismissed Kepler Wessels on the final day of that amazing inaugural Test between the West Indies and South Africa in Barbados. He edged a delivery from Courtney Walsh wide to my left and I dived and caught it two-handed about ankle height. I always try to get two hands to the ball. It is safer. My West Indies colleague Carl Hooper stands out as one of the best slip fielders in the world today. He is very focused on the ball when the bowler is about to deliver and rarely drops anything. His concentration level is exceptionally high.

Following our setback in the Britannic Assurance Championship match at Worcester we took on Nottinghamshire, another of the outsiders for the title, at Edgbaston and we lost by an innings and 43 runs, our first defeat of the season. I made my first duck in championship cricket in the second innings which brought my average down to double figures. The only consolation for me was that the successful bowler was my great friend Jimmy Adams. I tried to cut the first ball I received – always a risky business – and with the ball keeping low was bowled. Jimmy was embraced by the whole of the Nottinghamshire side. At twenty-six he is a very thorough, painstaking cricketer who is learning all the time. I believe he will be a regular member of the West Indies side for some years to come. He has so much to offer.

The Nottinghamshire innings of 597–8 off 166 overs was notable for an unbeaten 220 by the England all-rounder Chris Lewis, the highest total by a number 6 against Warwickshire according to the statisticians. The cynics among the critics said that he comes good when touring sides are about to be picked and this was another example of it. But in my view Chris is a top cricketer who is capable of winning matches both with the bat and the ball and also in the field. If he was qualified to play for the West Indies he would have a good chance of being selected.

I do not know him well enough to know why his form seems to fluctuate. The fact that he shaves his head ought not to count against him. He should only be considered for his cricketing ability, which is immense. He must have been disappointed when he was left out of both England tours that followed, although he was called up as a replacement for England in Australia when McCague, White and Gough were all injured.

Our first innings 321, with Grame Welch making 84 not out, up to then his best score, was not enough to avoid the follow-on and we were bowled out for 233 in the second innings. Graeme joined the staff as an eighteen-year-old from Durham in 1990 and had to wait four years for his début. When he was given his chance he proved to be a useful all-rounder, a medium-paced swing bowler with a lot of ability with the bat.

Warwickshire gained some revenge in the Sunday League match, running up the highest Sunday total in twenty-six years, 294, and setting Nottinghamshire a target of 7.37 an over. Neil Smith, promoted to open with Dominic Ostler, figured in an opening stand of 92 in 12 overs to set us on our way. Neil's bowling improved during the season and so did his batting. I made some amends for my duck with 75 from 72 balls, my highest on Sundays. Nottinghamshire failed to reach our score by 72 runs and we stayed 4 points ahead of nearest rivals Worcestershire, the second-best one-day side of 1994.

Until last season I had never batted with a runner at any level of the game. But in Warwickshire's next Britannic Assurance Championship game, against Yorkshire at Scarborough, it was forced on me when my right knee started giving trouble. The left knee was already sore and the combination of the two meant I could hardly walk. It was very worrying. Martyn Moxon, the Yorkshire captain, set us a target of 199 in 49 overs on a good pitch, and as Andy Moles was the batsman out, he acted as my runner. Andy gives his weight as 'above average' in *The Cricketers' Who's Who*, 1992 edition, and is not rated as the quickest mover between the wickets. The players thought it was extremely funny. Andy did not have too much running to do because I was out for 17. Roger Twose, 86 not out, and Dominic Ostler, 40 not out, saw us to victory by 8 wickets with time to spare. Dominic's 186 in our first innings included a seven when a throw from the newcomer Alex Wharf hit the helmet parked behind the wicket-keeper.

Wharf was playing in his first county match and he had the satisfaction of claiming my wicket for 21 in the first innings. My footwork was restricted and I swished at a widish delivery, giving Richard Blakey a catch behind the wicket. Richard Davis, our slow left-arm bowler from Kent, took 6–94 in that match and impressed me as a bowler who has all the attributes needed to be successful in county cricket. I think he just needs to spin the ball a little more, then he would be top-class and a regular member of the side.

I had played in Festival matches at Scarborough before and always enjoyed the experience. It is a nice ground and a good batting pitch. My only reservation is about the signposting: it was one of the grounds where I found myself getting more and more confused the closer I got to it!

My injuries meant I was forced to miss the Sunday game, which was watched by a near-capacity crowd of 10,000. Instead I undertook the duties of 12th man. I had no worries about that; someone has to do the job. Unfortunately Yorkshire won by 54 runs while close rivals Kent and Worcestershire both won. In the match at Worcester Chris Lewis, dropped on 0 kept up his run of form by scoring 75 in his side's 148.

One of the first people I met at Hove in our next Britannic Assurance Championship match was the former England left-handed opening batsman David Smith. Some time earlier, a friend showed me a cutting of an interview he had given to the *Sunday Mirror* in which he urged me to 'quit moaning about the demands of county cricket and get on with it'. I asked him what he meant. Clearly ill at ease, he said: 'I wasn't having a go at you.'

The pitch was the most peculiar we had encountered all summer. It was green down the middle, which would suit the seam bowlers, and bare at the ends which would favour the spinners. They were obviously hoping for a result! The Test and County Cricket Board had insisted that pitches should last four days but a few counties were more concerned with winning matches. It is hard to prepare a pitch in England which doesn't enable the ball to seam about, much different to Trinidad. I think I learned a lot from playing on these kinds of surfaces.

I had a chat with Eddie Hemmings, at forty-five the oldest player on the county circuit. He is a very interesting character to talk cricket to and I asked him what he would do when he retired. He said he still wanted to keep playing but realized that might be difficult. He lived in Nottingham and commuted to Brighton to play for Sussex. He made a brilliant catch in that match but had little opportunity to take any wickets because the seam bowlers did most of the bowling. Tim Munton took 8 wickets for us as Sussex were bowled out for 131 and 127, and we won easily by 10 wickets.

I spent a lot of the time when off the field having treatment but was feeling fitter when our final home match, against Hampshire, started four days later. If we won that one we would win the title. Hampshire were not one of the stronger sides and they were without their opening bowlers Winston Benjamin and Norman Cowans, and we were confident that if the weather held we would be successful. Hampshire's first innings 278 was not a challenging total and when rain restricted the third day to 65 overs we made up for lost time by reaching 483–6 at almost 5 an over. It was a pleasing day for me because at 125 I became the only batsman that season to pass 2,000 runs, and my 191, my ninth century of the season, equalled Alvin Kallicharran's club record set ten years earlier. It was disappointing not to pass 200 – it was the second time that summer I had come close – but 191 is always better than 91.

Roger Twose's 137 was his third hundred of a very successful season and he deserved the highest praise for his all-round effort. On a flattish pitch with no bowler of great pace to contend with, I batted for much of the day without a helmet. I was out to a spectacular catch by Robin Smith at square leg. Shaun Udal, the England off-spinner, bowled short and I pulled the ball to Robin's left. He took off and held a brilliant two-handed catch.

The England squad was shortly to be announced for the tour of Australia and Robin was hoping he would be recalled. 'It's going to be tough to get back,' he said. He gave the impression that it would not be unexpected if he was excluded, but he must have been very upset when the two veterans, Graham Gooch and Mike Gatting, were preferred to him. I thought he was unlucky to be left out at the start of the summer after his 175 in the final Test in Antigua. The abiding rule of selection, in my view, is that class players should be the first to be chosen, and I have always believed Robin is a class player.

It was said that his technique against the spin bowlers was suspect and this would count against him in Australia, but Sydney is the only Test ground where the ball turns. It was not as though he was going to tour India, where spin bowling plays such an important part in the game. Robin is one of my best friends and I was sorry for him when it was announced on the Friday, the day we won the championship, that he was staying at home.

Hampshire needed to bat out 89 overs on the final day but the task was beyond them. They lost their last 7 wickets for 11 runs as Neil Smith, 5–65, bowled them out on a pitch responding to spin. There was a feeling of relief, as well as joy, among the players because it signalled the end of a long, punishing campaign. The cheque for £48,500 for winning the title was presented, plus a bonus of £6,600 for winning eleven matches, and went straight into the kitty to be shared among the playing staff.

Dermot Reeve held the trophy aloft and we posed for pictures on the balcony. During the day the crowd had risen to several thousand and there was a lot of noise from them as the ceremonies took place. Much has been said about poor attendances in county cricket but most of it is untrue. Certainly there were good crowds at most of Warwickshire's matches. Gates were up at Edgbaston and the atmosphere generated by the crowds definitely played a part in our success. There is nothing worse for a cricketer or an actor than to play in front of rows of empty seats. At away matches, too, we generally attracted reasonable crowds and secretaries reported that some of their biggest attendances were on days when Warwickshire were the visitors.

The players were shocked on that final day by the knowledge that only Keith Piper had been selected by England for a winter tour and that spurred them on. He was included in the A side for the trip to India. I felt Dominic Ostler, Roger Twose and Neil Smith also deserved selection and Tim Munton should have gone to Australia with the senior side. Not having a player chosen for England in the two series against New Zealand and South Africa had of course helped us, but it was astonishing that a side that won three of the four domestic honours was not represented in either series.

Warwickshire's greatest asset was team spirit and the way the players played for each other. When someone failed, a colleague would step forward to score the runs or take the wickets. There was an air of confidence among the batsmen. They were prepared to take risks to score quickly to enable the bowlers to have more time to bowl the opposition out. I think I might have provided a good example to follow because the 2,066 runs I scored in first-class cricket in 1994 came off 2,262 balls. Alex Davis, the Warwickshire and England scorer, reckoned that was twice the speed at which the average county scored.

Attitudes in county cricket are fairly negative, with the emphasis on occupying the crease and building up large totals in order to try and bowl the other side out on a wearing pitch. Young batsmen are told to play themselves in and not take too many risks. This accumulation of runs is not particularly entertaining for spectators and is probably the reason why crowds fell away. There was not too much excitement out in the middle. Warwickshire changed all that.

The authorities sought to improve standards by allowing counties to sign the world's best players from 1968 onwards and that made county cricket a better spectacle. Habits are still ingrained, however, and caution is still all too prevalent. I found it hard to accept that the counties were really in favour of banning overseas players from 1996 as was proposed by Lancashire. Their chairman Bob Bennett was upset at losing Wasim Akram half-way through the season because he had to take part in Pakistan's tour of Sri Lanka, and his county wrote to the other counties seeking support for a ban. Somerset backed the Lancashire chairman after losing Mushtaq Ahmed, and the whole concept of having foreign players in England appeared in danger.

This happened at a time when more and more English Premier League football clubs were signing foreigners. I could understand these counties being upset at losing their best bowlers, but to ban all eighteen overseas players would not benefit English cricket at all. Most of them are their side's best players. Courtney Walsh and Curtly Ambrose took most of the wickets for Gloucestershire and Northants, and Carl Hooper and I scored the most runs for Warwickshire and Kent.

If a mistake was made by the counties when they first brought in overseas players I believe it was that too many recruited bowlers instead of batsmen. That did not aid the development of young English bowlers because there were fewer opportunities for them. Against that, however, it must be said that young English bowlers would have learned a great deal from the likes of Andy Roberts and Malcolm Marshall. I believe supporters much prefer watching great batsmen scoring runs than great bowlers taking wickets.

Another reason for the proposed ban was that in the opinion of many chairmen too much money was going out of English cricket paying the overseas players and their agents. A figure of £500,000 a year was mentioned. That was a feeble excuse. Many of the overseas players are sponsored, and if they are paid more than the top English players they deserve it because they attract more members and more spectators.

The take from a Lord's Test these days exceeds £2 million, and with the TCCB having trebled its income from television there is more money coming into English cricket. I support Tim Curtis, the chairman of the Cricketers' Association, when he says the pay of cricketers should be higher. I accept that wages cannot be anywhere near the highest salaries paid in football, which attracts much bigger crowds. But the top players in cricket are well down the pay scale in sport and deserve better. No-one apparently earned more than £100,000 in 1994 and that is the basic pay of an average Premier League footballer these days.

I cannot claim to have transformed Warwickshire, because our success was due to a team effort with everyone making a contribution, but I would like to think my attitude to batting helped create an even more positive approach in a side which already played more positively than its rivals. When younger batsmen have seen me scoring fairly consistently, they may have been inspired to better things by my success. There are players now at Edgbaston who are better known to the cricketing public than they were a year previously.

If foreign players were to be excluded, county cricket would sink into mediocrity, I am sure of that. I know when the Test players are missing on international duty in the West Indies, younger players have the chance to show what they can do and many of them perform quite creditably. But when most of them are picked for representative cricket they are not ready for it. The selectors have to stick with the established players. Standards are falling in the West Indies and it is worrying.

England and South Africa are the only countries where overseas players are used on a regular basis and I do not believe it has harmed cricket in either country. The reverse is the case. I believe it is possible for the International Cricket Council to arrange schedules far enough in advance to prevent series being held during the English season. If they cannot do that, English counties will have to avoid giving contracts to players they know might be off halfway through the season. It should be fairly easy to find a solution to this problem without blanket bans.

When I first played county cricket I was sceptical about the standards. I did not think it compared too favourably with Red Stripe cricket, or cricket among the state sides in Australia, where the competition is shorter and more intense. I felt the players were coasting, because they knew a long, hard season was ahead of them. After my first season I still feel this is largely the case but I now have a lot of respect for the English players. Standards aren't that bad and in mitigation it is physically very demanding.

The championship is too big; too many matches are meaningless. Ray Illingworth, the chairman of the England selectors, has suggested two divisions of nine counties in each, with promotion and relegation. That would make it more competitive and provide the players with greater motivation, but I suspect it would force too many of the less rich clubs out of business. The best players would join the top counties and the smaller counties would wither away.

An alternative idea might be to divide the counties into three groups, which would provide plenty of local derbies early on, followed by national knock-outs and even play-offs. This would reduce the number of matches and give players more time to practise and work on their game. Once the daily grind gets under way, it is often impossible to get in a decent net practice. You are either playing or driving a car to the next venue. In any job you need a break occasionally, and in county cricket that doesn't really happen. I ensured I had a couple of trips back to Trinidad to recharge. I was to miss only two Britannic matches which was not a bad record.

One of the reasons why players sometimes lost motivation was because play went on too long. To be still on the field after 7 p.m. is clearly ludicrous but it happens in county cricket. Only a handful of people remain because the rest, having been there most of the day, want to get home for dinner. The 110-over requirement in a day is not really suited to the modern game, which relies more and more on quicker bowlers. I think it should be cut to 90, the same as in Test matches. To avoid being fined for having a slow over-rate, the fielding side rushes through the day hardly giving any thought to how batsmen should be attacked. Captains do not have much time to talk to bowlers to work out strategy. The result is that the quality of the cricket suffers.

One part of it which annoyed me was so-called declaration cricket, where the fielding side tosses up a few overs of bad bowling in an effort to force a declaration. This is against the true spirit of the game. Instead of trying to get someone out, you are giving him easy runs. The game goes into reverse. I was asked to bowl rubbish at Lord's when Middlesex were about to call off a run chase and play for a draw, and though I bowled an over of full tosses and it had the effect of getting the Middlesex batsmen interested in going for the target again, it offended my cricketing instincts.

There is no reward for a draw and perhaps the TCCB could change that so these artificial devices are not used to produce a result at all costs. I am totally against captains sitting down and agreeing the terms of a declaration. A declaration should be imposed, not agreed.

A crate of champagne was in our dressing-room after the defeat of Hampshire but it remained unopened. Next day we were at Lord's for the final of the NatWest Trophy and we needed a clear head. The Hampshire match ended at three-thirty which meant we had more time to get to London, but it was still after nine when I arrived. I was there to attend the annual dinner of the Cricket Writers' Club at Lord's and to receive the Peter Smith Award for making an outstanding contribution to English cricket. The prize was an engraved edition of *Wisden* which was later exchanged for an engraved copy of the 1995 edition, chronicling my feats.

On the way to 375 against England in Antigua, 18 April, 1994.

This came instinctively to me. I also wanted to wrap the pitch up and take it around with me but that was not possible! GRAHAM MORRIS

ABOVE: In the dressing room at the St John's Recreation Ground, Antigua, after my innings of 375. BEN RADFORD/ALLSPORT

LEFT: Taken into protective custody after breaking the world Test record of Sir Gary Sobers. GRAHAM MORRIS

The shot that nearly cleared the pavilion at Lord's. I have never hit a more effortless six. The bowler was John Emburey and the match was Middlesex v Warwickshire, 30 May, 1994. Keith Brown is the wicket keeper. GRAHAM MORRIS

ABOVE: My second favourite sport. Taking part in the Murphy's Pro-Am tournament at the Forest of Arden Golf Club, 1994.

STEPHEN MURPHY/ALLSPORT

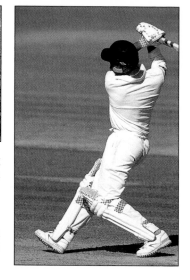

RIGHT: The shot that took me to 501 not out against Durham at Edgbaston on 6 June, 1994. PATRICK EAGAR

ABOVE: The first of several showers afterwards! GRAHAM MORRIS

RIGHT: Back in class at Fatima College after my two world records in 1994.

BELOW: With my mother Pearl on a return visit to Cantaro in 1994.

TOP LEFT: Struck in the face sweeping in a Sunday League game at Northampton. Three days earlier Curtly Ambrose hit me in the helmet, cracking it. TONY HARDACRE/*NORTHAMPTON CHRONICLE AND ECHO*

LEFT: Batting in the Benson and Hedges Final, 1994, when Warwickshire beat neighbours Worcestershire. PATRICK EAGAR

TOP RIGHT: Warwickshire win the County Championship, 2 September, 1994. CLIVE MASON/ALLSPORT

RIGHT: Batting in the NatWest Final which followed the next two days. It was the only trophy Warwickshire failed to win and I blamed myself for not batting longer. COLORSPORT

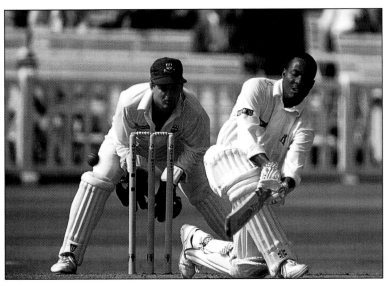

More celebrations after winning the Sunday League at Gloucestershire, 18 September, 1994. GRAHAM MORRIS

Signing autographs for young cricketers after giving a batting demonstration at a coaching session in South Africa. THE ARGUS, CAPE TOWN

CHAPTER EIGHTEEN

DEFEAT AT LORD'S

I KNEW WORCESTERSHIRE IN THE 60-OVER NATWEST FINAL WOULD present the greatest danger to our chances of winning all four major honours, and so did the rest of the team. Our great Midlands rivals were unlucky to lose the toss which cost them the Benson and Hedges Cup and that experience would make them more determined to make it all square. We remained favourites but so much depended on the toss, particularly on an early September morning.

Our path to the final had been fairly straightforward with only the semi-final against Kent presenting us with problems. We outclassed Bedfordshire in the first round, beat Leicestershire easily in the second and thrashed Somerset by 8 wickets in the quarter-final at Taunton. The Somerset game must have been very disappointing for a large crowd. They saw their team bowled out for 124 in 50.2 overs, with Neil Smith our leading bowler with 4–26. As he had in the county match, Somerset skipper Andy Hayhurst adopted a very defensive approach. On the basis of these two games, he has one of the most negative approaches to captaincy I have seen. The match was almost over when I went in after only 21 overs. With rain imminent, I decided to hit out from the start and lofted the first delivery I faced over the Press box stand for six. I blocked the second, took three off the third and was out to Adrianus Van Troost off the fourth. Van Troost is very sharp and he certainly put a lot of effort into that one, which swung back late and struck me right in front, leaving the umpire in no doubt.

The draw for the semi-final gave us a home tie against Kent who must have still been smarting over the way we put them out of the Benson and Hedges Cup in that controversial bowl-out at Edgbaston. They would be very keyed up to make sure that they, not us, reached Lord's. Some of their players were running into form and that would make it harder for us to stop them. Martin McCague was taking so many wickets that he forced his way into the England party for the Australian tour and Carl Hooper was having one of his best seasons with the bat. I knew Carl would be desperately keen to come out on top this time. Like me, he made his first-class début very early, at the age of eighteen, and he scored a century in his first match for Guyana, against Barbados at Kensington Oval. At school in Georgetown he started out as a fast bowler but showed more potential as a batsman and took up slow bowling. He works hard to keep fit, jogging and skipping and playing a lot of squash. And also like me, he found it hard to establish himself as a regular at international level. Now, of course, he is one of the key players in the West Indies side.

Mark Benson won the toss and asked us to bat first on a good pitch. He obviously thought his batsmen were capable of chasing any score we might get and our 265 was definitely reachable with players such as Carl Hooper in their batting line-up. Andy Moles took the sheet-anchor role, his unbeaten 105 including only two boundaries. It was up to the stroke-players to raise the tempo at the other end, but except for Roger Twose with 49, the rest of us failed. Mark Ealham, the Kent all-rounder, was swinging the ball and almost caught me at 21 when he got his right hand to a checked drive. 8 runs later I mishit a slower ball straight back to him and he just managed to hold on to it.

Tim Munton bowled Benson early on, only for Trevor Ward, one of the more aggressive young English batsmen, and the reliable Neil Taylor to swing it back Kent's way with a second-wicket stand of 124. With less than 5 an over needed, Kent were in control. But Warwickshire refused to buckle and when Dominic Ostler raced round the backward square leg boundary to hold a spectacular diving catch off Taylor, 64, we felt we could still win. Excellent spells by Paul Smith and Dermot Reeve saw Kent lose 3 more wickets in 4 overs, including Ward for 80.

As long as Hooper was there, Kent, I thought, had the upper hand and we did our best to keep him from the bowling. We were helped when Ealham turned down the chance of a run and wickets fell with Hooper looking on helplessly at the other end. Keith Piper took a splendid catch to dismiss Graham Cowdrey, throwing himself upwards to his right to where a first slip would normally have been. Steve Marsh went to another of Piper's brilliant stumpings which, like the running out of McCague, was decided by the third umpire, and suddenly Hooper found himself running out of partners. After scoring 44 off 49 balls he lost patience and hit a slower ball from Reeve high into the covers for Neil Smith to take an easy catch. The margin of victory was just 8 runs, the same as at the Oval in the other semi-final where Worcestershire beat Surrey.

The expectations of our supporters were high on the day of the Final and we were determined not to disappoint them. The forecast was not good, putting even more importance on the outcome of the toss. When Dermot Reeve lost it, there was a sense of panic in the dressing-room as if the match was already lost. The previous eight Finals had all been won by the team batting second, and Tim Curtis invited us to bat first in very overcast conditions.

I tried my best to create a positive feeling in the dressing-room by cracking a few jokes. Bob Woolmer reminded us we were the best side in the country, capable of beating anyone under any circumstances. Our worst fears were confirmed, however, once Tom Moody and Phil Newport bowled their opening overs. The ball darted around all over the place and most of the time we were unable to put bat to it. Conditions for batting were far worse than they had been in the Benson and Hedges Final. We found ourselves 17–2 after 10 overs, and I had so much difficulty early on trying to get accustomed to the conditions that I needed 25 deliveries to get off the mark.

Normally, when I am bogged down, I try not to let it worry me. If I am dropped, or if there are a few close chances with a lot going my way, I just carry on. If you think about it, in a matter of just one ball you could be back in the dressing-room contemplating your dismissal. On that day, it did not matter how bad or out of touch I looked. I knew that the longer I stayed there, the easier it would become, even when the ball seemed to dominate the bat.

There was a loud leg-before appeal which was turned down, and an even louder appeal for a caught-behind by wicket-keeper Steve Rhodes. When it was turned down Rhodes said something and I raised my arms in the air as if to say 'Take it easy, you guys'. Mine was the wicket they wanted. I realized that and the tension was on a high. At the end of the over umpire David Shepherd reprimanded Rhodes for his comments. If it had been in a Test match the ICC Referee might have fined the England wicket-keeper. As I have explained, I believe in walking but I was sure I was not out on that occasion.

I have never been more determined not to give my wicket away and I played with great circumspection. In terms of watchfulness and responsibility, it was probably the finest one-day innings of my career. Paul Smith, hero of the Benson and Hedges Final, helped me add 50 for the fourth wicket before skying a catch off Moody to Gavin Haynes at mid on.

Shortly before lunch the rain came with Warwickshire 88–3 off 29 overs. A reasonable total was still a possibility but we needed to resume in the afternoon when conditions might have been easier. But the light rain persisted and play was abandoned for the day. It meant we had to face another 10.30 start in atmospheric conditions ideally suited to Newport, Moody, Neal Radford and Steve Lampitt. The odds were really stacked against us.

The next morning it was little different from the first day. The ball was moving around still and the advantage remained with the bowlers. Trevor Penney helped me add 60 before Radford had him lbw with one that kept low. I hit Richard Illingworth for six and at 81 was aiming for the century which would have given us a better chance. I realized it depended on me. I had to stay there.

Gavin Haynes bowled on the leg stump and it was almost a replay of the shot which got me out in the Benson and Hedges Final. Trying to drive to mid on I realized I had to turn my wrists to get the right amount of bat on the ball and clipped it straight to Graeme Hick on the midwicket boundary. It was the wrong shot to the wrong ball and I felt very despondent. Haynes is just an up-and-down bowler. Despite claims from the Worcestershire camp that they had set a trap for me, I had got myself out. Deep midwicket is a normal fielding position in one-day cricket. You would expect them to have a fielder there at that stage of the game.

Our total of 223 was maybe higher than we could have expected, but to have a chance of winning we needed 30 or 40 more runs. We also needed a good start with the ball, and it came at 29 when I caught Damien D'Oliveira off Tim Munton for 12 and Dermot Reeve bowled Tim Curtis at the same score. Dermot repeated his Benson and Hedges tactic of bowling Tim Munton for a long opening spell, but the breakthrough against Graeme Hick and Tom Moody did not come, Hick surviving a confident caught-behind appeal off Gladstone Small.

At tea Worcestershire were 84–2 and we still had a chance. The Quadruple was still on. After tea, however, we disintegrated and for the first time in the season our cricket became a shambles. The first over after tea, from Roger Twose, cost 12 runs, and the tally off the first 5 overs was 45. Paul Smith made the mistake of banging the ball in far too short and Moody hit him over the Grandstand roof out of the ground. In another over the West Australian hit his former team-mate for three successive fours. At the end of it Paul was taken off with figures of 0–54 in 7 overs.

It became a rout as Hick hit a six off Twose into the Grandstand and Worcestershire won by 8 wickets with 10.5 overs to spare. Hick made 93 in 101 balls and Man of the Match Moody 88 in 112 balls. Neither of these players had established himself at the very highest level of Test cricket but in county cricket they had impressive records. They can destroy bowling as they did that afternoon at Lord's.

Graeme Hick has changed his style and now adopts a more orthodox stance. This has helped him but I still think he has something to prove. When the ball is coming through at great pace he is not the same commanding player, and until he scores consistently against the best teams in the world there will be questions asked about his claims to greatness. I personally think he is a good player. Unfortunately for him, he had the pressure of being considered a great player and the saviour for English cricket even before he had started his Test career, and this label was created by his achievements in county cricket. He was not allowed to settle in to Test cricket and his early failures were horribly criticized.

Both Lord's finals in 1994 were disappointing one-sided events and, as 28,000 people paid a large amount of money to attend each, I think the TCCB should consider improving the conditions of the pitch to prevent this happening again. The trouble is that it is very difficult for the groundsman at Lord's to produce a pitch suitable for a one-day final which takes place towards the end of the summer. On both occasions there was moisture in the pitch, and combined with the atmospheric conditions it meant the side batting first had almost no chance of winning. Since then, the pitch used for the NatWest Final has been dug up and relaid.

I believe the Board should consider moving the Nat-West Final to another venue if things do not improve in future years. The Oval nearly always produces a faster, bouncier pitch at the end of the season which enables stroke-players to play their shots and entertain the crowd. The Surrey v. Worcestershire semi-final in the NatWest Trophy was one of the finest one-day matches seen in English cricket. The snag is that the capacity at the Oval is only 15,300, or just over half the capacity at Lord's. Surrey are seeking to add another level around the terraces to raise that figure to more than 25,000, but that may take some years to achieve, although, having said that, I don't think I would get much support for the Oval from the county players, who look at a Lord's final as one of their main goals during the summer.

The pitch for a one-day game should be similar to one being used on the third day of a Test match – in other words, a flat pitch with some pace in it that does not give too much assistance to the bowlers. That was not the case at Lord's. On the Saturday morning I was trying to play outside the line to Tom Moody's deliveries but still missed the ball because it moved so much. That does not make it a fair contest.

Other suggestions to improve matters include making it a two-day game with an innings starting at 2 p.m. on each day, reducing the number of overs from 60 or 55 to 50, which is the standard around the world, or requiring the side batting first to suspend its innings after 25 overs to let the opposition bat for 25 before resuming and vice versa. Making it a two-day game would not, I feel, satisfy either the sponsors or the public. The appeal of one-day cricket is that the match finishes in a day. It is one-day cricket, not two-day cricket.

Reducing the number of overs, especially in the Nat-West Trophy, to 50 seems a more attractive proposition. With the number of overs in Test cricket now 90 a day and county cricket burdened with 110 a day, it is unrealistic to expect the two sides in English cricket's prestige Cup Final to play a total of 120 overs at the end of the season when the light starts to fade from 7.30 onwards. The idea of splitting innings in two has been tried in Australia, but I think it has little to recommend it. If conditions were favouring the bowlers at the start, as at Lord's, it wouldn't alter that aspect of the game.

The Warwickshire players were desperately disappointed about losing at Lord's but it made us all the more determined to succeed in the Sunday League and become the first county to win three competitions. I felt more upset than any of them. If I hadn't played that shot I might have been able to score enough runs to give us a total to bowl at. If Hick and Moody had been under greater pressure, the outcome could have been different, despite the handicap of virtually having the first 15 overs lost to us.

The morale of the players could have suffered when we met Hampshire in a rearranged Sunday League match the following Tuesday, a game we had to win to retain our chance of lifting the Sunday League trophy, but fortunately there were no after-effects. We won easily. With rain threatening we needed to score at a fast rate to match Hampshire's 197–4 with Robin Smith scoring 68 in 84 balls, but we managed to do it. I hit 56 off 56 balls, and when rain caused play to be abandoned at 147–4 off 28 overs we won on a faster scoring rate of 5.25 to Hampshire's 4.93.

CHAPTER NINETEEN

THE TREBLE

JUST ONE MORE TROPHY REMAINED TO BE WON, THE AXA
Equity and Law League trophy, and as I understand is common in cricket's Sunday League the outcome was not
decided until the final day, Sunday 18 September. I had
the final county match against Gloucestershire off, only the
second BAC game I had missed, and joined my colleagues
at 12 a.m. at Bristol for the 1 p.m. start. Again I was late
and again *The Times* reported this the following day.
When I am feeling in good form I try not to do too much
and after a brief warm-up on the outfield I settled down to
sign a few autographs.

The rest of the players were totally relaxed. Gloucestershire were bottom of the table, having won only four
games, and we felt we would win. We knew we had
to win but didn't feel under any pressure. Our one

concern was the weather. A call to the local weather bureau revealed that rain was expected in early evening, not early enough to halt the game. Someone from the Gloucestershire dressing-room claimed their information was that rain was expected earlier. Courtney Walsh, Gloucestershire's captain, won the toss and predictably asked Dermot Reeve to bat. The pitch was expected to play on the slow side and both sides included two spinners. Warwickshire preferred Richard Davis, who had taken 6 wickets in the county game, to Paul Smith who was 12th man.

Warwickshire made their worst start of the summer, losing Neil Smith, promoted to opener, Dominic Ostler and Roger Twose without a run being scored off the bat in the first 6 overs. It meant that I was batting from the second over but I did not have the feeling we would be bowled out cheaply. I knew I had to play a responsible innings and settled down to play myself in and not take any chances.

My second boundary must have alarmed the thousands of Warwickshire supporters in the packed crowd. It passed just over the head of Bobby Dawson at square leg. Trevor Penney came in third wicket down and was fortunate when he spooned a simple catch to Courtney Walsh at midwicket off the second delivery he faced and Courtney dropped it. Another wicket then and we might have been in real trouble. Trevor and I added 68 for the next wicket and the crisis passed.

As so often happened to me in one-day matches I was out to a loose shot, when I had reached 38. Mark Alleyne bowled outside the off stump, and as I aimed to drive the ball through extra cover it caught the top edge and flew high into the air down towards the third man boundary. Mike Smith, the bowler who had dismissed

Ostler and Twose, ran in hard to try and catch it. The Warwickshire supporters in that part of the ground must have been holding their breath while the home supporters were willing Smith to catch it.

Smith dived forward and jumped up holding the ball in the air, claiming the catch. The other Gloucestershire players rushed to embrace him. I had no reason to doubt that it was a fair catch and left the crease. Later, some of the other players told me that on the replay it looked as though the ball had bounced on the ground.

The BBC, who were televising the game, showed it in slow motion and their experts decided there was a lot of doubt about the authenticity of the catch. It did not worry me unduly. I leave it to the fielder; if he claims a catch then I accept his word. I do not believe fielders cheat on something like that and often the fielder is the only person who can definitely say whether it was a clean catch or not. Even with the increased rewards in top cricket I don't think anyone would risk the dishonour that would follow. I have not seen it happen since I started playing cricket.

Dermot Reeve joined Penney and both batsmen batted sensibly as they added a further 75 runs to the total in only 11 overs, profiting from some loose bowling from the slow bowlers Mark Davies and Martyn Ball. Trevor's 55 in 69 deliveries was another excellent innings from a player who grew in confidence during the season. Our total of 183–8 off 39 overs was, we felt, slightly above par, and at no stage during Gloucestershire's innings did we feel it might not be enough.

Kent would have taken the title had they beaten Surrey at the Oval, and we knew we had to make sure we settled the issue at Bristol. The organizers had hired a helicopter to take the trophy and medals to the ground where the competition winners were playing, and at tea, with Surrey having been put in and ending their innings at 205–8, they must have been hedging their bets. Our advice would have been to press on down to Bristol!

Dermot Reeve, who had scored a 52–ball 50, opened the bowling himself in partnership with Tim Munton, and Tim made his usual speedy inroad having opener Tony Wright lbw for 3. At 30–1 they were saying it was one of Gloucestershire's best starts and with 27 overs left the hopes of the home supporters were being raised. Reeve took himself off and brought on Gladstone Small, and once again Gladstone made a breakthrough, having Tim Hancock caught behind by Keith Piper for 7. Matt Windows, who made 47, and Dawson, 29, added 50 in 11 overs, but at 93–3 Gloucestershire lost the next 5 wickets quickly to Gladstone, who took 3–25, Neil Smith, 2–28, and Richard Davis, 2–28, and were all out for 137 in 37 overs. It was fitting that last man Smith should be caught by Tim Munton at mid on.

The players raced to the stumps to claim souvenirs as the crowd rushed on. I was one of the first players off. I felt a great sense of pride, not in my own achievements in the competition because I felt I had not contributed much, but in the performances of my colleagues. They had all worked so hard on their game during the season and deserved this great moment of success that no other county has ever achieved in the history of cricket. We wanted to have a few moments in the dressing-room, which was filling rapidly with supplies of champagne and canned beer, but Maria Bogdanowicz, the girl from the TCCB, insisted we go up to the top floor of the pavilion for the presentation ceremony. 'There will be drinks up there for you,' she promised.

Like motor-racing drivers, we yanked off the corks

of the champagne bottles, shook the bottles and sprayed the contents over each other and the supporters below who chanted 'Are you watching, Ray Illingworth?' The ceremony was shown live on BBC TV. Mr Illingworth and his selectors had picked only Keith Piper from our squad for one of the thirty-three places on the winter touring parties and it had rankled with the players, as I have said.

The crowd then broke into a chant of 'There's only one Brian Lara'. It was a very happy moment not only for me but everyone connected with the club. We had finished with thirteen victories in our seventeen matches, one more than Worcestershire who finished second after beating Durham by 26 runs at New Road. Kent failed to reach their target at the Oval by a 24-run margin and finished third. That must have disappointed Carl Hooper, whose tally of 773 runs was the highest in the competition. In the previous season Warwickshire had ended up in tenth place, and the only other time they won the Sunday League title was in 1980.

Opening the bowling in the match at Leicestershire when they last won it was a nineteen-year-old Gladstone Small, the only survivor in the current side. Dennis Amiss opened the innings and Bob Willis and John Snow were key bowlers. Willis was the newly appointed captain and, except for the success on Sundays, it was not a very successful season. Warwickshire were fourteenth in the championship and made early exits in the Benson and Hedges Cup and the Gillette Cup, failing to qualify for a bonus of £5,000 offered by the Supporters Association for winning the treble.

Winning the Sunday League in 1994 brought us £31,000 in prize money, plus £375 for each of the thirteen matches we won and £187.50 for the one game that did not end in a result. The total was £36,062.50, or £2,121.32 for each of the seventeen matches. Added to the prize of £48,500 for winning the Britannic Assurance Championship plus £600 for each of the eleven matches won, plus £31,000 for winning the Benson and Hedges Cup and an additional £2,175 in first- and second-round bonuses, and £15,000 for being runners-up in the NatWest Trophy, the total prize fund for the season came to £139,337.50. It was shared out among the players.

By the standards of golf, motor-racing, tennis and a number of other sports, it was not much of a bounty. A golfer can win £139,000 or more in a single tournament. A Wimbledon winner receives much more. This can be understood because most of these sports are individual ones. If one person had to represent his country at cricket, then that person's earning power would also be high. But then again, that isn't much of an excuse because football is a team sport and players are still being traded for millions of pounds. Perhaps with improved marketing, the position could improve and the wages of the players be brought into line with those in sports that do not receive so much media coverage. Until that happens, cricketers will have to continue being the poor relations. Despite this, it is a good life, an enjoyable life, and to us cricketers, especially in the West Indies, the emphasis is not so much on the money but on pride, recognition and love of the game. But unless you win the pools, it is not a job which usually earns you enough to retire when you come to the end.

CHAPTER TWENTY

THE INDIAN EXPERIENCE

THE TOUR TO INDIA BETWEEN OCTOBER AND DECEMBER 1994 WAS not a particularly enjoyable one for me. First of all it was postponed for more than a week after a much-publicized outbreak of plague in Surat. Then there was a misunderstanding when I turned up at Piarco Airport to catch a flight to London to join up with the rest of the team, only to discover that the ticket I was expecting was not there. It meant I had to wait until the next day's flight and I arrived late. The West Indies Board of Control decided to fine me 1,000 US dollars.

I was not in the best shape for what proved to be a very arduous tour. I was still pretty tired after my season in England and I put myself under a lot of pressure both on and off the field. I felt that everyone wanted to see how well I performed after my achievements earlier in the year, and I thought I had to prove that I could still score a lot of runs at the highest level. Unfortunately, the pitches were slow and not conducive to stroke-play, and I felt they were not proper Test pitches. They were prepared to suit the Indian spin bowlers and blunt our fast bowlers. We were already weakened by the absence of Curtly Ambrose, who had been advised to rest his shoulder after years of non-stop cricket around the world.

We lost the one-day matches 6–2, and during the game against New Zealand in Goa I was fined 50 per cent of my match fee and banned for one match by ICC referee Raman Subba Row for showing dissent. Apparently it was only the second time a cricketer had been suspended under the ICC code of conduct. Aqib Javed of Pakistan was the first after an incident in New Zealand in 1993.

Courtney Walsh, our skipper, decided to leave himself out of the one-day match in Jaipur as he was not fully fit, so I took over the captaincy of my country for the first time. It was a great feeling to be leading the team out and I wanted to impress and do a good job. Unfortunately, luck was not on my side. I lost the toss, dropped a catch and the Indians totalled 259–5 in their 50 overs, with Sachin Tendulkar making 105. I was out for 47 to a delivery which kept low, and towards the end our batsmen panicked a bit so we lost the match by just 5 runs.

We knew it would be tough in the three-match Test series because we had some inexperienced players and our bowling was not as formidable as it had been on previous visits. The conditions were weighted against us. In the First Test in Delhi, we were well beaten on a poor pitch and might well have lost the second in Bombay but for the decision of the Indian captain Mohammad Azharuddin to delay his declaration. Jimmy Adams batted magnificently throughout the series, scoring more than 500 runs and averaging 173. One–nil down going in to the last Test in Chandigarh we knew we had to be at our strongest to avoid becoming the first West Indian side to lose a series since 1980, when a side captained by Clive Lloyd lost 1–0 in New Zealand, mainly as a result of a number of questionable umpiring decisions.

We were in determined mood when we assembled for a team meeting the night before the match started. Courtney told us, 'I have never played in a losing Test series and I'd rather lose 2–0 than go home 1–0 losers. It's a proud record and whatever else has gone on we don't want to be the team to surrender it.' To our surprise, the pitch was a good batting surface and we made the most of it. Jimmy Adams was the mainstay of our first innings 443 with an unbeaten 174, and Walsh, Kenny Benjamin, Cameron Cuffy and Anderson Cummins shared the wickets as India responded with 387, Manoj Prabakhar scoring a patient 120.

Our opener Stuart Williams was ill when our second innings began and I was asked to open with Phil Simmons. I had opened on numerous occasions in one-day matches but not in a Test match. I was disappointed not to have scored more runs in the tour so far but, perhaps because of my poor record over the last few weeks, I batted in this second innings with a much freer mind. I told myself that things could not get much worse and played in a much more relaxed manner, as I usually do. I was no longer putting pressure on myself. I was also helped by the fact that the West Indies needed quick runs so I had to get on with the job and not think too much about my form. Thankfully, we were able to achieve our objective and Courtney declared at 301–3, after we had scored at around one run a minute. I was 9 runs short of my first century of the tour when I tried to steer the spinner Venkatapathy Raju through the slip area and got a faint edge to the wicket-keeper Mongia. Realizing I was out I walked straight away, before the umpire had made his mind up. My decision to go was featured prominently in the Press but I have always believed in walking if I felt I was out.

Courtney's declaration left India seven hours in which to make 358 and we were confident they would not take any risks. There were 15 overs remaining on the afternoon of the fourth day and Courtney and Kenny Benjamin extracted a lot of life from a docile pitch. Navjot Sidhu was bowled by Courtney for a duck and Prabakhar retired after a vicious delivery from our captain lifted and smashed into his nose through a gap in his visor. He needed five stitches in a gash on his nose.

That delivery proved decisive. Next day the Indian batting collapsed and we won by 243 runs. It was hailed as an astonishing comeback and a triumph for the kind of cricket which has made the West Indies side the best in the world for such a long period. David Holford, the team manager, said it was the worst tour he had gone on, and I agreed with him. I was glad when it was over and I was able to head off for Australia to appear in a charity match at the Bradman Oval in Bowral, the birthplace of Sir Donald Bradman. Some of the world's greatest players, including Michael Holding, Andy Roberts, Joel Garner, Bobby Simpson, Greg Chappell, Doug Walters, Jeff Thomson, Dennis Lillee, Barry Richards, Sunil Gavaskar, Graeme Pollock, Jeffrey Dujon, Abdul Qadir and Gary Sweet, the actor who played Sir Don in the Bodyline TV series, took part and it was a memorable occasion.

Around 18,000 people paid more than £100,000 to watch the Bradman XI beat the World XI by 6 runs.

The money went to a trust fund which is paying for the Bradman Museum, coaching schemes and scholarships. The game was shown live on Channel 9 in its entirety but sadly Sir Don, who was not well at his home, was unable to be present. I was honoured to be invited and it was particularly satisfying to be able to bat for a while at the same time as Graeme Pollock, the legendary South African left-hander. I was dismissed, caught behind, by the Australian woman cricketer Zoe Cross. Having started the year by breaking two world records, I found it amusing that I ended it being bowled out by a woman.

From Australia, I made a brief trip to the USA before returning home for a short rest prior to the tour of New Zealand in the New Year, which preceded the home series against the Australians and the tour of England. 1994 had certainly been an extraordinary and hectic year.

CHAPTER TWENTY-ONE

STANDARDS OF BEHAVIOUR

CRICKETERS ARE NOW UNDER GREATER SCRUTINY THAN AT ANY time in the history of the game. Up to ten TV cameras are focused on them during Test matches, and anyone who misbehaves can expect to be charged with misconduct by the ICC match referee, who sits with the third umpire with a TV set in front of him. I have no argument with that. I think the leading cricketers have to set an example to youngsters and the vast majority do so.

But I question whether the process of punishing players may have gone too far. The subject was highlighted during the Third Cornhill Test between England and South Africa at the Foster's Oval in August 1994, a match Ray Illingworth, the chairman of the England selectors, said contained some of the most aggressive, most exciting cricket he had ever seen. When the England captain Mike Atherton was given out lbw by umpire Ken Palmer, he clearly thought the ball had brushed his bat before hitting the front pad on the line of the off stump. He touched his bat with his fingers, suggesting he had made contact with the ball before it hit his pad, and as he made his way towards the dressing-room he shook his head in disbelief. I did not think it was a blatant case of dissent; Mike looked to be showing disappointment on legitimate grounds. Most batsmen react like that at certain times; their emotions just get the better of them. As he said afterwards, 'We are human beings not robots.'

Atherton had already been fined £2,000 for the 'dirt in the pocket' affair in the First Cornhill Test at Lord's and ICC referee Peter Burge had warned him about his future conduct. If that hadn't happened, I do not believe Mr Burge would have found Atherton guilty of dissent at the Oval. The case was heard after the close of play on the Friday night and Atherton was fined £1,200, half his basic Test match fee. It was a very harsh punishment and I think if that is the method the ICC is adopting, then the game is going to suffer. In applying the rules strictly, umpires sometimes make bad mistakes and they are allowed to do so without any punishment, but maybe they should be under the same amount of scrutiny as the players.

That Test match, although it was full of fines, was still remembered for the great bowling spell by Devon Malcolm during the South African second innings. This was fuelled by the first-ball bouncer which Fanie de Villiers, the South African pace bowler, bowled at him, hitting him in the grill of his helmet. Devon is normally a very calm, easy-going individual but he said to Fanie and his team-mates: 'After that, you're history!' And they were, with Devon taking 9–57, one of the best returns of all time in Test cricket. Conditions were ideally suited to Devon: it was a hard, bouncy pitch and he was able to obtain a lot of pace. When his rhythm is right Devon is as fast as any bowler in the world. Bowling a bouncer to a fast bowler and hitting him in the helmet is not a course of action I recommend!

De Villiers was also fined by Mr Burge and I felt that was a harsh decision, too. Thinking he had Graeme Hick caught behind the wicket by David Richardson, he ran down the pitch with his arms aloft, and when the umpire ruled not out he dropped his arms in exasperation. That kind of thing happens a lot in Test cricket and I was surprised that Mr Burge fined him 25 per cent of his basic match fee.

De Villiers is one of the game's characters. He is always smiling and has a great rapport with the spectators. By the time he was fined 70 per cent of his match fee along with his colleagues for not meeting the fifteen overs an hour requirement he came out of the Oval match with about £20 profit, or £5 a day! I can see no alternative to having a minimum number of overs in Test cricket, even when both sides are operating with four pace bowlers as happened in that match. Otherwise spectators are being short-changed. But I believe the fines are too steep and need scaling down. To be docked 70 per cent of one's income for falling fourteen overs short during two innings is a drastic penalty.

More than £13,000 in fines was collected from the players in that Test match, which I think is an enormous amount. Hopefully the money is utilized, maybe in the development of young cricketers around the world, which is a praiseworthy objective. But if these standards had applied in previous generations, many players would have been paying out money to play the game. Their fees would have gone in fines! I think standards of behaviour these days are higher than at any time, yet more money is being taken from the players in fines. Discipline had to be tightened because there were a number of unsavoury incidents, players kicking down the stumps and the like, but I feel things may now have gone too far. With so many former players becoming ICC referees – each of the nine Test match-playing countries can nominate up to four each year – there is a danger of inconsistency. I gather the ICC intend to counter that threat by reducing the number of referees to six and they will be expected to be consistent in their judgements.

I have to confess I showed dissent when I was given out stumped in the first Test between Australia and the West Indies at Brisbane in December 1992. I escaped punishment because I think the referee, Raman Subba Row, the former England Test batsman and ex-chairman of the Test and County Cricket Board, accepted that I wasn't out. I had reached 58 when I failed to make contact with a leg-side delivery from Greg Matthews, the Australian off-spin bowler. I was out of my ground when Ian Healy, the Australian wicket-keeper, who is one of the most competitive of cricketers, dived to retrieve the ball and threw himself towards the stumps. I was an inch or two out of my ground when the off bail fell but I was convinced that it was Healy's glove that hit the base of the stump and caused the bail to fall, not the ball. And it was quite apparent that he did not have the ball in that right glove when contact was made. Umpire Terry Prue, standing at square leg in his sixth Test, was clearly unsighted because Healy's body was between him and the stumps. But to my utter dismay he signalled that I was out. I stood there dumbfounded. I said to Healy: 'Tell the umpire what happened.' He said in a news conference afterwards that he had told Mr Prue that his glove had hit the stumps and he had no idea where the ball had gone. But I didn't hear that. I felt like crying. I was batting well and my first Test century was looming. The West Indies had made a poor start and were 58–3 before Keith Arthurton and I added 112 for the fourth wicket. It was a turning-point in the innings.

After a long delay, long enough for me to be considered as a dissenter, I left for the pavilion. The next day Mr Prue issued a statement accepting that the Australian players had stated that the wicket was broken by Healy's gloves but at no time did the players inform him of that fact. He was obviously disturbed about the implication that he had disregarded what they had said and hadn't reacted. The TV evidence showed clearly that I should not have been given out. At the time the Australian Board were not using the off-field camera. Maybe if they were I would not have been given out.

When the ICC approved the use of the off-field camera working with the third official they limited decisions to run outs, stumpings and hit wicket. The only other disputed area they were allowed to consider was whether a boundary had been recorded when a fielder was making a stop close to the ropes, and if a stroke had resulted in a six or a four. Personally, I would like to see the TV evidence extended to all forms of dismissal. It would help the umpires out in the middle clear up doubts if at all possible. I realize there are some decisions, like whether a batsman nicked the ball on to his pad, or edged the ball, particularly down the leg side when pad and bat are in close proximity, that are impossible, but the overall effect would be beneficial. And it would add to the drama. There is mounting excitement in the crowd when they are awaiting the verdict from the TV camera.

The next day, my partner in that fourth-wicket stand, Keith Arthurton, was on 78 when he edged a delivery from Steve Waugh to Healy, who took the ball suspiciously close to the ground. Prue was unsure if the ball had carried and consulted his fellow umpire Steve Randell at square leg. Mr Randell ruled that the catch had been taken on the half-volley (and therefore not out), which again brought the Australian players' reaction and behaviour almost to the point of boiling over. Keith added a further 79 runs to record an unbeaten 157, his maiden Test century. Those extra runs gave the West Indies their lead of 78 runs on the first innings.

In their second innings Australia were able to overcome that lead, as David Boon's fourth successive hundred in Tests in Australia, 111, enabled his side to reach 308, leaving the West Indies a target of 231 in 63 overs. We felt the pitch at the Gabba was good enough for us to win the match but made a disastrous start, losing the first 4 wickets for just 9 runs. Craig McDermott captured 3 of them and I was one of his victims, for 0, caught at slip by Mark Taylor.

Our skipper Richie Richardson saved us with a brilliant innings of 66 in our total of 133–8. His second scoring stroke, with the total 4–3, was a hook for six off Bruce Reid, and he raced to his fifty in only 77 deliveries. At tea we were still needing 133 in 31 overs with 6 wickets standing and our hopes of victory were revived. Carl Hooper's dismissal for 32 convinced Richie that the task was beyond us and he switched from attack to defence, with Ian Bishop blocking away at the other end.

There were numerous loud appeals from the Australians as the tension mounted during our second innings. When Steve Randell, one of the Australian umpires, turned down an appeal from Merv Hughes when Richie was 47, the umpire exchanged words with the bowler. Allan Border weighed in, pointing to his shins as though to indicate he thought the ball had kept low. Randell rejected another lbw appeal shortly afterwards and again Border had words with him.

Randell, standing in his twelfth Test, reported both Border and Hughes to Subba Row for breaches of the ICC Code of Conduct. Border refused to attend the hearing and in his absence was fined half his match fee, just under £1,000. It was the heaviest imposed up to that time and Border was most unhappy about it. Subba Row issued a statement saying, 'All players should adhere to the proper standards of behaviour which should prevail in Test and international cricket.'

When Atherton was fined at the Oval some critics thought he would have to resign the captaincy, but he wasn't the first Test captain to be punished for dissent. Mr Subba Row also fined Hughes 10 per cent of his match fee for his part in the episode. Hughes said it was 'a spur of the moment thing, the classic case of the bowler always thinking he is right'. The controversy did not in any way affect the good relationship between the two sides. Richie said: 'It is competitive out there, but friendly. That is the way I like to play.'

The Australians have been criticized for their enthusiastic appealing. So have the Pakistanis and the Indians. Some players tend to place umpires under undue pressure, especially for close-in catches where the fielders all seem to rush to congratulate the 'catcher' before the umpire has made his ruling. It is said to be an attempt to influence the umpire into giving the batsman out. I don't see anything wrong with that, if the fielders genuinely believe a catch has been made. Of course, they are entitled to show their emotions because it is an emotional game after all. On the other hand, I know there are players and cricket teams that tend to try to manipulate umpires' decisions, especially if they are playing at home, and I do have a problem with that. England were criticized after the Headingley Test against South Africa in 1994 for a series of appeals of this nature and Kepler Wessels, the South African captain, thought it had gone too far. Umpires must show their authority throughout the game and they ought not to be swayed by any actions of the fielding side.

I have to admit I have been fined on one occasion and, as I have said, suspended for a one-day international match whilst I was in India during our tour at the end of 1994. We were playing against New Zealand in the triangular series involving ourselves, New Zealand and India. Matthew Hart, a left-arm orthodox spin bowler, was bowling. I went down the wicket to hit one of his deliveries over mid-off but missed. Adam Parore, the New Zealand wicket-keeper, fumbled with the ball and I honestly thought I got back into my crease before he removed the bails. Without hesitation the umpire lifted his finger, signalling that I was out. I thought this could not be happening. The third umpire was available and he could easily have referred the decision to him. I do not know how to explain my feelings then but my hands seemed automatically to make the signal the umpires use when they are in doubt and asking for the third umpire to make the final decision. Doing this also meant that I delayed my walk back to the dressing-room. The end result was that the umpire in question made an official complaint to the match referee, Mr Subba Row, who in turn fined me 50 per cent of my match fee. He also imposed a one-match suspension. I could have done without losing my earnings, but at that time I was already completely exhausted and I did not mind a match off.

You have heard about sledging and this is something that I definitely do not condone on the cricket field. The Australians are very famous for it and I think the ICC have been right in trying to eliminate that sort of behaviour. I have a short anecdote which is not about sledging but about aggressive confrontation between two players. It happened during our tour of India, between Kenny Benjamin and Sachin Tendulkar. At the start of the tour we were playing on a lot of easy-paced pitches where Tendulkar seemed to be on top form, scoring a lot of runs. Maybe Benjamin had kept those punishing periods in mind, because during the First Test match at Bombay he bowled Tendulkar a bouncer, and went up to him and said, 'The one-day series is over. This is the real stuff.' I suppose Benjamin got his own back, but during the Second Test he tried another short-pitched delivery which only got up to hip height and Tendulkar pushed it back past him for four. He then walked over and stood next to Benjamin and said, 'This is not Bombay.' For me this is a comical incident and shows the sort of aggression that makes cricket the game it is. It is not something that should ever be taken away.

One episode, however, which did disturb me was when I was docked 500 TT dollars, or about £65, for allegedly criticizing Gus Logie when he was captain in a one-day match against Jamaica. What happened was that Gus, who was one of my idols when I was a boy, brought on a new bowler when only a few runs were needed for Jamaica to win and the bowler was hit for 22. I said to wicket-keeper David Williams that I did not think that was a good idea and he told Gus Logie. The outcome was that I was told not to criticize my captain and a fine was imposed. I was sore about it at the time but it did not affect my relationship with Gus or David Williams. I am sure such comments are made on cricket fields all over the world.

My life is now in the public eye off the field as much as it is on it and this is shown by one incident I was involved in. It concerned a matter over an altercation in public when I was out with Dwight Yorke and another friend in Port of Spain. Someone tried to be aggressive towards my friend and I stepped in to tell him to stop behaving in such a manner. Because I was involved the police were called, and we found ourselves in the police station being given a few words of advice. I would hardly describe it as a dressing-down, especially as I was the innocent party, but what it proved to me was that when you are a well-known figure you have to try to avoid confrontations in public. Since then I have been careful to try and do just that.

CHAPTER TWENTY-TWO

MY NEW LIFE

THE YEAR 1994 WAS A TREMENDOUS ONE FOR ME AND I HAD SET MY goal of establishing myself as an outstanding Test cricketer. This sudden great belief in myself stemmed from the 277 I scored at the Sydney cricket ground against Australia in 1993. I had a taste of success then and I thought that with continued dedication I could be a force to be reckoned with in world cricket. For my performance in Australia I was named my country's Sportsman of the Year in 1993, and achieving that was one of my main goals. Cricket is the main sport in my country and the sports awards are normally won by cricketers. I did not only want to receive this award in 1993 but continue every year to maintain my position as the top sportsman in my country.

That small taste of success and what was to follow needed a lot of level-headedness. I suppose the way my parents brought me up would be exposed to a lot of scrutiny because of the amount of attention placed on me. This attention did not remain on the cricket field but extended into my private life and I don't think I can thank my parents enough for keeping me on the straight and narrow path throughout my early and vulnerable years. Looking back at my early days I have never had to pay any money to my coaches or to the people who have played a great part in developing my cricket. They helped me through the goodness of their hearts and saw this as their contribution to the game. I became very grateful for their dedication, and what I have achieved must have given them great satisfaction. I know I have mentioned some of their names before but I very much want to thank them all for their great support.

My emotions before and after 18 April will always remain with me. I suppose it is one record that every batsman will be looking to break in his cricket career. It has brought great joy, good financial benefits, and yet it has placed a lot of strain on my life. As expected, endorsements quickly followed the high level of success that I achieved during that unbelievable period when I broke the two world records. I appreciate every single endorsement but the great relationship between my first sponsor, Angostura Bitters Limited, and myself stands out in particular. They are the ones who supported me financially from the beginning but they also gave me the opportunity to pursue my cricket by helping me to overcome all the material obstacles that would come my way. Cricket is not one of the more glamorous sports which attracts a great number of sponsors. The individual players cannot compare their on- or off-the-field earnings with those of other sportsmen. This is a sad story because I honestly think cricket, which obtains a lot of television time, should benefit a lot more in the sponsorship market.

Nowadays cricket faces tremendous competition from other sports and the present players need to play their part in selling the game to the next generation. One of the things I would love to see is the game of cricket spreading to other countries and most definitely America. America is the one country which has the ability to turn it into a mass sport. There are millions of people living in America with origins from the West Indies, India, Pakistan, not to mention England, all of which are cricket-playing countries. If we could introduce the sport into American schools there is no telling what sort of impact it might make.

I arrived in England expecting the spotlight to be mainly on my cricket but the Press seemed to be hungry for a lot more. If it was not my private life it was the commercial side of Brian Lara. Sometimes I sit back and read sensational stories, a lot of which are untrue, about the new cricket wonder boy. One of the more inventive ones came during my signing up with Mercury Asset Management, one of Britain's leading investment houses. My signing and press conference took place at the Tower Hotel, next to the Tower of London. When I arrived, I was surprised at the number of journalists and photographers present. There must have been more than forty and the photographers were lined up like a firing squad.

MAM wanted me dressed as a City gent and I wore a grey, pin-stripe suit and was fitted up with a bowler hat, a briefcase and, despite the fact that it was a very hot, sunny day, an umbrella. The resulting pictures were carried in most of the newspapers the next day, some on the front pages. If one of the objectives of MAM was to improve their market awareness it had to rank as a conspicuous success. I was asked how much the deal was worth and I replied: 'I am very happy with the terms but cannot say what they are exactly.' Richard Royds of MAM was also evasive. But somehow some of the journalists heard a figure of £500,000 mentioned and most of their stories the next day said that was the sum I was making and, together with my other endorsements, I had become a millionaire.

Unfortunately this was not the case. This opened my eyes to how much of a big news story I was for the Press and how they can distort facts and figures. All this success on the cricket field and the publicity off it meant that I became a very easily-recognized person. At the beginning it was nice to know you could walk through London and people recognized you but later on I became very self-conscious. Sometimes I thought it was not the greatest thing to be a celebrity. One day I sat and asked myself what I was going to do with my new life and one thing that stuck with me was that, no matter whatever else happened, I did not want to lose sight of my goal of becoming a great cricketer.

The endorsements will come and go and I suppose all will depend on how well I perform on the cricket field. I cannot accept every offer and I have to make sure nothing interferes with my cricket, but I was amazed at the range of companies that approached me to endorse their products last year. For example, I now have a range of Brian Lara jewellery which is developing quite well at home. I suppose I have a lot of examples from around the world to look and learn from, such as Michael Jordan, Andre Agassi and Greg Norman. They seem to be controversial, colourful individuals who are all associated with a range of products, yet they maintain a high level of achievement in their own sports.

What also means a lot to me are the spectators. Whatever the sport and wherever it is being played around the world, it would be nothing without the spectators. They have needs, they want to be entertained and see good sportsmanship, and they also need little things such as autographs and we as sportsmen should always keep this in mind. Joey Carew once said to me, 'Never forget those people you meet on the way up because you might need them on the way down.' I try my best never to turn away a reasonable request, and if kids ask for an autograph I try my best to oblige. Maybe to them I am a role model and role models play a very important part in the development of young people.

The three international awards I won in 1994 capped my year. Firstly, I won the Panasonic ITV Sports Personality of the Year, which is something I will always cherish as Michael Jordan had won the previous year. Although he is not a West Indian, he has always been one of my greatest sporting idols. His achievements, the way he handles the good and bad sides of this success, have always impressed and influenced me. During my disappointing tour of India, I was proud to receive two further awards, one from the *Daily Express*, and one from the BBC for their Overseas Sports Personality of the Year. This sort of recognition is great but can also be very frightening because it gives you the feeling of responsibility to keep performing at the highest level at all times. This has made me keep focused on my long-term goals which have been a comfort to me.

All these achievements would not have been possible, however, without the support of my team-mates, from the members of the Trinidad and Tobago team, through to those of the West Indies and finally on to the Warwickshire cricket team. All three teams gained a lot of success during 1994. Trinidad and Tobago were second in the Red Stripe Cup, the West Indies were triumphant over

England and came back and levelled the series against India, and Warwickshire had a historic year by winning three of the four possible trophies. Whenever I am available I play for my country, but I am always asked whether I will ever return to county cricket after my first experience of it. I must say that it was a very long, tiring season, the longest season I have ever been involved in. I played five months of cricket five, sometimes six, days a week. But during that time I gained a lot of friends and a lot of respect for the game, so in the end the possibility of success would definitely draw me back to county cricket.

On the way back to Trinidad from the West Indies tour to New Zealand, which was a most enjoyable, relaxed tour, I made a brief visit to Birmingham during which I agreed a new three-year contract with Warwickshire from 1996. I was delighted we were able to reach an agreement and I am keenly awaiting the start of next season. I would like to see Warwickshire win all four trophies, not just three!

In New Zealand, after rain ruined the First Test, we beat them in the Second Test at Wellington by an innings and 322 runs, their worst-ever Test defeat. We scored 666–5 decd, with myself (147), Jimmy Adams and Junior Murray making centuries, before Courtney Walsh skittled New Zealand out for 216 and 122, taking 7–37 and 6–18 for a match aggregate of 13-55.

I developed a love of golf in 1994 because it is a new challenge and a new sport, but also because it allowed me to have time on my own and get away from the pressures that were building up over the summer. Because I am worried that it could affect my cricket, I play the game right-handed. I was fortunate to be invited to play in a couple of Pro-Am tournaments, one of which was in the Forest of Arden. My four-ball on that occasion consisted of Rodger Davis, the Australian golf professional, Sir Gary Sobers, Ian Botham and myself. Actually we shot a ten under par 62 and were expecting to be up there with the leaders but to our surprise one group had shot 55.

Also during 1994 I visited a number of countries. One of the more memorable ones was South Africa, as I was able to go to the townships and play a part in helping to develop the cricket in those areas. I had played there once before, but to be asked specifically to come over and help develop their cricket was a great honour. I also shared the stage briefly with Prime Minister John Major who is a cricket fanatic and was there at the same time. I was very impressed with the progress of the new United Cricket Board in South Africa in developing the game throughout the country. I must say I saw some extremely talented young cricketers in the many town-ships who I feel will soon become outstanding cricketers if they are given the opportunity they deserve. Although walking down the street in London and being recognized can be a good feeling, walking through Soweto and being considered a hero felt a lot better and meant more to me.

After that trip I also visited Hong Kong for the sixes which was a total contrast to South Africa with its high-rise buildings and busy streets. Unfortunately I was only there for a couple of days so did not have the chance really to get the feel of the place.

I do love cricket and I pray that I can stay fit enough to play for a number of years to come. Unfortunately I don't see myself still playing cricket when I am forty. I admire those players who have done it, but hopefully I will have enjoyed myself enough to be able to bow out before then and enjoy the rest of my life.

CHAPTER TWENTY-THREE

MAN OF THE SERIES

THE WEST INDIES TOUR OF ENGLAND IN 1995 WAS NOT AS successful or as rewarding as most of us would have liked. It ended in a 2–2 draw, with the last two Cornhill Tests finishing in frustrating draws. I believe that suited both sides because neither wanted, nor could afford to, lose the series. The West Indies side had been beset by injuries and internal squabbling and we were all relieved when the campaign was over and we were able to go home.

Ray Illingworth, the chairman of the England selectors, voted me West Indian Man of the Series after topping the batting averages with 765 runs for an average of 85. In the final three Tests I scored a century in each match which was satisfying, but I still felt I could have done more for the team. By not making a hundred in the first half of the tour I laid myself open to criticism that I had become a flashy player more intent on playing to the gallery than building a match winning innings. Even Sir Gary Sobers put his name to an article in a newspaper which implied I was too reckless in my approach. I knew this was not true but I have to admit I let the pressure get to me and there were times when I felt like walking out and letting someone else take the brunt of the criticism.

But there were deeper problems affecting West Indies cricket, as opposed to my own position, and the catalyst came on Sunday, 30 July, when we held a team meeting at the Crown Plaza Hotel in Manchester following the defeat by England in the Fourth Test. Long team meetings have long been a feature of West Indies cricket. Players are encouraged to talk frankly and sometimes it can develop into a row. I had become very disillusioned with the way some players had been behaving. I felt it was undermining the side and I believed that Richie Richardson should have done something about it. When discipline goes, performances suffer. We had just lost in humiliating circumstances and the exchanges were frank, almost hostile.

I said to Richardson: 'You are always with the team, on and off the field, and you are doing nothing to change the behavioural pattern of the team.' He saw this as a criticism of his captaincy and replied: 'If everyone wants me to resign, I will, but I won't resign because of what someone says who has his own captaincy agenda.' That made me angry. I did not raise the issue because I wanted to take over from him. I did so because I believed West Indies cricket was suffering through lack of firm leadership.

'If you think I have hidden motives for what I have said, then I retire,' I said. I thanked the players and left. I didn't storm out and drive off in a cloud of dust as some people claimed. I slept on it and next morning told Wes

Hall that I couldn't remain in that kind of atmosphere and was leaving. He tried to persuade me to stay but I said it had gone too far.

I went off to stay with Dwight Yorke in the Midlands, leaving a telephone number with Mr Hall. I was away for two days. No more. Not a word leaked out about my absence. On the second day I was contacted by Peter Short, President of the West Indies Board. He spoke about my duty to the game and how much I was needed and I agreed to see him at the 300-year-old Castle Hotel in Taunton, where the team had arrived for their next match.

Wes Hall and Richie Richardson were present at the meeting and Mr Short told me if I didn't return I would be risking bringing West Indies cricket into disrepute. Mr Short also warned me that I would be in danger of breaking my tour contract. I outlined my views about the decline in standards and what I felt was needed to repair things. Eventually I agreed to return and apologised for leaving the team the way I did. I thought this would be the end of the matter, but both Mr Hall and Richie Richardson mentioned the affair in their tour report to the Board. Richardson described the way I spoke to Mr Hall at the team meeting as 'abominable'.

After the team returned home, it was reported that four players faced disciplinary action following incidents on the tour. To my intense dismay, I was one of them, along with Ambrose, Winston Benjamin (who had been sent home) and Carl Hooper. I was now branded with the people whose conduct I had complained about at that meeting in Manchester. I was being called a trouble maker. At their next meeting, the Board's disciplinary committee decided to fine us 10% of our tour fee. I was mortified. It was most unfair.

Subsequently I received a letter inviting me to tour Australia with the West Indies side from December. I wrote back saying: 'This fine has damaged my character and self confidence. It is with this in mind I now write to request that you release me from my obligation to travel with the team to Australia.'

My letter was called a bombshell in Trinidad and in other parts of the world, too. Mr Short was quoted as saying that he feared whether I would ever play again. I never gave that impression, though I suppose he might have believed that was the case when I said 'I retire' at the Manchester meeting. Michael Holding said I needed psychiatric help but that was not so. I was pent up and annoyed. I simply wasn't focussed to go to Australia. I needed a break. I had dreamed of playing for the West Indies since the age of six but for the past eighteen months I had felt the pressure building up. I needed to get away from it for a while.

I realised I might never be asked to captain the West Indies. That did not worry me. I would be happy to play under anyone who was able to restore the highest standards of discipline and get the side playing as a team, as in the old days. I am just one player. Despite what some people say about me I have only ever been dedicated to one thing, the West Indies cricket team. West Indies cricket is not just going through a talent problem caused by a shortage of players of class. There seems to be some other influence causing the decline. What we need is a better relationship between the Board and the players. A big rebuilding job is needed.

Though I did not return to Trinidad at the end of July from the England tour I did make a flying visit home, with permission of the management, to conduct some business relating to my house-building plans. The project was behind schedule and I felt I had to be there in person. It was unusual I agree, but necessary.

My trip was turned into a mystery by some newspapermen who suggested I had fallen out with the management. A Trinidad newspaper claimed that my land had been cursed by a voodoo man and I was surprised to find that this 'story' was used on the front page of the *Daily Telegraph*. I know we have fantasy cricket these days. This was fantasy journalism!

The other low point of that 1995 tour for me came on 2 July at Canterbury when I recorded the first pair of my career. The bowler, Dr Julian Barton DeCourcy Thompson, was not even a Kent regular. When the season started, he had taken just one wicket in his first class career at a cost of 120 runs. A house surgeon at the Royal Berkshire Hospital in Reading, he was only in the side because so many other players were injured. Yet he dismissed me in both innings and became famous for a couple of days! These things happen in cricket but when you reach a certain standard it is almost as though you are not allowed to fail. Your public expects more records, more success. The responsibility of preserving the long unbeaten run of the West Indies against England was seemingly on my shoulders. If I made big scores, the West Indies would win. If I didn't, they would lose.

It was all becoming too much of a burden for me, but my mood changed after I read an interview with the golfer Nick Price, the winner of the British Open in 1994. Explaining why he showed such poor form after his Open success, he said: 'What was missing was my desire. Actually I was grateful to be out of the limelight. I just wanted someone else to take the heat for a while. Every time I went out people would expect me to play well. It just wore me down. I had to get away from it because I felt my personality change. I got tired of people asking me to do things, tired of signing countless autographs every day, tired of saying the same things to the same questions all the time. I felt as if I was starting to resent the fact that people wanted stuff from me when I should have been honoured they wanted it at all. I am an easy going person but I just got fed up with it all.'

That was exactly how I felt. I could relate to him over this but whereas it was unlikely he would stay in that position for the rest of his career because there are so many other outstanding golfers on the circuit I am condemned to it for as long as I continue playing. I will never be allowed to forget that I am cricket's double world record holder. Wherever I go, someone will want to talk to me about it. Someone will want my signature.

Also Nick competes in a mainly individual sport. He can take time off if he wants to and miss a few tournaments. Tennis players, too, can do that. But mine is a team game and if I say I want a break it can cause resentment and I am branded a prima donna. There is always someone who can take your place. The treadmill goes on and it is not easy to step off. The pressure is on me every time I go to the crease.

The realisation that other leading sportsmen have had similar problems and came through them, as Nick Price obviously did, helped lift my depression. My form changed and the first century I made on the tour came at Old Trafford, followed by another one at Trent Bridge and a third at the Oval. Naturally I was pleased about that but I felt unrewarded because none of these performances won a match for my side, which is my objective when I go to the crease.

With Illingworth helping Mike Atherton to kindle a new, more aggressive spirit in the side, England played much better than my team. They made the most of their abilities, which is always the sign of good leadership. Man for man, Atherton did not have as good players as we had but whereas he got the very best out of them, we tended to under achieve. The togetherness and mental strength of previous West Indian sides simply wasn't there. We just didn't perform.

We arrived in England shortly after the 2–1 defeat at home by the Australians, our first reverse in a home series for 22 years. It was a result that ended our invincibility and dented our confidence. Ideally, we needed a few weeks off to regroup and reassess our strategy but there was no time.

Team manager David Holford and coach Rohan Kanhai, who were popular with most of the players, were dismissed and Wes Hall became manager and Andy Roberts the coach. Kanhai was particularly missed. He was a thinker about the game and a shrewd analyst of the opposition. I did not think the changes helped our cause.

The Australians won convincingly without being able to use the services of their best bowler, Craig McDermott. The dicipline of their other bowlers, particularly Paul Reiffel and Glenn McGrath, was such that none of our batsmen averaged more than fifty, a rarity in a series in the Caribbean. I topped the averages with a modest 44 from 308 runs.

The catching of the Australians was also decisive. Skipper Mark Taylor took ten in the four Tests, one more than wicket keeper Ian Healy and few could disagree with him when he said: 'Their tactics against us – the short pitched stuff – didn't work and that was the crucial factor. We knew it was coming and we handled it.'

Steve Waugh, mistakenly labelled suspect after this

type of bowling, proved to be his side's outstanding batsman and his 200 at Sabina Park helped his side clinch the series by an innings and 53 runs. Too great a workload was put on Courtney Walsh, whose 20 wickets at 21.55 represented a magnificent effort. The Lara v Shane Warne confrontation never really materialised. I was out to him only once, in the Jamaica Test and though he captured 15 wickets he finished bottom of his side's averages.

Few of the West Indian batsmen, myself included, were in any kind of form when the three match Texaco Trophy series started in England at the end of May. Normally these matches do not have much bearing on the outcome of the Test series that follows but there was one important difference this time. When the season started Atherton was under a certain amount of pressure. Illingworth and his fellow selectors had taken their time to re-appoint him. But the England skipper showed so much character and resolution in the Texaco games, particularly during his innings of 127 in the deciding contest at Lord's, that it set him up for the whole summer. Being voted Man of the Series boosted his confidence tremendously. He was a much tougher opponent when the real battle started at Headingley eleven days later.

Atherton failed in the first Texaco international at Trent Bridge, scoring only 8 before I caught him off the bowling of Courtney Walsh. England's 199 was well short of what was required on a good batting pitch and when Sherwin Campbell and I had taken the West Indies reply to 180-1 England were in danger of going down to one of their heaviest defeats in this form of cricket. Some slapdash cricket saw us lose five wickets, Sherwin being run out for 80 and myself and Richie Richardson falling to Darren Gough before victory was achieved by five wickets with 14 deliveries left.

Richie again won the toss in the second game at the Oval two days later and his decision to field led to England rattling up 306, the highest total ever conceded by the West Indies in a limited overs international. One of the reasons the total was so high was that Courtney Walsh was only able to bowl 5.2 overs before pulling up with a back injury.

Luck went against us all day. When Curtly Ambrose kicked the ball against the stumps Neil Fairbrother, who went on to score 61 in 52 balls, appeared to be well out of his ground but umpire Dickie Bird ruled him in without calling for the assistance of the off field umpire and the TV replay. Dickie was not to make that mistake again. Whenever there was an appeal for a run out in the Tests in which he stood he signalled for the TV evidence almost every time!

The West Indies needed a big score from someone in the top six of the order but none of us passed 40 as the newcomer from Lancashire Peter Martin bowled exceptionally well to take 4–44. He bowled me with a delivery which swung late and said afterwards: 'That was the most satisfying delivery I've ever bowled.' Peter was gracious about the help he had received, from Malcolm Marshall among others. Unfortunately he pulled a muscle shortly afterwards and was forced to drop out of the squad. If he had stayed in, he might have delayed the entry of Dominic Cork to the Test side.

Junior Murray's 86 kept our hopes alive for a while until he was run out by Fairbrother and England won by 25 runs with two overs unused. I play so many of these matches it is difficult to distinguish one from another but that particular game will be memorable for me because of my running out of Graham Thorpe. The Surrey left hander played the ball to deep square leg and was going for a second when I picked the ball up one handed more than seventy yards from the wicket and hit the stumps.

With both sides having won a match the third contest at a packed Lord's two days later was the decider. Again, Richie won the toss and his decision to ask Atherton to bat was undoubtedly the right one because it had rained overnight and conditions suited the bowlers. Curtley Ambrose had an inspired opening spell, constantly beating the outside edge of Atherton's bat. He was to finish without a wicket as England recovered from a slow start to reach 276–7.

Conditions were easier when the West Indies batted but once more we disappointed and 6.4 overs remained when the last wicket fell at 203. The captain was not too upset. 'We lost all three of these matches last time we were here and that had no bearing on the Test series,' he said. It was worrying, all the same, that none of our batsmen were in good form so close to the start of the series.

As it turned out, that did not matter so unprofessionally did England's batsmen and bowlers perform in the four chilly days the opening Test lasted in Leeds. Their bowlers, with Devon Malcolm leading the way, bowled far too erratically and most of the batsmen got themselves out playing the cut shot before they were set. It is a risky shot to use early on when the pitch has regular bounce. At Headingley it was suicidal.

From the West Indies viewpoint, the success story belonged to Ian Bishop whose control and swing earned him match winning figures of 5–32 in England's rain interrupted first innings total of 199. Ian had been carefully nursed back to fitness after a second major back operation and we were overjoyed he was able to prove that he remained one of the game's top fast bowlers.

With Illingworth insisting on six specialist batsmen

Robin Smith was asked to open and that proved a mistake. Robin has been England's most successful batsman against the West Indies attack when going in three or four. I know how he must have felt. I have opened in one day matches but in Test cricket you need a sound defensive technique first and foremost. The opening position is one for specialists.

Smith's promotion meant that the Atherton-Stewart opening pairing, so effective on the last tour of the Caribbean, was broken up, Stewart coming in at five because he was preferred to Steve Rhodes as the wicket keeper. The Surrey captain kept superbly but his contribution with the bat was only 6 runs in two innings. England lost six wickets for 15 runs in 7 overs.

The West Indies, too, had a makeshift opener in Carl Hooper and he fell to the first ball of the innings from Devon Malcolm, caught by Thorpe at slip. Devon's subsequent deliveries were so short they gave me ample opportunity to pepper the advertising boards. After four overs the score reached 40 before Atherton withdrew his fast bowler from the onslaught. Sherwin Campbell and I took the total close to 100 and the noisy crowd were probably enjoying it as much as we were.

I had reached 53 in 55 balls when I went down the pitch to drive Richard Illingworth's second delivery and the ball turned just enough to find the outside edge and provide Graeme Hick with a comparatively simple catch. It was an annoying way to go and I was angry with myself. A collapse at the end of the innings, the last five wickets going down for 39, saw us dismissed for 282, a lead of 83. It should have been much greater. Darren Gough, playing in front of his own supporters, broke down after 5 overs and was not able to bowl again in the match.

England's batting in the second innings was little better than in their first. Smith fell to the cut shot again and the total of 208 would have been much lower had we held our catches. Poor catching dogged us throughout the series. More went down than were held. In previous years that was never the case.

Faced with the routine task of scoring 126 to win, we lost Campbell to a fine diving catch by Atherton at 11 only for Carl Hooper and myself to race to the target in 19 overs, Hooper being unbeaten on 73. I had made 48 off 40 balls when I pulled Malcolm to leg for the winning runs. He bowled only 11 overs in the match and they cost him six runs an over . . . and his place in the side. He was not to reappear until the Oval in the final Test.

As our over rate was 12.7 Match Referee John Reid fined us 30% of our match fees. In my opinion, this ruling of the ICC that 15 overs must be bowled every hour is ludicrous. The circumstances of the match should be taken into account. If we had kept to the rate the game might not have gone into the fourth day, robbing a large crowd of their cricket.

Illingworth did not make the mistake of criticising his players too severely afterwards. 'We know we can play better than that,' he said. 'The players know it and they will. There is a fine margin between winning and losing. Batsmen getting a bit of luck for example. Brian Lara got three bottom edges in his innings which just missed off stump. That makes a difference.'

Illingworth's point about luck was borne out in the Second Test at Lord's, a closely fought match which ended with England winning their first Test against us at cricket's headquarters since 1957. When the final day started the West Indies were 68–1 needing 228 to win and most of the critics were saying that if I stayed there the odds were on us. I felt confident and so did my partner Sherwin Campbell who was to go on and make 93 in that second innings. The mood in our dressing room was optimistic. The pitch was playing better than it had done on the first two days.

I reached my fifty off 59 balls and cover drove Darren Gough for another boundary next ball. Then came the turning point. Gough ran one down the slope from the pavilion end and it was almost wide enough to leave. But I was committed to a shot and the ball nicked the outside edge of my angled bat. I followed its line and it was going fast and low, dropping about a foot in front of Atherton at first slip. Alec Stewart, confirmed as England's wicket keeper on the morning of the match when most people expected the job to go to Steve Rhodes, swooped to his left and held the ball left handed.

Regulars at Lord's claimed it was one of the greatest catches ever made at cricket's most historic ground. There was no luck attached to it. But I could easily have played and missed. As at Headingley, I walked off the field feeling that I had let down myself and my team. It was so frustrating to be playing so well only to have my innings cut short in full flow. I couldn't say it was negligence on my part. It was just something that happens in cricket.

We needed someone to stay with Campbell after that but no-one was capable of doing it as Dominic Cork, on his Test début recorded figures of 7–43, the best by an England player on début surpassing John Lever's 7–46 against India in New Delhi on the 1976–7 tour. Cork disclaims any likeness to Ian Botham but he has many similarities to the man whose picture he has on his mantelpiece at home. He is aggressive, loves to talk on the field, appeals in extravagant fashion and when he bowls, expects every delivery to take a wicket. He is the kind of cricketer who makes things happen. Once he establishes himself in Test cricket, I think he will also score a lot of runs. He emulated David Gower by striking the first ball he received in Test cricket for four, a sure sign of confidence. 'He would have been in the side the year before if he had been fit,' said Illingworth. The emergence of Cork and Gough as all rounders is good for English cricket. In the West Indies we have yet to find young bowlers of quality to replace our main bowlers.

Cork's stock ball is the outswinger but he has now mastered the inswinger and is also capable of reverse swing, as he showed when taking his hat trick at Old Trafford. One of his problems is that he bowls so close to the stumps that he is often warned for running down the pitch. He could find himself being ordered out of the attack if he cannot overcome this handicap.

In the final Test at the Oval I was disappointed to find him pitching the ball outside my leg stump as a defensive tactic. There is no law against this in Test cricket but I feel it is against the spirit of the game and umpires should have powers to warn offenders. The paying public do not pay out big sums to watch bowlers bowling a foot or more outside the leg stump to prevent batsmen scoring.

Cork's dismissal of Jimmy Adams for 13 was a decisive wicket at Lord's. It was an example of the way, like Botham, that he sometimes takes wickets he does not deserve. It was a widish delivery presenting little menace and Jimmy swished at it and gave Graeme Hick a routine catch. Richie Richardson was his next victim, for his second duck in three innings. Paul Weekes, substituting at short leg for Thorpe, made two fine catches to dismiss Keith Arthurton and Junior Murray and when Cork had Otis Gibson lbw for 14 and Campbell caught behind seven short of what would have been a deserved century it was virtually all over. As we had done so often in the series, the West Indies had failed to do themselves justice with the bat.

There was plenty of discussion before the match began about the pitch. Richie Richardson described it as the driest he had encountered at Lord's and there were fears that the cracks that were discernible at the start might widen. On the first two days several batsmen were rapped on the gloves leading our coach Andy Roberts to say at a press conference: 'I am fearful for the game of cricket with wickets like this. It is one of the worst I have seen in England. I think it was deliberately done, under prepared because they thought it would turn. But it is uneven and balls are taking off and hitting batsmen on the fingers.'

He said he thought the West Indies would score a lot on it and added: 'I wouldn't like to see us having to chase more than 150 in our second innings but I don't think that will be necessary because we'll get 500.' Next day he was reprimanded in a statement from Match Referee John Reid for criticising the pitch. Apparently the ICC rules did not allow officials to comment publicly on pitches. Yet it is a practice that goes on all the time.

Mr Reid was in action again later in the match after Gough and Ian Bishop exchanged words and as the two men turned away, Gough spat on the ground. Mr Reid said: 'The act of spitting indiscriminately is a filthy habit and it was an unfortunate coincidence that Darren Gough unthinkingly expectorated at the wrong time, giving the false impression that it was directed at Ian Bishop.' He was satisfied there was no breach of the ICC Code of Conduct.

This comparatively trivial incident underlines the problems cricketers face today, problems that were unknown in previous times. Every more we make, or nearly every move, is picked up by one of the many cameras now at Test grounds and there are countless people around the country ready and eager to ring up newspapers to tip them off about so-called incidents. Reporters at matches are asked to investigate them and if it is discovered that one newspaper is prepared to devote space to this trivia, the others usually fall into line. The next day something that may have gone unnoticed by most people present is built up as a major controversy. The Match Referee is called into action, players are interviewed and verdicts are announced. It is as though we are constantly on trial. No-one wants to see bad behaviour out in the middle but I really do think things have gone too far!

Winning the toss at Lord's proved a considerable bonus for Mike Atherton, even if he failed himself this time, bowled by Ambrose for 21. England's 255–8 at the end of an absorbing opening day was probably slightly up on par especially as the pitch was expected to deteriorate. As it turned out, that was not so. Robin Smith, back at number 5, was his side's mainstay in his 100th Test innings scoring 61 in just over two hours. His partnership of 11 with Graham Thorpe, who made 52, was full of aggressive shots. Cork, 30, and Peter Martin, 29, enabled England to close on 283.

Our response was once again inadequate. Sherwin Campbell went for 5 in Gough's opening over and I was lbw for 6 to provide Angus Fraser with his 100th Test wicket. Dropped catches were a feature of the match and both Adams, who came back to form with 54 in 220 minutes and Richie Richardson, 49 in 109 minutes, were reprieved. Richie showed a lot of restraint as he played his side out of trouble, leaving Keith Arthurton with an opportunity to put us on top with a responsible innings of 75 in our first innings of 324, the first time we had passed 300 in eight innings.

Our lead of 41 proved useful as England lost both Atherton and Stewart for 51 and Thorpe retired to hospital after an unintentional beamer from Courtney Walsh struck him in the helmet. Courtney bowled several of these deliveries during the tour. They were attempted slower balls that went wrong. Each time he apologised and each time the batsman accepted his apology.

Graeme Hick now proceeded to play his most important innings of the summer, striking out boldly against top class fast bowling and racing to his fifty off only 67 balls. Hick is one of England's most criticised batsmen chiefly because he never appears to have the appetite to face short, fast bowling. That day at Lord's he proved his critics were premature. Ian Bishop eventually ended his innings when he went round the wicket and bowled him for 67.

There was no means of upsetting the concentration of Robin Smith, who was still there in the gloom when the umpires called a halt with the home side 155–3, 114 ahead. Mark Ramprakash, a young batsman who was to score 2258 first class runs to top the averages that summer, was out third ball on Sunday morning for a duck.

It was his second of the match and was to cost him his England place. He was caught by substitute Stuart Williams at third slip and was so shocked he stayed at the crease for a short time. I felt desperately sorry for him. The new batsman was Thorpe and he received a huge ovation. The circumstances provoked a partisan atmosphere in a ground which is usually quiet and I am sure that helped inspire Thorpe, who went on to score 42, and Smith, whose innings of 90 was one of the most physically demanding he has surely played. Smith was struck a number of times and needed treatment from physio Dave Roberts yet stuck it out unflinchingly. He batted six hours before Ambrose brought one back into him and he was lbw ten short of his century.

England's last four wickets fell for 21 and their second innings total of 336 meant we were left four sessions to score 296 to win. It was an acute disappointment to us that we failed to make the target. England's victory to make it 1–1 in the series was hailed with big headlines. I was amused by the comment in the *Sydney Morning Herald*. 'If even the Poms can beat them it takes a bit of the gloss off our win,' it said.

Before the Third Test at Edgbaston I gave more interviews than I had given in the whole of the series up to then. The interviewers wanted to know if I felt I would score that elusive first Test century in England on the ground where I had compiled my record 501 not out the year before. I said I hoped so but cricket has a habit of frustrating the best of intentions. The pitch did not appear to us to be the usual Edgbaston type of pitch. It was hard but the ends were shaven and in the central areas there were tufts of grass.

Questioned about this odd looking surface, Wes Hall said he had no comment to make on it. 'We'll play them in the car park if necessary,' he said. He had a point there because when Curtly Ambrose delivered the first ball of the day halfway down the pitch it soared over Mike Atherton's head and cleared wicket keeper Junior Murray by several feet to fly to the boundary. It might as well have been bowled on the concrete in the car park. Umpire Ian Robinson of Zimbabwe signalled four wides and Atherton looked shocked. Afterwards he was to describe the pitch as 'diabolical' without incurring any censure from Mr Reid. Two batsmen, Jason Gallian and

Richard Illingworth, had broken fingers and half a dozen more needed treatment.

With their greater height and pace, the West Indian bowlers were lethal on it and the game was over early on the third morning after only 172.2 overs had been bowled. It was the second shortest Test in terms of balls since 1912 and it was also England's first defeat inside three days at home since the West Indies won at Old Trafford in 1966.

England were bowled out for 147 in 46.2 overs and it might well have been quicker had Ambrose not pulled up with a groin strain after bowling only 7.5 overs. Thorpe was out to a brutish delivery from Ambrose but I felt some of his colleagues contributed to their downfall. The exception was Robin Smith, who played on after taking a number of blows on the back, arm and gloves. He topscored with 46 and was also leading scorer in the second innings when England were rushed out for 89, their lowest in a Test at Edgbaston. Courageously as he performed, he still made it worse for himself by sometimes taking his eye off the ball and ducking. None of the other batsmen were able to stay long enough with him to force Richardson to use his part time bowlers. Courtney Walsh and Ian Bishop took fifteen wickets between them, Bishop becoming the 14th West Indian to pass 100 wickets.

England's four seamers were unable to obtain as much bounce and we found it relatively easy to make 300 in our only innings. I was 21 not out when the first day ended at 104–1 and was disappointed to be lbw without scoring in the morning to Dominic Cork. The Derbyshire bowler bowled just the right line with a little movement from leg to off to beat the bat and it was something I had to put right in subsequent encounters. I think I managed it!

Cork also dismissed Sherwin Campbell, who topscored with 79, Carl Hooper, who made 40 and Jimmy Adams,

10, to add four more wickets to his growing haul. Campbell's performance earned him the Man of the Match award from Michael Holding and justifiably so. He is a quick learner and I was delighted that Durham signed him for the 1996 season.

Richie Richardson overcame his problems with a dogged 69 in 242 minutes. He forsook his normal approach to block his way out of trouble. He took 32 minutes to get his first run and was becalmed on 7 for no less than 75 minutes. Atherton dropped him at 25 – one of several dropped catches by both sides. The England captain needed to play a similar innings but he made only four before Courtney Walsh bowled him with a shortish delivery which cut back almost a foot. Alec Stewart, who damaged his injured right index finger while keeping wicket, was unable to bat and Gallian defied a broken finger to come in at six. Gallian lasted just two balls.

The packed crowd who had paid £300,000 booed when it was all over after 13 overs but it was harsh to apportion the blame on England. The way the pitch played penalised them far more than it did us. Not that we had much sympathy. We needed the victory to take a 2–1 lead and restore confidence after losing to lowly Sussex by an innings and 121 runs in the previous match. That was a game I was not too disappointed to miss.

There were further ructions when the management decided to send Winston Benjamin home for indiscipline. They were upset that he had declared himself unfit to play when senior bowlers like Ambrose and Walsh were clearly struggling with injuries and were being pressed into action when it would have benefited them and the team to have a rest. It is highly unusual for a player to be sent home from a tour. Fortunately there was so much happening at the time it received only minimal publicity. But it was an episode that did not help the team's overall well being.

Our performance in the Fourth Test at Old Trafford reflected the disarray in our camp. We lost by six wickets to an England side which showed six changes. Lancashire skipper Mike Watkinson was given his Test début on his own pitch at the age of 34 and even more surprising was the recall of John Emburey at the age of 42. Emburey failed to take a wicket but his sound advice to Atherton was one of the factors in England's success.

Richie Richardson won the toss but indifferent batting on a pitch of even bounce led to us being dismissed for 216, less than half the total we should have made in the conditions. I was determined to bat as long as I could and was most unhappy to miss a straight one from Dominic Cork when I was 13 short of a century. The next highest scorer was Jimmy Adams with 24.

Several batsmen were out to loose shots and I agreed with Angus Fraser, who captured four wickets, when he said: 'The West Indies were cock-a-hoop after winning at Edgbaston and probably believed the series was there for the taking. They wanted to stamp their authority on the game from the start. Fortunately for us, they didn't. They were going for almost everything and when they connected it was going past the fielders with some oomph. We just had to try to put the ball in the right place. They are not the most patient of players.'

Cork, who again had me leg before with a ball which straightened slightly, said: 'It's nice to get him but I wouldn't say he is my bunny!'

There was an amusing moment in the 100th Cornhill Test when Dickie Bird, who officiated in Cornhill's first Test in 1978, stopped play because of excessive glare. It took some time to discover that it was coming from a B and Q greenhouse next to the Indoor School. Apparently it had happened once before and the groundstaff had to cover the windows with the black sightscreen used for Sunday matches before play could resume.

There was another long stoppage later when the England captain complained he was being dazzled by reflected sunlight from an executive box at the same end. Dickie went off the pitch to tell the occupants of the box to do something about it but they were totally mystified. Eventually someone discovered the glare was reflected from the windows in the Press Box at the other side of the ground. The boxholder said to Dickie: 'Come and have a drink old lad.' As it was a very hot day with the temperature in the high eighties, the world's most experienced umpire must have been sorely tempted. For some reason we were not having drinks intervals at this time, probably because of the poor over rate of both sides.

Graham Thorpe showed the kind of application needed with a brilliant innings of 94 in England's reply of 437. He richly deserved a century for the way he stood up to some aggressive bowling but was out the next ball following a Mexican Wave in the 21,000 capacity crowd. We realised we had to make a supreme effort in the field to get back into the match and Thorpe and Robin Smith, who made an equally courageous 44, had to withstand long periods of hostile bowling. Dickie Bird thought Courtney Walsh overdid it at one point, warning him under the new interpretation of the law regarding unfair bowling. Courtney was very indignant because the three deliveries complained about were not bouncers and the batsman had no difficulty in countering them.

England had a huge slice of luck on the Saturday morning when they resumed with a lead of 131. Dominic Cork, unbeknown to anyone else on the field including the umpires, stepped back on to his stumps and dislodged a bail when setting off for his first run of the day. As he was on 3 at the time and finished 56 not out it was a key incident in the match. When he got back to that end after an all run four, he calmly replaced the bail and no-one asked any questions. The incident was only picked up when Richie Benaud spotted it on television. I believe Richie Richardson appealed but neither umpire saw how the bail came off and was not able to make a ruling.

With a deficit of 221 to make up we batted a little more responsibly at the start of our second innings and eighty minutes went by before the first wicket went down, totally unnecessarily. Keith Arthurton, standing in for Carl Hooper who had a fractured finger, called for a risky single and was sent back by Sherwin Campbell. Angus Fraser at mid off had an easy task to run him out. I had made only one when there was a concerted appeal from the England players for a 'catch' behind by Jack Russell but I knew I hadn't touched it.

Campbell, 44, and Jimmy Adams, 1, fell to Mike Watkinson, who turned the ball more than Emburey and when the fourth day's play began on another hot and humid day we were still 62 behind. Richie needed to play the kind of innings he played at Edgbaston but was out to Cork's fourth delivery of the day in a cruelly unlucky manner. It was a widish delivery and as he lifted his bat the ball clipped the inside edge, diverted on to his pad and cannoned into the stumps.

Junior Murray was next in and shuffled across his stumps as Cork's next delivery held up slightly to have him lbw. Hooper was the new batsman and he had been the third victim in Cork's only hat trick up to then, in a Kent v Derbyshire match the previous season. The tension was as stifling as the weather. No English bowler had taken a hat trick in a Test since Peter Loader, also against the West Indies 38 years previously. As Cork prepared to bowl, Loader was caddying for a friend on a golf course in Perth, where he lives. He heard that Cork had emulated his feat when he returned home later and sent his congratulations.

The ball which had Hooper lbw was similar to the one which accounted for Murray. It was straight, well pitched up and would have hit. Cork, arms aloft Botham style, fell back into the arms of his jubilant colleagues. He had become the eighth English bowler to take a hat trick and the 20th in Test history.

It was now left to me to prolong the innings as long as possible with the aid of the tailenders. Atherton spread out the field when I faced the bowling, making it more difficult but I managed to go past the elusive 100 mark. I felt I was timing the ball as well as I have ever done and was disappointed when on 145 I struck the second ball of Fraser's new spell with the second new ball to Nick Knight at deep mid wicket. Knight made a fine catch. He is an excellent all round fielder.

Our total of 314, with Cork taking eight wickets in the match, meant England needed only 94 to win. After he was out in the first innings, Thorpe said he wasn't assuming anything 'because I was at Trinidad and know what happened there.' With England cruising to 39 before Atherton needlessly ran himself out there seemed little chance of a miracle happening but when Knight and Thorpe fell in successive overs we suddenly sensed we had a chance. Craig White departed and at 48–4 England were struggling. More so after Robin Smith deflected a ball from Ian Bishop into the side of his face and had to retire to hospital. Robin had a depressed fracture of the cheekbone and was out of the series. Surprisingly considering he puts his name to a make of helmet which has a visor, he was not wearing a visor at the time.

One newspaper tried to imply our bowling was intimidatory but Robin rejected that by saying it was a complete accident, which it was. Jack Russell came in and played exactly the right innings for the occasion. He went for his shots and his unbeaten 31 off 39 deliveries saw England through to a six wicket win to square the series at 2–2.

Before the Fifth Test at Trent Bridge, we lost the services of Jimmy Adams who was struck in the face by a ball from Somerset's Dutchman Adrianus Van Troost. Jimmy had a depressed fracture of the cheekbone like Robin and though he turned up at Trent Bridge and said he hoped to be fit for the Oval Test there was no chance of that happening. Sadly, his sight was affected for some time afterwards. Curtly Ambrose was injured along with Carl Hooper and we brought in Raj Dhanraj, my Trinidadian colleague, Stuart Williams for Hooper and Shivnarine Chanderpaul for Adams.

Dhanraj was our leading wicket taker up to then but unfortunately did not bowl as well at Trent Bridge as he had done on the rest of the tour and his 55 overs cost 191 runs without a wicket. He constantly overpitched, especially against Graeme Hick who celebrated his recall in place of Robin Smith with an unbeaten 118 in England's first innings of 440. Dhanraj's sole contribution was to run out Atherton for 113 with a direct throw on the first day. Kenny Benjamin, bowling straight and up to the bat, captured five wickets for 105 and together with his 5–69 that earned him the Man of the Match award.

When I went in at 77–1 I felt in good form and the runs came in a torrent. While Sherwin Campbell played the anchor role at the other end, I passed my fifty in 43 deliveries and at 86 I recorded 500 runs for the series. My hundred came off 118 balls and I was beginning to think this could be a really big one. The pitch was easy paced, as England chairman Ray Illingworth wanted, the outfield was as fast as any in the Caribbean and the ball was doing little through the air or off the pitch. My placements almost invariably found the gaps and I enjoyed myself more than at any time that summer. Campbell's dismissal for a five-hour 47 brought in Richie Richardson without a helmet and Richie proceeded to outscore me, hitting 40 off 45 deliveries.

My 150 came with my 28th four, a pull off Cork but to my chagrin I was out almost immediately afterwards, edging a long hop outside the leg stump from Cork and Russell making a diving catch to his right. The fourth day began with the West Indies on 334–5 and a draw appeared certain when we closed on 417, 23 behind. Yet another player was put in hospital when Nick Knight, fielding very close on the off side, was struck in the head by a powerfully hit shot from Kenny Benjamin. Nick was not wearing a helmet because, like most close fielders, he believes there is less chance of being hit close on the offside than on the leg. Tailenders are unpredictable, however, and I would not recommend the practice myself. Amazingly, there was no serious damage and Nick was able to bat on the final day, albeit for only 21 minutes.

If Ian Bishop hadn't ricked his ankle we might have won on the last day because at lunch England were 155–6, only 178 ahead with tailender Richard Illingworth suffering from a broken finger. England were only 212 ahead when Watkinson was joined by last man Illingworth. Almost immediately Watkinson hit a ball from Courtney Walsh straight to Sherwin Campbell at mid wicket and Sherwin dropped it. If the chance had been accepted, the West Indies would have been left chasing 215 in 40 overs, an achievable target in the conditions.

Watkinson, 82 not out, went on to help Illingworth, 14 not out, add 80 for the last wicket, England's highest for the 10th wicket in 15 years to save the match, Atherton declaring at 269–9. Set to score 292 in 20 overs, we made a gesture by sending me in first along with Campbell and I made just 20 off 30 balls when Russell caught me, cutting against Fraser. Players of both sides were relieved when a halt was called at 5.30 with out total 42–2.

It was on to the Oval with everything to play for. I agree with former West Indies wicket keeper Deryck Murray that six Tests is one too many. These commercial decisions are made without consulting the players. I am sure not many would agree with an extra Test.

Around 70,000 cricket lovers paid a record £1.5m to watch the five days of the Final Test and most of them must have suspected the match would end in a draw. The pitch was even more bland than the one at Trent Bridge and the batsmen were on top almost throughout. Perhaps if our bowlers had all been fit we might have achieved victory just as we did in 1976 chiefly through the efforts of Michael Holding. But Ambrose was suffering the effects of a long, hot summer, Bishop still had trouble with his ankle, Courtney Walsh played on with several niggling injuries and Kenny Benjamin did not bowl at all in England's second innings claiming he had a bad back.

Ambrose, in probably his last big match in England, still managed to generate a lot of pace and his 5–96 off 42 overs in England's first innings of 454 was a herculean effort. Near the end of the final day he bowed out, leaving the field to generous applause as he waved farewell. Afterwards when Jimmy Adams was filming him for his video of the tour, someone said: 'Is that your swansong Curtly?' And Curtly said: 'That's it, full stop.' He pulled the studs from the soles of his boots in a symbolic gesture. Even though he had problems with fitness, he still managed to take 21 wickets in the series at a cost of 24.10, giving him a total of 258 wickets at 21 apiece in 59 Tests. He was one of the greatest bowlers of all time.

The game may have been meaningless in many ways but it provided a landmark in the career of my great friend Courtney Walsh. Courtney was becoming increasingly frustrated at not being able to take the 300th Test wicket of his career. In England's first innings, he was angry when the Indian umpire V.K. Ramaswamy warned him for bowling three short deliveries in a row to England's number 3 batsman John Crawley. In our view there was no suggestion that this constituted dangerous play, especially as the Lancashire batsman had no difficulty dealing with these deliveries. At the end of the over, Courtney snatched his sunhat away from Ramaswamy, earning him more criticism on the back pages of some newspapers.

All that was forgotten when 35 overs after he captured his 299th wicket, Courtney found the edge of Mike Watkinson's bat and he became the 10th Test bowler to pass the 300 mark and the third West Indian behind Malcolm Marshall (376) and Lance Gibbs (309). At 33, Courtney should catch Gibbs but I suspect he might find Marshall's total beyond him. As Courtney Browne made the catch which gave Walsh his 300th wicket the Jamaican captain collapsed to the ground on his knees. I doubt if there has ever been a greater trier, or a more wholehearted cricketer, to represent the West Indies. We were all delighted for him and it was especially pleasing that his mother was there to see him do it. It was her first trip outside Jamaica.

Late on in the second day Dominic Cork, going for a quick single, ran straight down the pitch at Ambrose and Ambrose warded him off with both hands. It did not look a serious incident but Match Referee John Reid still felt it was worth investigating and there was an hour long hearing at the close of play. Mr Reid finally ruled that the collision was accidental and he also exonerated Ian Bishop and Kenny Benjamin for kicking the ground in exasperation. Mike Atherton was also to kick the ground after being dismissed for 95 in his side's second innings. His case was not investigated.

If we were to win we had to score quickly and Stuart Williams did just that taking five boundaries off Devon Malcolm in nine deliveries. What might have been one of the quickest Test centuries of all time was brought to an unsatisfactory end when Ramaswamy decided that a ball from Malcolm had struck Williams on the glove when he had made 30 off 40 deliveries. The TV evidence failed to confirm that contact was made with the glove. It looked more like the batsman's arm or sleeve. It was not the first time in the series that had happened to a batsman and it was a sign of the high standard of behaviour in the series that there was no dissent from the batsmen.

I played at and missed the first ball I received from Cork, was hit on the pad by the second and then settled down to play one of my best innings in England. I felt in the same confident mood I had been in at Trent Bridge. The boundaries, 26 fours and a six, came in rapid succession. It was unfortunate that Sherwin Campbell went for 89. He thoroughly deserved what would have been his first Test century.

The pitch had similarities with the one in Antigua when I scored my 375 and it crossed my mind that I might be given a chance of raising that total. At 179 I didn't quite get to the pitch of a delivery from Malcolm and gave Angus Fraser an easy catch at mid off. That was one of the few times I had hit the ball in the air during the four and a half hours I spent in the middle. It was my 7th Test hundred in my 31st Test and my fifth against England and it took my tally of runs for the series to 765, a total only exceeded in England by Don Bradman, with 974 in 1930, Mark Taylor, 836 in 1989 and Viv Richards, 829 in 1976.

Richie Richardson became the third player to be dismissed in the 90s when he was out for 93 but Carl Hooper contributed 127 and Chanderpaul 80 as we scored 692, our second highest Test total. There was to be a fourth in the nineties, Atherton with 95, and apparently that was only the second time it had happened in Tests.

Ambrose and Walsh put all they had into a final assault on the last day but Atherton, England's Man of the Series, defied them and England ended at 223–4 as the match petered out in a draw. Under their new management, England showed a lot of character, particularly Atherton, but I still feel they have some way to go before they have a side capable of beating the best in the world. Cork is a fine acquisition and Darren Gough may well turn out to be another one once he regains full fitness. The batting, with Robin Smith back in his rightful position, Graeme Hick scoring more consistently and Graham Thorpe showing his class, is more settled but Illingworth needs to find several more talented young players to strengthen his squad.

Jack Russell performed magnificently with the bat and at 32 may have a year or two more. The natural successor to him, in my opinion, is Warwickshire's Keith Piper, who had a wonderful season for his county in 1995.

The West Indies side needs rebuilding and I believe I can play a significant part in the task of re-establishing the side at the top of the world league. First we need to find some young fast bowlers to take over from Ambrose,

Walsh and the Benjamins, and that will not be easy.

Morale has to be restored. There is a lot of work to be done.

STATISTICS

BRIAN LARA FACT FILE

FULL NAME: Brian Charles Lara
BIRTHDATE: 2 May 1969
BIRTHPLACE: Cantaro Village, Santa Cruz, Trinidad
SCHOOL: Fatima College, Port of Spain
CLUB SIDE: Queen's Park CC, Port of Spain
FIRST–CLASS TEAMS: Trinidad and Tobago, Warwickshire
TYPE: Left-hand batsman, right-arm legspin bowler
FIRST–CLASS DÉBUT: 1988 Trinidad and Tobago v. Leeward Islands,
                        Pointe-à-Pierre
TEST DEBUT: 1990 v. Pakistan, Lahore
ONE–DAY INTERNATIONAL
DEBUT: 1990 v. Pakistan, Karachi

CAREER STATISTICS UP TO 1 MARCH 1995:

FIRST-CLASS RECORD

BATTING   88 matches, 141 innings, 4 not outs, 7,737 runs, 501 not
            out highest score, average 56.47, 23 hundreds, 28 fifties
BOWLING   281 balls, 223 runs, 1 wicket, average 223.00, best 1-22
CATCHES   110

TEST RECORD

BATTING   21 matches, 34 innings, 0 not outs, 1,975 runs, 375 highest
            score, average 58.08, 4 hundreds, 10 fifties
BOWLING   24 balls, 0 maidens, 12 runs, 0 wickets
CATCHES   33

ONE-DAY INTERNATIONALS

BATTING   80 matches, 80 innings, 7 not outs, 3,057 runs, 153 highest
            score, average 41.87, 4 hundreds, 23 fifties
BOWLING   4 overs, 0 maidens, 22 runs, 2 wickets, average 11.00, best
            2-5
CATCHES   45

CAREER EXTRAS

Captain, Trinidad and Tobago Youth team, 1987-8; captain, West Indies
Youth team to Australia, 1988; captain, West Indies B team to Zimbabwe,
1989; captain, Trinidad and Tobago team in Red Stripe tournament, 1990 and
1994; West Indies Cricket Annual Cricketer of the Year, 1991; Trinidad and
Tobago Sportsman of the Year, 1993; awarded Trinidad's Humming Bird
medal in 1993 and Trinity Cross in 1994

TEST MATCHES

Against	Venue	Date	1st Innings	2nd Innings
Pakistan	Lahore	6 Dec 1990	44	5
South Africa	Bridgetown	18 April 1992	17	64
Australia	Brisbane	27 Nov 1992	58	0
Australia	Melbourne	26 Dec 1992	52	4
Australia	Sydney	2 Jan 1993	277	
Australia	Adelaide	23 Jan 1993	52	7
Australia	Perth	30 Jan 1993	16	
Pakistan	Port of Spain	16 April 1993	6	96
Pakistan	Bridgetown	23 April 1993	51	
Pakistan	St John's	1 May 1993	44	19
Sri Lanka	Moratuwa	8 Dec 1993	18	
England	Kingston	19 Feb 1994	83	28
England	Georgetown	17 March 1994	167	
England	Port of Spain	25 March 1994	43	12
England	Bridgetown	8 April 1994	26	64
England	St John's	16 April 1994	375	
India	Bombay	18 Nov 1994	14	0
India	Nagpur	1 Dec 1994	50	3
India	Chandigarh	10 Dec 1994	40	91
New Zealand	Christchurch	3 Feb 1995	2	
New Zealand	Wellington	10 Feb 1995	147	

ONE-DAY INTERNATIONALS

WORLD CUP

Against	Venue	Date	Innings
Pakistan	Melbourne	23 Feb 1992	88*
England	Melbourne	27 Feb 1992	0
Zimbabwe	Brisbane	29 Feb 1992	72
South Africa	Christchurch	5 March 1992	9
New Zealand	Auckland	8 March 1992	52
India	Wellington	10 March 1992	41
Sri Lanka	Berri	13 March 1992	1
Australia	Melbourne	18 March 1992	70

TEXACO TROPHY

Against	Venue	Date	Innings
England	Lord's	27 May 1991	23

Against	Venue	Date	Innings
India	Perth	6 Dec 1991	14
Australia	Melbourne	12 Dec 1991	11
India	Adelaide	14 Dec 1991	29
Australia	Sydney	18 Dec 1991	19
Australia	Melbourne	9 Jan 1992	22
India	Brisbane	11 Jan 1992	4
Australia	Brisbane	12 Jan 1992	69
India	Melbourne	16 Jan 1992	11
Pakistan	Perth	4 Dec 1992	59
Australia	Perth	6 Dec 1992	29
Australia	Sydney	8 Dec 1992	4
Pakistan	Adelaide	12 Dec 1992	15
Australia	Melbourne	15 Dec 1992	74
Pakistan	Sydney	17 Dec 1992	3
Pakistan	Brisbane	9 Jan 1993	10
Australia	Brisbane	10 Jan 1993	10
Australia	Sydney	16 Jan 1993	67
Australia	Melbourne	18 Jan 1993	60

OTHER ONE-DAY

Against	Venue	Date	Innings
Pakistan	Karachi	9 Nov 1990	11
Pakistan	Sharjah	17 Oct 1991	5
India	Sharjah	19 Oct 1991	45
Pakistan	Sharjah	21 Oct 1991	0
Pakistan	Karachi	20 Nov 1991	54
Pakistan	Lahore	22 Nov 1991	18
Pakistan	Faisalabad	24 Nov 1991	45
South Africa	Kingston	7 April 1992	50
South Africa	Port of Spain	11 April 1992	86*
South Africa	Port of Spain	12 April 1992	35
South Africa	Port Elizabeth	11 Feb 1993	13
Pakistan	Johannesburg	13 Feb 1993	0
South Africa	Cape Town	17 Feb 1993	14
Pakistan	Durban	19 Feb 1993	128
South Africa	Bloemfontein	23 Feb 1993	111*
Pakistan	Cape Town	25 Feb 1993	26*
Pakistan	Johannesburg	27 Feb 1993	49
Pakistan	Kingston	23 March 1993	114

Against	Venue	Date	Innings
Pakistan	Port of Spain	26 March 1993	95*
Pakistan	Port of Spain	27 March 1993	5
Pakistan	Arnos Vale	30 March 1993	5
Pakistan	Georgetown	3 April 1993	15
Sri Lanka	Sharjah	28 Oct 1993	5
Pakistan	Sharjah	29 Oct 1993	14
Pakistan	Sharjah	1 Nov 1993	14
Sri Lanka	Sharjah	3 Nov 1993	42
Pakistan	Sharjah	5 Nov 1993	153
Sri Lanka	Bombay	9 Nov 1993	67
South Africa	Bombay	14 Nov 1993	7
India	Ahmedabad	16 Nov 1993	23
Zimbabwe	Hyderabad	21 Nov 1993	4
Sri Lanka	Calcutta	25 Nov 1993	82
India	Calcutta	27 Nov 1993	33
Sri Lanka	Colombo	1 Dec 1993	89
Sri Lanka	Colombo	16 Dec 1993	65
Sri Lanka	Colombo	18 Dec 1993	29
England	Bridgetown	16 Feb 1994	9
England	Kingston	26 Feb 1994	8
England	Arnos Vale	2 March 1994	60
England	Port of Spain	5 March 1994	19
England	Port of Spain	6 March 1994	16
India	Faridabad	17 Oct 1994	10
India	Bombay	20 Oct 1994	6
India	Madras	23 Oct 1994	74
New Zealand	Goa	26 Oct 1994	32
New Zealand	Gauhati	1 Nov 1994	69
India	Calcutta	5 Nov 1994	1
India	Visakhapatnam	7 Nov 1994	39
India	Cuttack	9 Nov 1994	89
India	Jaipur	11 Nov 1994	47
New Zealand	Auckland	22 Jan 1995	55*
New Zealand	Wellington	25 Jan 1995	72
New Zealand	Christchurch	28 Jan 1995	34*

375 – HIGHEST TEST SCORE

Score	Mins	Balls	Fours	Sixes
50	150	121	7	–
100	228	180	16	–
150	324	240	22	–
200	436	311	27	–
250	511	377	32	–
300	610	432	38	–
350	721	511	42	–
369	748	530	44	–
375	766	538	45	–

501 – HIGHEST FIRST-CLASS SCORE

Score	Mins	Balls	Fours	Sixes
100	144	138	14	–
150	201	193	22	–
200	224	220	30	2
250	246	245	37	5
300	280	278	44	7
350	319	311	49	8
400	367	350	53	8
450	430	398	55	9
501	474	427	62	10

BRIAN LARA – A RECORD RUN OF SCORES

Score	For	Against	Venue	Balls	Fours	Sixes
375	West Indies	England	St.John's	538	45	–
147	Warwickshire	Glamorgan	Edgbaston	160	20	2
106	Warwickshire	Leicestershire	Edgbaston	136	18	–
120*	Warwickshire	Leicestershire	Edgbaston (2)	163	22	–
136	Warwickshire	Somerset	Taunton	94	14	2
26	Warwickshire	Middlesex	Lord's	48	3	–
140	Warwickshire	Middlesex	Lord's (2)	147	22	1
501*	Warwickshire	Durham	Edgbaston	427	62	10

INDEX

Australia: one-day matches in, 51–6; test matches, 66–74, 81–6, 206–9; World Cup, 1992, 54; World Youth Cup 24

Hair, Daryl, 70

Hall, Wes, 223, 227–8

Hammond, Wally, 98, 99

Hampshire, 46–7, 173–4, 189

Hancock, Tim, 194

Hanif Mohammad, 98, 99, 135, 140, 143

Hart, Matthew, 210

Harvard Clinic, Port of Spain, 17, 18

Hayhurst, Andy, 120, 183

Haynes, Desmond, 30, 132; v Australia, 71, 73, 82; v S. Africa, 63, 66; v India, 36; v Pakistan, 37–8, 40, 90, 91; Red Stripe Cup, 40–1; one-day internationals, 51, 52, 56

Haynes, Gavin, 163, 186

Haynes, Rob, 28, 30

Headley, George, 16, 137

Healy, Ian, 71, 206–7, 227

Hemmings, Eddie, 172

Hemp, David, 113

Hero Cup, 58–9

heroes, 10–11

Hick, Graeme, 76, 79, 141, 162, 163, 186, 187, 231, 234, 237, 245, 250

highest-paid players, 106

highest test score in Australia, 85

Holder, Roland, 24, 27, 30

Holding, Michael, 11, 15, 224, 240, 247

Holdsworth, Craig, 67

Holdsworth, Wayne, 24

Holford, David, 227

holiday, 148–50

Hollioake, Adam, 147–8

hooking, 15

Hooper, Carl, 23, 25, 26, 39, 84, 91, 182–4, 195, 223, 231–2, 239, 243–5, 250; one-day internationals, 52, 56

Houghton, David, 25

house, 111

Hove, 172

Hoyte, Ricky, 28

Hudson, Andrew, 62, 64

Hughes, Merv, 68, 70, 208, 209

Hutton, Len, 98, 100

Illingworth, Ray, 178, 195, 221, 226, 228, 230–2, 234, 238–9, 246–7

Illingworth, Richard, 45

Imran Khan, 37, 40, 92

India: test against, 35–6; tour to India, 197–201; Hero Cup, 58–9; World Cup, 1992, 53

injuries, 43–5, 51–2, 123–4, 155–9; risks of, 14; to Ian Bishop, 41; to Desmond Haynes, 132

ICC Code of Conduct, see standards of behaviour

intimidatory bowling, 13–15, 211

Inzaman-ul-Haq, 24; maiden century, 91–2

Jaipur, 198

Jamaica, 22–3, 26–7, 30, 35

Johnson, Glenroy, 27

Johnson, Richard, 119, 131, 132

Jones, Allan, 155

Jones, Dean, 56

SUMMERS WILL NEVER BE THE SAME
A Tribute to Brian Johnston
Edited by Christopher Martin-Jenkins & Pat Gibson

'I understand there are some men who do not like cricket, but I would not like my daughter to marry one'
Brian Johnston

Brian Johnston, who died in January 1994, was one of the best loved figures on radio. His unique broadcasting style won him a special place in the hearts of listeners everywhere.

Although 'Johnners' became known as the voice of cricket, he was also a national figure as the presenter of *Down Your Way*. His many other broadcasting credits include presenting for television the Queen's Coronation and the Boat Race.

Most of all, Johnners will be remembered for his schoolboy humour. Specially revised and updated for the paperback edition, this volume of tributes includes anecdotes and memoirs from over sixty colleagues and friends – including John Major, Sir Colin Cowdrey, Richie Benaud, John Paul Getty, Lord Whitelaw, Tim Rice, Lord Carrington and Jonathan Agnew – as well as short extracts from Johnners's own publications and transcripts of some of his most famous broadcasts.

0 552 99631 9

BOYCOTT: THE AUTOBIOGRAPHY
by Geoffrey Boycott

Captain of Yorkshire and England, yet discarded by both when still at his peak, Boycott has been at the top for over twenty years. As a boy growing up in a Yorkshire mining community, he played cricket in the back streets with a manhole cover as a wicket, displaying even then the gritty determination which drove him on to become one of the greatest run-getters in Test history. Such brilliance, together with his steely courage when facing the fastest and most terrifying bowlers in the world, has led many to feel that he is the greatest batsman of our time. Boycott talks frankly about his often fiery relationships with such great cricketers as Illingworth, Trueman and Close, and about his love-hate relationship with Yorkshire cricket. He discusses his key partnerships with team-mates such as Denness, Brearley and Botham. And he speaks here for the first time about why he chose to opt out of Test cricket for three years in the mid-1970s.

'An admirably honest insight into one of sport's most complex characters'
Daily Telegraph

'Marvellously good, full of passion and observation'
Guardian

'Misguided, mishandled, criticised and crucified – and only because he's different'
Brian Clough

0 552 99318 2

A SELECTION OF SPORTS TITLES
AVAILABLE FROM CORGI BOOKS
AND PARTRIDGE PRESS

THE PRICES SHOWN BELOW WERE CORRECT AT THE TIME OF GOING TO PRESS. HOWEVER TRANSWORLD PUBLISHERS RESERVE THE RIGHT TO SHOW NEW RETAIL PRICES ON COVERS WHICH MAY DIFFER FROM THOSE PREVIOUSLY ADVERTISED IN THE TEXT OR ELSEWHERE.